"I know that you w... ...s friends, and offered them their freedom if they would kill her in her chains."

Julian clapped his hands. "Bring in the vampire."

Naked to the waist, wearing a leather gauntlet that extended from his shoulder and was strapped over his chest, Angel was brought into the arena.

"If you kill him, Slayer, all your friends go free. If you refuse, they die. Horribly."

The amphitheater was abuzz. Boos and cheers mixed in a chorus of reaction to the scene played out in the arena. In the din, Buffy stared at Angel.

"We won't fight."

"Buffy, if you have to kill me, do it."

"Part them," Julian commanded in a ringing voice.

Two vampires roughly pulled them away from each other. Angel looked over the head of his handler and stared hard at Buffy.

Then he hefted his sword.

Buffy the Vampire Slayer™

Buffy the Vampire Slayer
  (movie tie-in)
The Harvest
Halloween Rain
Coyote Moon
Night of the Living Rerun
Blooded
Visitors
Unnatural Selection
The Power of Persuasion
Deep Water
Here Be Monsters

The Angel Chronicles, Vol. 1
The Angel Chronicles, Vol. 2
The Angel Chronicles, Vol. 3
The Xander Years, Vol. 1
The Xander Years, Vol. 2
The Willow Files, Vol. 1

Available from ARCHWAY Paperbacks and POCKET PULSE

Buffy the Vampire Slayer adult books

Child of the Hunt
Return to Chaos
The Gatekeeper Trilogy
  Book 1: Out of the Madhouse
  Book 2: Ghost Roads
  Book 3: Sons of Entropy

Obsidian Fate
Immortal
Sins of the Father
Resurrecting Ravana
Prime Evil
The Evil That Men Do

The Watcher's Guide: The Official Companion to the Hit Show
The Postcards
The Essential Angel
The Sunnydale High Yearbook
Pop Quiz: Buffy the Vampire Slayer

Available from POCKET BOOKS

BUFFY
THE VAMPIRE
SLAYER™

The
EVIL THAT MEN DO

NANCY HOLDER

An original novel based on the hit TV series created by Joss Whedon

POCKET BOOKS
New York   London   Toronto   Sydney   Singapore

An *Original* Publication of POCKET BOOKS

POCKET BOOKS, a division of Simon & Schuster Inc.
1230 Avenue of the Americas, New York, NY 10020

™ and copyright © 2000 by Twentieth Century Fox Film Corporation. All rights reserved.

ISBN: 0-671-02635-6

First Pocket Books printing July 2000

10 9 8 7 6 5 4 3 2 1

POCKET and colophon are registered trademarks of Simon & Schuster Inc.

Printed in the U.S.A.

This book is for Nicole Kallas,
and her daughter, Caroline.

Acknowledgments

My sincere thanks to my editor, Lisa Clancy, and her assistant, Liz Shiflett; to Joss Whedon, Caroline Kallas, and the entire cast and crew of *Buffy;* to Debbie Olshan at Fox; my agent, Howard Morhaim, and his assistant, Lindsay Sagnette. For their love and support, thanks to my husband, Wayne, my sister, Leslie, my friends Stinne and Karen, my baby-sitters, and my dearest daughter, Belle. And of course, a big thank-you to Christopher Golden.

The
EVIL THAT MEN DO

Prologue

Hellsapoppin'. . . .

The cemetery was going up in flames as the hooded figure soared through the air and slammed its boots directly into the center of Buffy Summers's chest. With a grunt of pain, she smacked against the stone wall so hard that for one startling moment, she thought her heart had exploded.

The breath was completely knocked out of her. But Buffy had no time for pain, or injuries. Not if she wanted to live.

Her attacker was bent on killing her, of that she was certain. Buffy didn't have a chance to suck in air, even to think, as she instinctively fought back a rain of punishing blows. First to her face, then to her midsection, even to her thighs and kneecaps. The punches and kicks came hard and fast.

She fought back with every trick in her Slayer's repertory. Pushing away from the cemetery wall, she whirled in the air with a vicious roundhouse kick that caught the faceless figure across its throat. She followed that with a double-fisted blow to its solar plexus and jammed her fingers in and up below the rib cage.

Nothing seemed to faze it. It came back at her, hardly winded, and rammed its fist into her abdomen. Buffy doubled over, but managed to headbutt it as hard as she could.

They kept at it, maybe for five minutes, maybe for five hours. Buffy was way beyond tired. But gradually she began to get used to its fighting style, and she blocked more of its blows. Her open hand stopped a sock to her jaw. Then she used the meat of her hand to undercut the figure's chin, and threw in a quick jab to its cheek.

Still, way too many blows were hitting home. Sweat streamed down her face and arms as she kept up the killing pace. It was blazing hot in the cemetery, and the heat was sapping her energy. The trees were on fire and the ground smoldered. The headstones gave off steam, shattering into pieces that sizzled as they fell. It was hot as Hell.

And Buffy should know.

As she did a 360 in the air and landed a good solid kick on the side of its head, a strong wind whipped through the crackling branches and scattered burning leaves that darted and flickered like sparks. With a whoosh, the figure's robe burst into flame. It didn't seem to care. Still, Buffy seized the moment and rushed the figure, slamming it to the ground.

It didn't fight her.

Buffy's hands blistered as she grabbed at the dark fabric across the figure's face.

She tore the mask away.

Then suddenly, the figure was no longer beneath her.

Buffy called out, "Hey!" and whirled around.

Across the cemetery—which now was eerily silent and not on fire at all—the figure stood in a strange aura of flickering black flame. It slowly pulled its robe away from its chest.

A human heart pulsed in the cavity.

"Evil dwells here," the figure whispered.

Then it stepped from the ring of black flame, revealing at last its face to Buffy.

She caught her breath.

Her own face stared back at her. The eyes were narrowed, the mouth hard, cruel.

The laugh, however, was hers.

Then it stepped back into shadows, laughing, and vanished.

In the hot winds that blew across Sunnydale, Buffy Summers dreamed. She moaned in her sleep and threw a protective arm over her face. Perspiration beaded her forehead.

The Santa Ana gale forces whipped through the pines outside her window, making them scratch against the siding and the open frame. It might not make sense for someone with as many enemies as Buffy had—many of whom could levitate, fly, or simply prop a ladder against the two-story house on Revello Drive—to sleep beside an open window.

But Buffy trusted her instincts. She was the Chosen One, she who must go up against the demons, the vampires, and the forces of darkness. With her Watcher, Giles, she trained to do her job as if her life depended on it. Which it did. Most Slayers had a notoriously short life span. Buffy herself had buried a dear friend who had been a Slayer—Kendra, who had been called because the Master, Buffy's first foe when she had come to Sunnydale, had actually succeeded in killing Buffy . . . for a very short time.

Death was part of the Slayer's business. A very big part.

So was evil. And the hooded figure was very real evil, and very near, no matter that it came to Buffy in a dream.

For the dreams of Slayers were rarely simple flights of fantasy. They foretold the future, revealed the present, clarified the past.

The nightmares of Slayers were even more telling.

When Buffy realized she was dreaming, she bolted upright with her hands in fists and her shoulders tensed, ready to defend herself. The things that walked her dreams were often things that could hurt her.

And which she in turn could hurt.

She listened carefully for sounds the night did not usually own. The blistering wind blew hard, sounding almost like surf. As it rose and fell, like waves, the scraping of crickets lent a counterpoint to the rapid beating of Buffy's heart.

"Evil dwells here."

Buffy frowned. What was that supposed to mean? That everybody had some evil in their heart?

This is news?

Even Buffy had bad secrets, done things she wasn't particularly proud of. You couldn't wrestle with the dark on a nightly basis without a bit of shadow creeping into your soul. That was the cost of doing business.

In a Slayer's case, the cost of staying alive.

She scanned her room—gaze sweeping over her umbrellas, her butterflies, her stuffed animals, especially Mr. Gordo—and saw nothing unusual. Nothing out of place. Still, she kept her guard up. The dream had seemed so real. Buffy's dreams often did. Usually did.

Tense and alert, she wiped her forehead and got out of bed. She wore a white spaghetti-strap baby T-top and a pair of satin boxers her mom had brought home from the gallery gift shop. Circles of blue and black coiled around yellow stars. The design was called *Starry Night*, and the lunatic who had done the original painting had also cut off his ear.

Some people are so versatile.

Like Buffy herself. She smiled faintly as she crept across her floor and opened the door to the hallway. She could slay, and she could now also salsa dance, thanks to Oz, of all people. Oz, with his bowling shirts and his cool band, had his secret side as well. Besides being a werewolf.

He danced very well.

But she was digressing. The dream was the thing to deal with. Giles wanted her to write her dreams down, but that took too long and besides, she always remembered them in perfect detail. And it was more important at the moment to find out if some hooded evil Buffy twin with her heart hanging out of her chest was tiptoeing through the hallways of Buffy's own home.

There! At the end of the corridor, a figure stood motionless. Buffy rushed it, ready to inflict major damage, when she realized about halfway to her destination that it was her mother, looking very apprehensive and very sleepy.

"Honey?" Joyce Summers queried muzzily. "Is something wrong?"

Buffy shook her head. "Couldn't sleep."

"Oh." Her mom still looked just as apprehensive, and only slightly less sleepy. "And so you were going to attack me?"

"Not you," Buffy blurted, then shrugged with a little laugh. "Just my demons. Slayer in-joke there. Which is," she added quickly at her mother's look, "not so funny."

Joyce frowned. "Is there a demon in the house, Buffy?"

For a guilty moment, Buffy thought she meant Angel. Then she realized her mom was just spooked, so she firmly shook her head.

"No, Mom. It's all clear. Go back to bed."

Joyce cocked her head. "What are you going to do?"

Buffy smiled sheepishly. "Attack. The rest of that quart of Cherry Garcia ice cream."

"Not if I get there first," Joyce shot back. She darted around Buffy and loped down the hall.

"Mom!" Buffy shouted, tearing after her.

She was the Slayer; she could have easily outdistanced her mother. There was not a human alive she couldn't best in a skirmish. But she fussed and fumed all the way to the kitchen for her mother's benefit, only to find Joyce pulling out two bowls and two spoons, and the prize—the half-empty carton of Cherry Garcia.

Buffy sat at the table and watched her mom dish out the ice cream. A wave of longing for this kind of life all the time, this normal mom-and-teenaged-daughter life, swept over her.

"I've been thinking, Buffy," her mom said, in a very serious tone of voice.

"Yes?" Buffy croaked, struggling to hide her emotion.

"From now on . . ."—she turned around dramatically—"we only buy half-gallons. Quarts are for wimps. And *we* are not wimps."

"No, we certainly are not." Buffy thrust out her chin. "This house is wimp free."

"And . . ." Joyce turned back to the ice cream. Facing away from her daughter, she said a little uncertainly, "And you're sure everything is okay?"

"Just peachy," Buffy assured her.

In the morning, she'd have to tell Giles about her dream. Because Buffy had the sense that things were not *completely* peachy.

But that was not something she was going to tell her mother at three-thirty in the morning.

If ever.

She walked.

Down the dark passageways, a candle in her hand, she crept silently. If she knew he was following her, she didn't let on.

She rarely slept, haunted as she was by what he had done to her. He wished he could regret his actions, but they had been necessary at the time. Her obsession with butchering Slayers had made them both into targets. The primary mission of each succeeding Chosen One was to avenge the death of the Slayer before her. For centuries.

The madness that ensued, well, that was . . . unfortunate. He wished he had the heart to feel worse about it than he did.

Now she unsheathed a long, vicious dagger. He knew what was coming, and his own bloodlust rose. She and he were creatures born of a ruthless and brutal age—the time of Roman Empire—and his passion for the Games had never abated. To see another writhe in torment, to know their life hung by a thread that he could cut—there was no greater excitement. Save one . . .

"Slayer," Helen hissed. The knife edge gleamed in the candlelight.

In the darkness, someone whimpered. Helen laughed to herself, the low, flat laughter of the mad and the damned—she being both—and held the knife in the flame of the candle.

"Slayer, I come. I challenge you."

"I—I—lady, I'm not a Slayer," the voice babbled. It was a young girl. She would be their seventh victim since arriving in this strange little town. Within the fortnight, they must kill eighteen. Seven was the first magickal number, the first requirement to set the Transformation into motion. Eleven was the next. And eighteen, the last, which must occur on the Night of Meter, the very next full moon.

"You are the Slayer, and you must die for your betrayal," Helen whispered, moving toward the voice. "But first, you must suffer. Horribly."

Julian smiled in anticipation.

"The first cut I dedicate to Angelus," she whispered.

Rage filled him. He had tried to tell himself that it was merely a coincidence that Angelus was here, in the same town that had become home to the reigning Slayer. That the gods had chosen to send the Urn of Caligula to this place had been a portent he and

Helen could not ignore. That the stars would align in the correct position at the next full moon was indeed a sign.

If the rites were correctly performed, they would unleash the power to rule this world.

But the matter of Angelus . . . that was a different affair entirely.

He had learned that Angelus had changed. He had no idea if that would please or distress Helen.

He did know that he would kill Angelus at the first opportunity.

There was a scream. Julian had heard hundreds of Helen's victims scream. Thousands. And among them, more Slayers than could be counted.

Slayers were her passion. She had destroyed them in many ingenious ways—through various forms of torture, starvation, even freezing them to death. Drowning them.

"Beg me for your life, Chosen One!" Helen shouted. "Beg me on your knees."

"Please, lady, please!"

Julian came up to Helen and put his arm around her waist. His darling was very tall and muscular. Her long black hair spilled down her back to brush her hips. She wore an exquisite white gauze toga, leaving nothing to his imagination. After all these centuries, she still stirred him. She looked like a goddess, which she would soon become, if all went according to plan.

"My darling," he murmured.

The girl in the cell had once been very lovely. Now her nose was broken and some of her teeth were missing.

"Mister, help me," she pleaded, cowering as Helen ran the knife through the candlelight again.

"I had a dream, Julian," Helen said, staring at her captive. "This very Slayer faced me, young, fresh-faced, and full of virtue. A Slayer is a noble creature, chosen by the Fates for a special purpose. A goddess brought to earth for the benefit of mankind.

"A Slayer is a lie."

"Indeed, my darling." It would do no use to explain to her that this child was no Slayer.

"The first cut," she said, then smiled and turned to him. "For you."

Julian felt the renewed flare of rage, knowing she was thinking once again of Angelus. But he hid his anger behind a very pleasant smile.

"Helen, you are all heart," he said sincerely.

"A heart where evil dwells," she replied, touching his face. Then she glanced over at the girl. "And soon, I will take her heart. The pure and sacrificial heart of a Slayer. And our Dark Mother will rise, and turn us into gods."

"That is true," he said, simply.

10

Chapter 1

Buffy the Vampire Slayer

LIFE GOES ON, BUFFY THOUGHT SADLY, AS WILLOW Rosenberg looked up from the computer in the school library and grimaced. *Or not.*

"Another one, Buffy," she said unhappily.

They sat in the gloomy stillness of the large, musty room. The books that Giles loved so much were dusty from disuse. Very few Sunnydale High students ever used the library, making it the perfect Slayer's HQ. Over the years, it had become Buffy's home away from home, but never a refuge. She'd gotten wind of more dire prophesies, end of the world scenarios, and various other forms of bad news here than she ever wanted to think about.

And here was more.

It had been a week since Buffy's first bad dream. She had had a similar one every night, and she was slagged. But what was worse was that the homicide rate in Sunnydale had risen very sharply in that week, and the murders were brutal in the extreme.

And there seemed to be no way she could stop them.

Standing behind Willow, Oz put his hand on her shoulder as the two studied the computer screen. "You might not want to click on that window." To Buffy, he added, "The one labeled 'Autopsy Photos.'"

Nevertheless, Willow clicked. "Not if you want to keep your breakfast," Willow said, growing pale. She touched Oz's hand and he squeezed her shoulder. "Skip it, Buffy."

"No. I have to look." Buffy got up from her chair and steeled herself. "So I'll know what I'm dealing with."

"You still won't know," Oz said. "Trust me on this one."

Buffy cleared her throat and he moved aside.

She stared at the screen. Felt everything inside her heave. She tried to swallow, and couldn't. Without really seeing where she was going, she managed to sit back in her chair.

The library doors opened, and Xander called cheerily, "Anybody for lunch?"

Rupert Giles came out of his office, looked at Buffy, and said to Willow and Oz, "You two go on ahead."

Willow spoke for both of them. "We're not hungry."

"Still," Oz murmured, taking Willow's hand.

Willow looked puzzled. Then she glanced at Giles, raised her brows, and said, "Oh. Yes. Going now."

They walked away, leaving Buffy with her Watcher. He perched on the edge of the study table and folded his hands, leaning toward her with an expression of concern on his face.

She folded her arms over her chest and said, "You're going to tell me those murders are not my fault. Again."

"Yes. Until you believe it." He cocked his head. "Buffy, I truly believe these recent killings are the work of a madman. A garden-variety, mortal madman. Not a supernatural madman. The police should be good for something, don't you think?"

She guffawed bitterly. He shrugged, took off his glasses, and polished them.

"Giles, evil is evil. How can you separate it into stuff I handle and stuff I don't? Did you see those pictures?"

"Yes." He regarded her. "You're exhausted, Buffy. It's dangerous to put yourself at risk taking on burdens which don't belong to you. Heaven knows you have enough responsibilities. I want you to stay out of this."

She frowned at him. "But Giles, how can you say this is something normal? It's so *not.*"

"Nevertheless," he said, and then his phone rang. He went into his office to get it.

Buffy took the opportunity to make a break for it. She called out, "I'm catching up with the gang," and hurried out of the library.

Oz and Willow were holding hands and Xander was trailing behind them. They all looked pleased to see her, and she brightened a little.

Willow said, "Need to talk?"

Buffy shrugged. "Naw. I'm fine." She looked at each of them in turn. "Really."

They looked back at her. "Okay," Willow said, but she looked a little hurt.

* * *

School was out, and she was free.

She was only eight years old, and she was not supposed to ride her new two-wheeler any farther than the entrance to the reservoir. But the shiny lavender-and-pink bicycle was like a magic pony that could take her anywhere in Sunnydale, and she wanted to see the water.

The license plate on the front of her bike said *Lindsey* in strawberry-colored letters. The pink and white plastic streamers fluttered from the handlebars as she excitedly pumped the pedals.

She zoomed past the gate and waved at Mr. Bitterman, the chubby man who worked there. He and his wife knew her mom and dad from church. Her daddy said they did not get along very well.

"Hey, Lindsey, new wheels?" he asked. He was sweating in the heat.

"Yup."

She skidded to a stop, nearly falling off, and put her foot down just in time. Then she carefully flipped down the kickstand and parked.

She started to head for the little building where the bathrooms were, but he hurried over and said, "The toilets are closed today. We had a backup."

"Ew," she said.

He chuckled and crossed his arms over his chest, watching her as she meandered down to the water's edge, stepping over pebbles and some reeds that had washed up.

"It'll be getting dark," Mr. Bitterman said. "You should go home."

"Not for a long time," she answered, but he was an adult, so she had to do what he said.

"Go on, now, honey." He gave her a smile and walked toward the bathrooms.

As she turned to leave, something caught the glint of the long afternoon sun. She bent down to retrieve it from the shallow water. It was a pretty little bottle with sparkles on the top. It was empty.

She held it up and inspected it. It wasn't quite empty. There was some kind of blue liquid inside.

Maybe it's perfume.

She popped off the top.

Hurry, sundown.

Jordan Smyth was on sched and in control. He was jamming. He was fresh. This was a new gig, and so far it was *très* cool.

He scratched his shaved head as he followed Willy the Snitch down to the basement of the Alibi, Sunnydale's ragtag loser bar. The lightbulb on a string over his head caught the glint of the signet ring Brian Dellasandro had given him in partial payment for the wicked high he had sold him. Never mind that the initials were "M.D." Jordan figured Brian had swiped it from his little brother, Mark.

Jordan practically whistled as he and Willy wound through the tunnels to the secret rooms that were carved like caves out of the rock.

And there they were, just like before, the blond Englishman with the goatee and his beautiful, dark lady. The one they called the Queen. They had some candles going, very Goth, and he chuckled at their need for drama.

The Englishman turned and smiled at the visitors. "Good evening."

"Hiya," Willy replied, with a little bob of his head.

"I, uh, got customers upstairs." Willy was afraid of his new renters. He was sorry he'd let them move in down here. But Jordan knew better. These were really fine people.

As in, useful.

"Yes, leave us," the blond man said, dismissing the bartender.

Willy scampered away. Jordan joined in the looks of contempt on the faces of the couple.

The man looked Jordan over. "Willy was right to bring you to us."

Jordan had done a few illegal things for Willy, bought stuff for some of the bar patrons, fenced stuff for others. Half of it, Jordan didn't even know what it was. Willy had suggested he work for "the newcomers," and now Jordan realized it was because Willy wanted to put as much distance between them and himself as possible. Which was stupid. These people were rich.

The Queen touched his forehead, tracing her long fingernails down to the corner of his mouth. Jeweled rings glittered in the candlelight.

"You gave the Madness Potion to our contact?" the woman said.

Jordan nodded, chuckling to himself at her use of the word "potion." Drugs were drugs no matter what fancy name you gave them. He was cool with that. He'd dealt before, and he'd deal again.

What he didn't mention was that he had also sold one of the vials to a customer of his, name of Brian Dellasandro. In return, Brian had given him the ring. But they didn't need to know about his private side deals.

The man looked pleased. "Now Sunnydale will scream."

Jordan wasn't sure what that meant, but he let it go for now.

The man smiled at Jordan again. "There's an art gallery in town. It has something that belongs to us. Something that was stolen from us a long time ago."

Jordan squared his shoulders proudly and tugged at the row of earrings in his left ear. It was an old habit and he didn't care at all about breaking it. He had a lot of habits.

Some of them were expensive.

He announced, "I've done time for robbery."

The man's smile grew. "I know."

The Queen wrinkled her nose at him. "We have a group here. It's like a family. Part of the reason we came here was to look for people who might fit into our family." She flattened her hand on his chest. He caught his breath. Her fingers were ice-hot.

"People who need people. People like you," she continued.

Her voice was calm and sexy, and it wrapped around Jordan like a silken scarf.

"I've got a family. On the streets," he said, raising his chin. He was Jordan Smyth—with a Y—and he didn't need anybody. Needing was for losers.

The blond man snapped his fingers. Some weird scarred guy came out of the darkness with two cups filled with something that smelled a little rank. The man handed one of the cups to Jordan and kept one for himself. Jordan looked down. The liquid was thick and kind of brownish-red. His stomach rolled. It looked like blood.

"So, are you two, like, boyfriend and girlfriend?" Jordan asked contemptuously, to hide his fear.

"One thing you'll learn in our family," the man said, "is that there's a lot of room in our hearts for many people. Many different kinds of relationships."

Then the Queen trailed her fingernails down Jordan's stomach. Jordan reacted, he couldn't help it, but he kept the mental part of himself away from her. He was a good-looking guy. Maybe not too lucky, up until now. He'd gotten himself kicked out of Sunnydale High, but he still hung around. Nobody would have much to do with him, though. They were all too busy trying to make it, not realizing most of them were going to end up in a dead-end life in this dead-end town.

Not him, though. He had just gotten himself connected.

"Will you break into the gallery for us?" the man asked. "I'll reward you. Well."

He shrugged. "Sure."

He got the gun out of the storage cabinet in the garage.

Take them out.

He loaded it.

He lurched down the hall.

He opened the bedroom door and aimed the weapon at the first sleeping body.

He pulled the trigger.

Kill them.

Stuff splattered all over him.

His mother jerked awake with a shriek, saw what he had done, and started screaming.

None of it registered: not that this was his mother,

or that he had just blasted his father into the dead zone. He pulled the trigger again, and as her body was thrown against the wall by the impact, he pulled it again and again.

The modest three-bedroom, two-bath Dellasandro house sat on the outskirts of town in a tract called Sunnydale Estates that had not made it. For some reason, no one wanted to live there. As a result, only a few houses were built, and they were far apart from each other. The Dellasandro house was surrounded by empty lots, where kids congregated to drink and make out until either Brian's father chased them away or the police drove by and made them scatter.

By two-thirty on this Friday morning, they were all long gone. So the gunfire went unheard and unnoticed throughout the sleeping town of Sunnydale.

As did Brian's shuffling, stiff-legged gait as he headed mindlessly toward town.

There was nothing in his brain but fury; nothing in his heart but rage. He wiped his mouth, barely aware that he had a mouth. His Hellboy T-shirt and blue sweatpants were splattered with blood and gore, but he didn't notice as he cradled the gun across his abdomen. He was barefoot, but he didn't feel the warm sidewalk.

The hot winds blew, and perhaps he was aware of them, for he threw back his head and howled like a wolf. Then he laughed deep in his throat, a feral, edgy laughter that was nothing like the pleasant laughter of Brian Dellasandro, a popular boy, an excellent student.

Portions of his mother's brain were matted in his chestnut brown hair.

It was a long walk to the school, but it was only two forty-five A.M.

Brian would arrive well in time for first period.

"Take 'em out," he whispered to himself.

His finger caressed the trigger and he trembled with the need to empty a clip into the calico cat trotting across the street. At the next corner, a few pieces of stray lava rock from Mrs. Gibson's front yard cut into the soles of his feet. Then he stepped on a broken beer bottle as he stumbled from the curb, but he didn't so much as blink.

He staggered on, leaving a trail of blood.

Overhead, the pink moon was tossed by the winds and the stars were sizzling. When Brian looked up at them, they jittered and blurred, and they told him to kill anything that moved.

"You talked to Mr. Giles about your dreams," Joyce Summers ventured, as she and Buffy sat in the kitchen in the middle of the night.

Buffy was not into talking about it. "Yeah."

They finished their bowls of ice cream in silence. Then Joyce suggested microwaving some popcorn.

"What's with these munchies?" Buffy asked, smiling finally, as her mother rooted for the last envelope of low-fat butter flavor.

"Look, we forgot about the vanilla wafers," Joyce said, displaying the box like a spokesmodel. "Shall we bag the popcorn and stick with sugar?"

Buffy shrugged, amused. "Sure."

As her mother opened the box, Buffy glanced at the clock and stifled a yawn. It was almost four. But she didn't want to go back to bed. Bed meant sleeping.

Sleeping meant nightmares. There really was no point.

"Good grief, it's already so hot," Joyce said. It's going to be a scorcher today. Remember in L.A. when . . ."

But Buffy wasn't listening. Someone was moving past their house. Somebody walking way too fast, and not in a straight line. Drunk maybe.

But maybe not.

"Mom, stay here, okay? Stay in the kitchen," Buffy said, getting to her feet.

"Buffy?" Joyce asked, but did as Buffy requested as her daughter unlocked the kitchen door and walked out into the yard.

It was a little girl in a nightgown. Buffy vaulted down the driveway and over a bush. She landed in front of the girl.

"Hi," Buffy said cheerily. "Sleepwalking?"

A growl tore out of the girl's throat and she launched herself at Buffy. Buffy grabbed her hands, which were drawn into claws, and said, "Whoa, jump back, little frog! Wake up!"

The girl fought and struggled, baring her teeth as if she wanted to rip Buffy's face off. She didn't look like a vampire. Her skin was pink and her teeth were just regulation humanoid teeth. But one never knew.

Buffy shot a glance around her perimeter for a weapon, and broke a fairly sizable branch off the bush she had jumped over. It wasn't sturdy, but in the hands of the Slayer, even a No. 2 pencil could turn a vampire into dust.

"Back off, okay?" Buffy said. "I don't want to hurt you."

The girl raked Buffy's cheek with her fingernails. Buffy batted her hand out of the way and threw her to the ground. Straddling her, she held the branch over her head while she pressed the girl on her back with a firm hand over her carotid artery.

There was a pulse. *That rules out vampire. But not much else . . .*

Then her mom was at the door, shouting, "Buffy, stop! That's Lindsey Acuff!"

Buffy didn't let go of the branch, but she didn't impale the girl with it, either. The girl thrashed and struggled, and Buffy was afraid she was going to have to knock her out.

"Whatever's come over her?" Joyce rose. "Let's take her inside."

"Good idea." Buffy kept her eye on Lindsey. "You get the door and I'll carry her—"

"Ouch!" Joyce cried out.

"Mom?" Buffy said, turning her head to see what had happened.

In that moment of distraction, Lindsey pushed Buffy away, leaped up, and rammed into Joyce. With a wild scream, she bit Joyce hard on the shoulder. Then she bolted and tore down the sidewalk for all she was worth.

"Hey!" Buffy shouted, but concern for her mother reluctantly took precedence over catching the girl.

Buffy bent over her, to find her mother holding the wound as blood seeped between her fingers. She looked a little gray. She said, "I'm sorry I distracted you. I stepped on a sprinkler head."

"It's okay, Mom," Buffy said, easing her mother to a standing position and slinging Joyce's arm over her shoulders. "My bad. I should have paid better attention."

"My God." Joyce's voice was shocked, breathy. "My God."

"It's just another night on the Hellmouth," Buffy said grimly, as she slowly walked her mother to the open kitchen door. But it wasn't, not when her mother was involved.

She really hated this place. Exiled from Los Angeles for burning down the gym at her old school, Hemery High, Buffy had not loved moving to this "one-Starbucks town," as Xander had once put it. But her mom had snagged a great opportunity in the form of the town's art gallery, and they had to live *somewhere*. How were either of them to know that the Chosen One had been destined to end up in a town called *Boca del Infierno* by the Spanish explorers who settled there? The mouth of Hell was what it was, a mystical convergence that both drew and expelled demons and all other manner of ooky bad guys.

Thus preventing the Slayer from wasting her time with frivolities like going to school on any kind of consistent basis; dating anyone who didn't like the notion of their girlfriend running out of the Sun Cinema in the middle of *Shakespeare in Love* without being able to explain; shopping, or being anything like she had been in L.A.: Fiesta Queen, a cheerleader, a party animal, and a shallow, spoiled brat.

"Honey, go after her," Joyce urged.

"No way," Buffy said. "I'm staying put."

There was a silence. More than once, Buffy had put the safety of her mother ahead of all other considerations. Though neither one of them talked much about it, Buffy had been forced to make that choice more often, now that her mom knew she was the Chosen One. Which was why she should never have told her. But it couldn't be helped, at the time. So much had happened so fast. But it was harder on Buffy for her mom knowing than when she had thought her daughter was some violence-prone slacker who came home all bruised up and bloody from gang fights.

In the kitchen, Buffy pulled a chair out with her foot and eased her mother down into it. Joyce was wobbly and shaken.

Buffy headed for the phone. "I'm calling nine-one-one."

Joyce shook her head. "No, honey." She waved a limp hand toward the kitchen cabinets. "I restocked the first-aid kit again. Just go get the Betadyne and bandages."

Buffy pulled her mom's bathrobe away from the wound, then made a face when she saw the teeth marks through her nightgown. "I don't know. This looks stitch-worthy."

"It's not fair, you know," Joyce said, wincing as Buffy examined the damage. She touched the scratches on Buffy's cheek, putting on her worried-mom face. "I scar, and you don't. Come to think of it, I wrinkle and you don't."

"I will, if I live long enough," Buffy shot back, then didn't smile because it wasn't funny. She might not live long enough. "Anyway, I think we should go get that checked."

"Oh, Buffy." Joyce sighed. "Let's just make some popcorn."

Buffy waited a beat. Then she realized her mother was serious.

"Well, it's nice to know your appetite isn't affected

by a near-death experience," Buffy shot at her, crossing the kitchen to retrieve the first-aid kit.

But Joyce wasn't listening. She was looking out the kitchen window. "What got into her?" She grimaced and touched her shoulder.

"Whatever it was, I hope it didn't get into you," Buffy said. *Or me.* Lindsey had dug her nails into Buffy's cheek pretty deeply. "I'm going to see Giles first thing."

Joyce nodded as she unbelted her bathrobe and bared her shoulder. "Good idea, honey." She exhaled.

"As soon as you're taken care of, I'll go look for her," Buffy promised.

"Oh, no," Joyce protested, but Buffy knew she wanted her to go. She knew she would worry about the little girl for the rest of the night.

She also knew her mother didn't want her to go out into the dark and battle the ugly things there. But as her old friend—*not*—the British sorcerer, Ethan Rayne, would say, *If wishes were horses, beggars would ride.*

Since becoming the Slayer, Buffy had ridden some pretty wild horses. Including black stallions that breathed fire.

Joyce caught her breath as Buffy applied the disinfectant. Buffy's stomach tightened as her mind cast back, remembering a night very like this. It was the first night she had invited Angel into her home. Not knowing he was a vampire, knowing only that he was this handsome, mysterious guy she'd nicknamed Danger Man, who appeared from out of nowhere to warn her about various dire goings-on. He had given her the large silver cross she had on.

When he had been injured helping her out in an

attack, she had brought him home and dressed his wound. Had seen the tattoo on his back, the mark that revealed him to be none other than Angelus, one of the most vicious vampires who ever lived. But to Buffy, he was Angel, the only vampire to have his soul restored, the only vampire who wrestled with demonic passion and human compassion. And she had grown to love him with all the need of someone who knew she would probably die young.

Then things had gone so wrong. . . .

"May I have some water, Buffy?"

Joyce's words were slurred around the edges. Buffy scrutinized her as she got a glass and filled it with water from the faucet. She handed the glass to her mother and stood over her while she slowly sipped.

"Mom, I'm still thinking Dr. Greene. You know, the ER." Buffy took the empty glass. "More?"

"No, thank you. I just want to rest," Joyce insisted, getting to her feet. Her cheeks reddened slightly. "They always ask so many questions at those places. Remember when I thought I'd fallen on a barbecue fork?"

Buffy would never forget. Angel's sire, Darla, had fed on her mother and practically killed her.

"They ask questions," Buffy said harshly, "but they don't really care what the answers are."

Joyce reached out and smoothed Buffy's hair. "Don't worry, Buffy. I'm sure I'll be fine. I don't want to go, all right?"

"Not all right," Buffy said, then grinned lopsidedly. "I think I know where I got my stubborn streak, though."

"Exactly. From your father."

Joyce put a protective arm around her daughter and urged her from the kitchen.

"I locked the door," Buffy said.

"Thank you, sweetie."

They climbed the stairs. Buffy watched uncertainly as her mom opened her bedroom door, and gave Buffy a little wave to show her she was all right.

"Sweet dreams, Mom," Buffy said.

"Don't go out," Joyce said suddenly. She shivered. "I have this feeling. Stay home. She'll be found."

Buffy smiled tightly. "Sorry. But Slayers take, like, this Girl Scout oath. It's very boring and long, but . . ." She shrugged. "You know I have to, Mom."

Joyce kissed her cheek, held her for a moment. "Come home safe to me," she said.

Buffy waited until her mother went into her room and shut the door. Then she went into her own room and opened up the drawer where she kept her slaying supplies. *What to take,* she pondered. *Holy water? Sure. A couple of good, sharp stakes? Why not?*

Brass knuckles? Too clunky.

As she loaded up, she looked over at the open window and, despite the heat, pulled it shut.

Most of the time, Slayers had very good instincts.

And on occasion, very bad dreams.

"Good morning, lemmings," Xander Harris cried out to a gaggle of Cordelia Chase's fashion-forward galpals as they set about ignoring him. "Lovely day for a mass suicide, isn't it?"

He slammed his locker shut and galumphed along the hallowed halls of Sunnydale High, searching for the Buffster. Willow and Cordelia had actually planned to come to school together. Some kind of bonding thing, he guessed, although the notion of those two chewing the fat made his ears spontaneously combust. True, they all had a lot of past to deal with, and he figured it was best dealt with in a group format, darn it. However, the girls had not consulted him about their morning plans, so, here he was, same old Xander, riffing off the snobs and the elitists and getting absolutely no credit for it.

He burst out of the building and onto the quad. The day was already boiling. Pretty soon, the fountain would be gushing steam.

"Morning, morning, morning," he said pleasantly, to guys who had flushed his head in the toilet in ninth grade; and stolen his Nintendo in seventh grade; and beaten him up for his lunch money in fourth grade; and laughed at him for three weeks straight when he barfed during nap time in kindergarten.

And who had cackled with feigned glee when Cordy had flounced off yesterday after some imagined insult—okay, it had been a real insult, but he hadn't guessed she'd actually get it—and told him he had always been and always would be a loser.

Ah, Sunnydale. You have to love the stability of small town life.

The warning bell rang. Ten minutes until first period. *Let the day begin.*

He started across the quad, didn't notice the tree root stretched out in front of him, and stumbled over it. Losing his balance, he dropped to one knee and anticipated some kind of putdown from someone who happened to see, mostly out of habit and not so much because such things bothered him anymore.

Instead, he heard a series of strange popping noises.

It took him a few moments to recognize them for what they were: gunfire.

On the quad.

At school.

For a split second he knelt, frozen. Some of the other students reacted as well, but most looked idly around, the way you might when someone's car backfires, and continued on with their conversations.

Then years of playing backup to Buffy's slayage activities kicked into high gear. He leaped up and said, "Run for cover! Someone's got a gun!"

"Harris, you are so twisted," Brad Thurman, one of the big, brainless football jerks, flung at him as he sauntered past.

"Thurman, for once—" Xander said, starting toward him.

Then suddenly Thurman was on the ground, screaming. Blood was spurting from the center of his thigh, right through his jeans.

Artery, Xander thought. He ripped off his shirt as he ran to him, no clue where the bullets were landing, fell to his knees, and started winding the fabric around Thurman's leg. The guy was in serious trouble; the blood was coming too fast.

Xander grabbed the jeans leg of someone running past, saw it was one of Thurman's teammates, and said, "Sit down and press your hand over this. I'm going to get help!"

The other guy, a bulky jock, shook his head as if he couldn't believe what he was hearing.

"No way, dude. Someone's freakin' shooting at us! I'm not sitting out here."

"This is your friend and unless you help me, he's gonna die," Xander shot back. "Now, *sit down.*"

The jock shook his head. Xander narrowed his eyes in disgust as the guy took off.

"Harris," Thurman gasped. His mouth worked but no more words came out.

"It's okay, Brad," Xander said, finishing tying the tourniquet. One Halloween he had been magickally turned into a soldier, and he still remembered his field medicine. Plus he'd helped keep Buffy in one piece after the occasional totally brutal battle.

"But remember this when you get out of the hospital, okay?" he added, fighting to hide his alarm as Thurman's eyes began to go glassy. "You owe me so big time."

Thurman exhaled. His eyes closed and his head fell to one side. For one awful moment, the entire world was telescoped down to Xander and this guy who was usually a huge pain in the butt, but who, at the moment, looked pretty much like a seventeen-year-old with his whole life ahead of him. Except for the fact that if he wasn't already dead, the rest of his life could probably be measured out in seconds.

Xander knew what death looked like.

"Hey, Brad, don't cheese out on me," he said to Thurman over the pops and shrieks, giving the guy's leg a gentle shake as he kept pressing on the gushing wound. "Cuz I intend to collect on this debt. Lifesaving, that's huge."

Thurman's eyes weren't closed all the way. He was staring blankly at the grass, which was pooling with his blood.

"Damn it," Xander gritted.

Around the two of them, kids shrieked and collided in utter panic. The popping kept going; a chunk of the fountain broke off and fell into the water. A window shattered.

Xander didn't want to leave Brad Thurman. But if he'd learned anything since Buffy had come to Sunnydale, it was when to cut your losses. There was nothing he could do for the guy; there would be no glory or even sense to staying with him just so a minister could say Xander Harris had died a hero as they lowered his coffin into the busy underground of Restfield Cemetery.

The quad was a battlefield. People were going down right and left. Mr. Carey, the new civics teacher, leaned his head out of his classroom on the second floor and cried out, "Kids! This way!" Then he shouted and grabbed his arm, crumpling to his knees.

Xander whirled around in the opposite direction, trying to see where the shot had come from. Somebody had to take out the maniac who was doing this, and it didn't look like Buffy was on duty. So, that left Riker . . . or was he Worf? Whatever. Looked like he was the only Slayerette available for the job.

He was grateful beyond words that Willow and Cordy were together, and he hoped like anything that they hadn't arrived at school yet.

Cautiously, he ran back to the fountain and shielded himself behind it. Several more pieces had been shot out of it and the water was streaming from the broken base and onto the grass.

Then this kid, Stevie, who was, like some brain or something who had skipped a half-dozen grades, scrambled up beside him. He was white-faced and his eyes were enormous.

"Stevie, get the hell out of here," Xander said.

Stevie shook his head. "I saw him." He pointed to the third classroom from the right on the second floor. "It's Brian Dellasandro."

"Get out," Xander said. "Brian? Have you been shot or something? No way!"

Bullets screamed around them. Stevie covered his face.

"Hey, man," Xander began, then blinked in amazement as Stevie straightened up and stood.

"What are you doing?" Xander shouted.

Something hit him; it happened so fast that Xander didn't even see it. Silently, Stevie went down in a terrible Peckinpah slo-mo ballet.

"Xander, here!" It was Giles. He stood at the back of the main building, directing kids back inside. He dashed across the lawn, half-crouching as he ran, and joined Xander at the fountain.

"He's been grazed," Giles said, inspecting his wound. "Let's carry him back into the main building."

"You got it," Xander said, taking Stevie's feet.

Stevie groaned.

They moved fast, carrying Stevie around the stairs. The gunshots came fast and furious. People were screaming, stampeding. More than once, someone slammed into Xander and almost knocked him down.

"The police are coming," Giles said. There was blood on his glasses.

"Yeah, yeah, that's what they always say." Something zinged close to Xander's ear and he almost dropped Stevie's left foot as he jumped.

They made it into the building. The halls were jammed with students stampeding for the main entrance. Xander couldn't remember when he'd been surrounded by so much noise and chaos. Once he and Willow had snuck into a rave, but that didn't even come close.

Someone slammed into Xander, knocking him off-balance. This time he did let go of Stevie's feet and the boy hit the floor hard.

Xander scrambled to retrieve him as someone else smacked into Giles.

"Let's go to the library," Giles suggested.

Xander nodded.

They got to the library's double doors. Giles backed through them and Xander rushed in after him.

The place was deserted.

"This must be depressing you," Xander said. "People are getting shot and they still don't think of the library as any kind of wonderful place to go."

Giles grimaced. "I'd say your jokes at a time like this are banal at best, but you've heard me say that before."

"Yeah, I have, but up until now, I thought it was a compliment," Xander said.

They carried Stevie over to the study table. Giles leaned over him, pushing up his blood-splattered glasses with a blood-splattered hand. His face was very grave.

"I'll call for an ambulance. Or a dozen." Xander moved for Giles's office.

"Good idea, though I'm sure they're en route," Giles replied. Then he added, almost under his breath, "Or else we're going to have a lot more dead students around here than normal. For a Friday, at any rate."

"Stevie said it was Brian Dellasandro who went postal," Xander said over his shoulder to Giles.

"That's preposterous," Giles replied.

"Actually, I'd say it's a pretty good guess," Xander said slowly. "Yes, a darn good guess."

In a gore-splattered Hellboy T-shirt and shredded sweatpants, Brian Dellasandro stood in the center of Giles's office with a semi-automatic pointed straight at Xander.

"Take 'em all out," Brian whispered.

He raised the weapon.

Chapter 2

EVIL DWELLS HERE.

There was cheering as she fought for her life. Seated in rings above her, thousands of people waved their hands and flung flowers down at her. Roses. The petals blurred and liquefied, raining down in a storm of overpowering scent.

Raining down in a storm of blood.

The sand around her feet was sticky with blood; she slipped and fell.

The axe in her opponent's hand came down . . .

. . . and Angel's head rolled in front of her . . .

"No," Buffy said in shock, blinking as she raised her head from the couch in Angel's living room. Someone had placed a pillow under her head and wrapped a goose-down duvet around her body.

Of course she knew who that someone had been.

Last night, she had told herself she had come here

35

only for the comforting presence of a friend. Lindsey Acuff had been nowhere to be found. A jog over to the Acuffs' house had revealed a police car in the driveway, lights flashing, and the sight of her mother and father through the kitchen window, fully dressed and very worn out, talking to one of Sunnydale's so-not-finest.

Lindsey's mother was in tears. Her father stood blankly with his arms around his wife. It was a study in grief which Buffy had, unfortunately, seen before.

The problem with being the Slayer was that you knew where a lot of the bodies were buried. Kids who went missing, kids who were thought to have run away—more often than not, Buffy had the information that could close the case file and give the parents if not peace, or answers, then at least a way to stop hoping.

Sometimes that was the best you could get. Hope could be the cruelest thing on earth.

Because the notion about coming to Angel for the comforting presence of a friend was pretty much a bogus lie. She had to face it: a tiny part of her still hoped that somehow she and Angel could be together. That was nothing short of crazy. She knew it, and she had resolved many times to give up hope.

But there were some battles even a Vampire Slayer could never win.

She knew that, told herself that, even believed that.

But hope still reared its ugly head when she least expected it.

Now, as she stirred, she realized she had completely blown it by seeking out Angel. She didn't feel any better. In fact, she felt worse. Not only had she violated her own rule about coming here, but she had probably kept her mother up worrying.

She crossed to the phone and dialed home. Her mom picked up on the first ring, and Buffy closed her eyes in shame at the tense, "Hello?" on the other end.

"Mom, it's me. I couldn't find her. I fell asleep at a . . . a friend's." She was about to say, *at Willow's,* but she made herself stop. Why lie? Her mother had no doubt called the Rosenbergs already.

"Yes, Willow let me know. You were already conked by the time she got to the phone. But it was sweet of you to ask her to let me know where you were."

"Oh," Buffy said uncertainly. She'd have to thank Willow big time, although she was sorry Willow had voluntarily fibbed. Willow really didn't like to lie. Plus, she was usually fairly bad at it. "I have to hurry. I'm already late for school."

There was a pause. Then Joyce said, "Should I call the police and tell them what we saw, Buffy? I don't know what to do. The Acuffs must be going crazy."

"I know." Buffy sighed. "Mom, trust me. Don't call. It would only make it worse."

"I suppose you're right." Her mother sounded frustrated. "I know you're right. But it's awful to know that she's out there somewhere . . . in that condition."

"Well, I'm hoping Giles can do something about it," Buffy replied, glancing around the room for her Slayer's bag and her sweatshirt. They had been carefully stowed beside the fireplace, her sweatshirt neatly folded and placed on top of the bag. "But if you try to explain it to people who don't understand, it could slow him and me down, do you see what I mean?"

"Yes." There was another pause. "I know this is old territory, honey. For both of us. It's just so hard to stand by and do nothing."

Buffy managed a faint smile. Her mom would have made a pretty awesome Slayer herself.

"Maybe whatever was wrong with Lindsey was a temporary thing," Buffy suggested. "Maybe she's her old self again. She fell asleep somewhere and she'll wake up and she'll get home." *And not end up in one of those hideous autopsy photos.*

"You're a good person, Buffy," Joyce said.

Buffy's eyes widened. "Huh?"

"To give me hope. That's very sweet. Now, go get ready for school."

They hung up. Buffy picked up her Slayer's bag and went down the hall to wash up in the bathroom.

There was a cup of freshly brewed coffee waiting beside the bathtub. Also, a note from Angel which read: *I'm awake if you want to talk.*

Buffy carefully put the note aside and started undressing. *Shower,* she told herself firmly. *Drink the coffee and go to school.*

The steam rose around her as she stepped in and stood under the hot spray. She knew Angel would hear the shower running, and she felt self-conscious as she closed her eyes and raised her face, trying to wash her weariness away. Not that he would ever barge in on her.

There was a fresh bar of soap in the dish, and half-used bottles of shampoo and conditioner. As she washed her hair, bits and pieces of her nightmare returned to her, and despite the heat, she shivered.

She rinsed and turned off the shower, realizing only then she hadn't checked to make sure there was a towel. There was one, freshly laundered, and hanging on the rack. *He thought of everything.*

She redressed in her sweats and T-top, wishing she had something else to change into.

When she was finished, she tiptoed back into the hall. Then she paused. Took a breath. Told herself firmly to move on.

Instead, she called softy, "Angel?"

There was no answer. Relief mingled with disappointment, and she moved on, to the living room. She collected her sweatshirt and let herself out.

In his bedroom, Angel lay with his eyes wide open and stared through the darkness. Buffy would never know how badly he had wanted to tell her to come in when she called his name.

But as soon as he had written her that note, he knew he wasn't asking her if she wanted to talk.

He was telling her what he really wanted.

And that was something he could never have again.

So he kept silent, and let her think he was sleeping.

Greater love hath no vampire, he thought ironically. And even though he was tired down to his bones, he knew he would have no rest that day.

"So, anyway, now you know my deepest, darkest secret," Cordelia said to Willow as she navigated wildly down the street. Mariah Carey was hip-hopping on Cordy's CD player. They had stopped at the Espresso Pump for lattes and girl time, and it was all a little much for Willow, especially this early in the morning.

"Uh-huh," Willow replied. "I must admit, I am a bit shocked. I would have never realized you knew where Sears was, much less that you actually bought a pair of shoes there."

"Well, we all have things. I'm sure even you have things. I mean, things you consider to be things, besides the obvious ones." Cordelia looked away from the road—*which, given her driving, won't make much difference,* Willow reminded herself, *so not to throttle up on the panic scale*—and narrowed her eyes. "I told you something. So, dish."

Willow chewed her lower lip. "Besides the lying to my parents almost constantly thing; and, well, stuff . . ." She trailed off. She knew that girls bonded by sharing secrets, but most of her secrets were about stuff Cordelia already knew. Like the Xander thing, and she sure didn't want to go there.

Suddenly, sirens pierced the morning, screaming up a short distance behind the Cordymobile. Willow jumped at least a foot and turned around to see not one, but several police cars in a line behind them. The nearest one was practically ramming Cordelia's bumper.

Cordelia only sighed and glanced into the rearview mirror. "What *now?*" she asked peevishly. "I swear, I'm always getting pulled over for nothing."

"By an armada?" Willow asked in a squeaky voice.

"Whatever." Which meant that Cordelia didn't know what an armada was.

As she aimed the car for the right-hand curb, swerving to miss another car that was inconveniently parked in the same vicinity, the police cars whined past. They were followed by two ambulances and a fire truck.

"Wow," Cordelia said. "What do you think's going on?"

Willow caught her breath. "Cordelia, what if they were going to the school?"

They traded glances.

"That could happen here so easily," Cordelia said. Willow nodded.

Without another word, Cordelia peeled out and jammed it.

All Willow said the entire way was, "Faster."

Xander.

Though she would rather die—really—than admit it, he was Cordelia's first and only thought as she screeched to a halt in front of the police barricade at the intersection in front of the school. There were police cars everywhere, and more barreling over the curb and parking on the grass. Blue and red lights strobed on top of cars with doors left open. Uniformed people were talking to people in suits who were talking on phones and gesturing to each other. A big black van was parked next to the steps, and a guy in dark gray body armor climbed out of it. He was carrying a rifle, and as he turned to go into the main entrance, Cordelia read SWAT written in yellow letters across his back.

Rolling down her window for the approaching police officer, Cordelia cried, "What's going on?"

"We're asking all students not yet in the vicinity to go home," the guy said. He had a bad sunburn that made him look like he had a rash.

"Well, we're pretty much in the vicinity," Cordelia retorted, trying to glance around him.

Willow leaned over and said, "Is there trouble?"

Duh, Cordelia thought, but waited for the cop's answer.

"We have it under control," the policeman replied stiffly.

Cordelia smiled the smile that could drop a quarterback at fifty yards. She said, "Gee, I hope you put sunscreen on this morning. That's a nasty burn."

He blinked at Cordelia and touched his face. She poured it on, sparkling all over, and he softened a little. *Yes,* she thought, and waited.

Sometimes it was so easy.

"Some kid went postal," the officer confided, dropping his voice. "Took out some school personnel. A couple students, at least. He's holed up in the library. Hostage situation."

Devon shut Oz's van door and said, "Okay, dude, so." He wasn't smiling and he wasn't pretending everything was good between them. He just looked at Oz as if the ball was in his court, and shrugged.

"Yeah." Oz started his van and backed out of the lot, leaving Devon to head to his own car, parked behind Sunnydale Chiropractic.

He got onto Route 17 and cranked up his CD player. Eric Clapton. A righteous musician who had seen his share of sorrow.

Oz ran his hand through his red hair and adjusted his seat belt over his brown-and-green bowling shirt. He was not the happiest camper in the whole U.S.A. Yesterday, he and Devon had agreed to a run-through of a new song Oz had written for the Dingoes, scheduled for tonight's practice. Then late last night, Devon called and asked if they could do it before school. Though not exactly a morning person, Oz had been cool with that.

He'd also been cool with the request to drive Devon to the chiropractor's office where his mom worked so he could take her car for the day, because his was up on blocks. And dealing, too, with the fact that all this took much longer than he'd expected, and he was monumentally late for school.

Given the fact of his fame as the student with the highest SAT scores ever to repeat his senior year, missing more school was not in his best interests. Still, he had kept his poise.

Devon had pretty much blown off the song, complete with some harsh comments on the second verse, and still Oz had stayed on idle. There was a difference between being dissed personally and someone criticizing your work. He understood that.

But then Devon had launched into his "Yoko" riff on Willow, blaming her all over again for Oz's fairly predictable absences from practices and the occasional gig. That was the real reason for the meeting, and that pissed Oz off. He felt ambushed; he was unprepared for the confrontation, even more so for the fact that the entire band was mad at him and yet no one had so much as given him a heads-up before this morning.

He thought he'd covered all this over six months before, with some vague confession about being enrolled in a "program." At the time, Devon had been understanding in the extreme, so sympathetic, in fact, that Oz figured he might have some kind of dependency problem of his own. But evidently Devon figured half a year of rehab was enough.

"You need to get it together, dude," Devon had insisted this morning. "Or you need to get out."

The thing was, Oz didn't exactly decide one day to become a werewolf. His cousin had bitten him, and lycanthropy was the gift that kept on giving. If you got bitten by a werewolf, you became one, too. And three nights out of every month, if you didn't chain yourself inside a cage in the school library, you stood a good chance of killing someone or getting killed yourself.

But this was all very hush-hush. Like Buffy, he had a secret mojo identity. Only his had nothing to do with heroics. His had more to do with the call of the wild side.

It was awkward, and it made for problems. Okay, so, life. But for Devon to essentially lie to him to call him on the carpet, that was uncool in anybody's book.

He checked the clock on the dash. Rate he was going, he'd make it to school by third period. Maybe Buffy would have detention, too. He smiled at that. It would be nice to have a one-on-one chat with her, see how she was doing. She was good people. She was a damn fine salsa dancer, too.

He reached down to scan the CD for "San Francisco Bay Blues," rounding a corner as he did so. His finger hit pause instead of forward, so he was momentarily distracted from his driving.

That was why he saw the overturned car that was blocking the road just a little too late.

Buffy got to the high school at exactly the same time that the ambulances peeled out for the hospital.

Cordelia nearly ran her over, but at the last minute squealed angrily to a halt and waited just long enough for Buffy to throw herself into the passenger side.

"What happened?" Buffy cried. "What's going on?"

"Well, Miss Slayer, you weren't here, so Willow tried to do this glamorous thing and she went into the library and got shot," Cordelia flung at her. "And Giles has a concussion and Xander—"

"Shot?" Buffy stared at her. "What are you talking about?"

Cordelia muttered, "Shut up. I need to concentrate on my driving. These ambulance guys really punch it."

"Cordelia," Buffy warned.

"Okay. Brian Dellasandro went nuts and shot half the school, and we waited for you to show, but he was killing all kinds of people. So Willow tried to make him think she was his cousin, Natalia, with magick. She went into the library to try to talk him out. Only it didn't work, so he knocked out Giles and Xander, and then shot her. So then the SWAT guys shot Brian."

She glanced at Buffy. "Willow's really bad, Buffy. She might die."

And I didn't show, Buffy thought miserably. *Because I fell asleep at Angel's.*

At the hospital, Willow's parents sat frozen in the waiting room, holding hands and barely acknowledging Buffy and Cordelia as they paced. No one would tell either of them anything. This was the time when being a relative or at least a legal adult paid off. Kids were basically ignored and told to wait. It wasn't like some TV show, like *90210,* where every sixteen-year-old practically ran corporate conglomerates without a shred of interference.

After an eon, Buffy's mother rushed in, saw Buffy, and threw her arms around her.

"Thank God," she said. "Thank God you're all right."

"Everybody but Willow is pretty much okay," Cordelia said. "Concussions. Some kid with them was grazed, but he'll live."

For a moment, Buffy let herself sink against Joyce. *This is all my fault. I as much as pulled the trigger. I may have killed my best friend.*

"Mom, find out about Willow," Buffy whispered.

Joyce gave Buffy a peck on the cheek and walked toward the nurses' station.

"I've said it before and I'll say it again," Cordelia murmured admiringly. "Your mom sure knows how to moisturize."

Buffy silently watched her mom as she talked to a blond woman in a white coat. Nurse, doctor, manicurist, Buffy didn't care, if the chart they were checking was Willow's.

The woman said something to Joyce, and Joyce smiled briefly at Buffy. Buffy assumed that was good news until Joyce came back over and said, "She's still in surgery."

Buffy walked over to the Rosenbergs, who were huddled together like Leo and Kate in the freezing Atlantic. She waited until they acknowledged her, and then she cleared her throat and said hoarsely, "I don't know if they told you, but Willow was a hero today. She went into the library to talk to Brian, and she didn't have to. She was trying to save Xander and Mr. Giles."

Willow's father, Ira Rosenberg, kept holding his wife's hands in his. He said, "If that school was a decent place, there would not have been a boy with a gun."

"Ira," Mrs. Rosenberg began, but then she burst into tears.

Buffy swallowed hard. There were times that Willow had kept her from going crazy from the pressure of being the Slayer. There were other times she and Willow could just be two girlfriends, talking about their boyfriends or lack of same.

"Your daughter," she began, then ducked her head. She wasn't used to talking about her feelings with adults. "She's the best." She knew that was a weak tribute, but it was the best she could do.

She sat with her mother, who kept murmuring, "Thank God you're all right." Buffy felt sick.

I wasn't there, she thought. *I didn't prevent this.*

Hours dragged by. Finally a doctor came out to talk to the Rosenbergs, who disappeared through the emergency room double doors. Buffy's heart thudded out of control as she waited for them to return.

After about twenty minutes, they did. Mrs. Rosenberg said to her, "Willow wants to speak to you."

Buffy nodded and followed a nurse through the doors.

Willow looked small and helpless in the bed. Her red hair was a shock of color against her pale skin and nearly white lips.

The nurse whispered, "She lost a lot of blood. Don't stay long. She's tired."

Buffy nodded and moved to the bed. She said quietly, "Will?"

Willow's eyes slowly opened. Tears welled.

"Buffy, I couldn't do it," she murmured. "I screwed it up."

"No, you did a great job."

A tear slid down her cheek. "It really hurts."

"I'll tell the nurse."

Willow grimaced. "Thanks. Great day you picked to be tardy."

It was supposed to be a joke, but it cut Buffy to the core.

"I'm so sorry, Willow. You don't know how sorry I am."

But Willow had drifted back to sleep.

The nurse came in and said, "You really should go. She shouldn't have so many visitors."

"She said it hurts," Buffy said.

"She has a morphine drip. I'll ask the doctor if we can increase her dosage," the nurse offered. She moved to look Willow over. Feeling helpless—*worse, useless*—Buffy left the room.

Instead of going back to the waiting room, she started peeking in rooms, searching for Giles and Xander. The place smelled like blood and vomit and disinfectant. They were smells Buffy was familiar with; when you were the Chosen One, you spent a good deal of time in hospitals.

And funeral homes.

After three rooms, she hit pay dirt, of a sort: Brian Dellasandro lay unconscious in a hospital bed, an astonishing number of machines hooked up to him. He looked really bad. Buffy realized that in all the chaos, no one had asked about him.

His younger brother, Mark, was hunched in a chair at his bedside. His face was streaked with tears.

When Buffy walked into the room, Mark jumped to his feet. He was a stereotypical nerd, skinny, with big glasses, the kind of kid bullies ached to punch out. He was fourteen but he looked like he was eleven.

Then he said, "Are you another doctor?"

She jerked slightly. "Hi. I'm Buffy. I go to school with you and your brother," she said.

Floods of tears streamed down his face. "He killed Mom and Dad," he said.

Buffy's lips parted in shock.

"I wasn't there. I couldn't do anything. I wasn't there," he sobbed. He waved her away and sank back into his chair, wailing with grief.

Buffy's heart thudded with the echo of his words. *I wasn't there.*

Chapter 3

"LOOK, XANDER, FREEDOM," BUFFY SAID BRIGHTLY TO Xander as she opened the passenger-side door of Cordelia's car with a flourish.

A sweet blue-haired Sunnydale Hospital Auxiliary volunteer helped Xander out of the wheelchair. "Freedom. Yang holy word. Do not speak it," Xander growled as he stood up easily and climbed in.

Buffy didn't know the pop-culture reference, but she smiled anyway. It was great to see Xander being Xander, all decked out in one of his signature too-big shirts and baggy trou, even if they had shaved part of his head to have a look-see at his concussion. In fact, the shaved-head part was kind of cool.

It was great because he was him, and Giles had returned fully to Gileshood.

But Willow, who was still in the hospital, was not shiny and new. She was very down, and very angry. She kept insisting she wasn't pissed off at Buffy for showing late, but Buffy couldn't believe her. Maybe because she was so furious with herself.

The same afternoon as the shootout, Oz's van had been found in the middle of a bend in Route 17 with the front end smashed in. There were flecks of black paint in the dents—evidence that he'd crashed into another vehicle, or vice versa—but no other vehicle was at the scene. Just his van with the driver's door open. And no Oz. No sign of Oz. No word from Oz, and it had been three days since he'd gone missing.

Buffy started looking for her salsa partner as soon as they found the van. What she discovered was that while Oz was well liked, he was something of a mystery to most of the people who knew him. No surprise there. When you had a deep, dark secret, it tended to put some distance between you and your nearest and dearest.

She talked to all the Dingoes, flaring when Devon told her about his "request" for Oz to get his act together or leave the band. Poor Oz. She couldn't even defend him except to say a few things about pressure and friendship. For Oz's sake, she'd stayed pleasant. Later, she took her frustrations out on a row of trash cans.

"You know, that's vandalism," Angel drawled as he leaned against the corner of an abandoned building on the other side of the alley. "And it's been on the rise the last week or so. Wonder why."

"This is my first trash can tantrum in a long time," Buffy insisted, ramming the nearest can as hard as she could, then whirling around and giving it a savage side kick for good measure.

"And no way would you do graffiti," he replied. "Which has also been increasing of late."

"Angel, *please.*" She stopped, smoothing back her hair and catching her breath.

He shrugged. "Someone's been spray painting the highways and byways. Their spelling is atrocious. I thought maybe you'd joined a tag team."

"We *so* need a teen club in this town," she said. "Sorry, my bad. We have the Bronze. The lovely, beautiful Bronze. Which I can spell, by the way."

"No news about Oz?" he asked, dropping the banter.

Buffy said nothing. He sighed and picked up the lid to the trash can, laying it on top of a small tower of peanut shells. They were on the bad side of town, which was half a block from the good side, as Cordelia had once told Buffy.

The overhanging streetlight cast hollows on his face, hiding his eyes, reminding her of her first dream in the Evil Dwells Here series. She shivered, and reminded herself that that dream was so cliché. Seeing your face on the bad guy . . . how many grade Z movies used that as the big shocker?

"My next stop is the Alibi. Again. I can't believe Willy doesn't know something."

Angel nodded. "I'll come with you. Again."

As usual, they caused a stir when they sauntered into the Alibi together. A few regulars discreetly moved farther away from the bar. Behind the bar, Willy himself also was less than happy to see them. That wasn't cause to stop the presses; he never looked very happy to see them.

"Hi," Buffy said brightly. "What's the haps since yesterday?"

The scummy little creep frowned and made a big

deal out of filling a glass with Diet Coke for Buffy, like he was really going all out to win her good graces. He looked questioningly at Angel, who shook his head. He wasn't into social drinking this evening. Just in getting answers.

Angel looked around the seedy establishment, which was frequented by the less-than-savory—or -human—population of Sunnydale. No vamps tonight; no demons, no spookables, as Xander called them. Just some very sad-looking people who could use some good news or a decent night's sleep. Or some methadone. The usual crowd for a place like this.

He crossed his boots at the ankles and leaned over the bar in a friendly, conversational way. His duster draped just so over his hip; if he were a human, he might have hidden a shotgun there for protection. But he and the Slayer didn't need any extra weaponry.

"You might have noticed an increase in petty crime recently. Tagging, overturned trash cans, that kind of nonsense. Do you know anything about that? Anyone new blow into town? A gang, maybe?"

Willy burst out with a laugh. "Right. A gang of leprechauns. They love to go in for that hard stuff. One-percenters, down the line."

"Excuse me?" Angel said, cocking his head. "Are you trying to be funny?"

"Especially since there have also been a lot of murders?" Buffy added.

Willy's eyes darted left, right. "Nobody new," he muttered guiltily. It was hard to decide if he was hiding something or not; he always sounded guilty, and with a guy like Willy, there was so much to hide you never knew if it was anything pertaining to you.

"You know, you should tell us if there is," Angel continued. "It's in your best interests."

"Really?" Willy's eyes gleamed. Angel almost laughed out loud; Willy actually thought they were going to offer him money.

"Really. What my colleague here is saying, is if you don't spill your guts, we will," Buffy chimed in pleasantly.

"My colleague puts it so well." Angel flattened his hands on the bar, making Willy jump. "So, tell me, Willy, do you feel chatty today?"

"I've got nothin'." His Adam's apple bobbed up and down. Angel noticed the vein on his neck pulsating just so. It occurred to Angel that he was hungry. *But not* that *hungry.*

He would never be that hungry.

"Absolutely nothin'," Willy babbled on.

"And nothin's plenty for you," Buffy finished. She looked at Angel as if to say, *Now what?*

"You realize of course that if we find out you lied to us," Angel said, then allowed his face to morph just slightly, and just so only Willy could see it, "if you lied, I'll decide to pay you back for nearly getting me killed."

Willy looked stricken. "I only gave you to Spike because that Slayer chick from Jamaica threatened me," he insisted.

"Don't start, Willy. It will only anger him," Buffy said kindly. "And you've never seen Angel angry."

"Yes, yes, I have," Willy assured her.

"Not really angry," Angel said. He made a fist and pounded the bar . . . very gently.

"You hear anything, you come clean," Buffy said. "Oh, and thanks for the Coke."

* * *

As soon as the Slayer and the vampire were gone, Willy wiped his hands and scurried toward the men's bathroom.

He was met in the hall.

He caught his breath and backed up a couple of steps.

"I didn't say anything," he said hoarsely. "I didn't tell them anything."

The beautiful dark woman only stared at him.

The blond man said, "Was that the Slayer?" He looked hard at the dark woman. "With *Angelus?*"

She inhaled sharply.

"Only we call him Angel," Willy said.

The blond man's face morphed. He was probably the scariest-looking vampire Willy had ever seen, and he'd seen his fair share. Then the man reached over to the men's room door and hardly without moving, ripped it off the hinges.

The dark woman flinched and bit her lower lip.

"Leave us," the vampire said. The dark vampire broad looked like she was about to wet herself.

"No problem." Willy darted back into the bar and poured himself a shot of gin. Threw it back and had another.

He figured it would take four or five more shots to stop the trembling.

Buffy walked despondently down the alley. "What do you think?" she asked. Her voice cracked.

"That you've got to get a better class of informants." He flashed her a wry smile. "I'm amazed no one's taken him out yet."

Buffy sighed and gave the nearest trash can a gentle nudge.

"The night's still young," Angel ventured. "Have you tried Restfield Cemetery?"

"Last night, yes. But not tonight."

"Let's go."

"Thanks," she said.

"I'm sorry he brought up Kendra," Angel continued.

"It's okay," she said tightly. "I've dealt."

"I know."

On the outskirts of town, the rooms were dark in the Dellasandro house. After the bodies were carted away, and the investigative teams combed the house for evidence, police tape was draped across the entrance. The kids began to congregate once more in the dirt lots surrounding the building. Stories began to spring up of people groaning and moving from room to room. If you listened real hard—after two or three beers—you might hear the crack of a shotgun followed by a scream.

Never mind that Brian had not used a shotgun.

It became a cool thing to run up to the front door and touch the tape. Then it became a cool thing to climb over the fence and peek in the windows. By the time the police got around to posting a guard, some drunk football players lobbed a couple pieces of burning wood onto the shake roof. Despite the efforts of the fire department, the house burned to the ground in record time.

Because it was an evil house, the kids whispered to each other.

Then the calico cat that lived a few blocks away—

Romeo Kitty—was found mutilated. And the dog farther on down the street, a poodle named Jewel, went missing. Her owner, an extremely obese woman named Mrs. Gibson—usually the butt of jokes and the recipient of many shouted insults whenever she called the cops to bust up the party—was so distraught that she tried to overdose. And no one, not even the biggest jerks in school, made fun of her ever again.

Jewel was discovered a week after Mrs. Gibson's suicide attempt in the canyon that abutted her backyard. Not a pretty sight; not a natural death.

Not coyotes, as the authorities tried to claim.

Mrs. Gibson moved. Some said she went to Philadelphia to live with her sister. Others, that she was carted away to an insane asylum, calling for Jewel.

But her vacant house became a tempting target, and soon there were reports of a figure or figures moving around inside it late at night.

Angry ghosts, some kids decided. But others murmured, *Mark Dellasandro.*

Where there was one psycho in a family, why couldn't there be two?

On Wednesday, Willow got out of the hospital, and Buffy went to see her. Oz had been missing for five days. Three to go until he changed.

Willow didn't look good: hair kind of oily and just clipped out of the way, no makeup, and a sweater that had seen far better days.

"I'm sorry I don't have some news," Buffy told Willow.

"You're not looking hard enough." Willow didn't

even glance up from the monitor on her desk. Willow was in hack mode, running through the Sunnydale police reports and checking out all the nearby hospitals' admitting records.

Buffy was stung. "Well, Will, I do spend a couple extra hours every night patrolling for Oz, and—"

"That's just stupid," Willow snapped, clearly exasperated. "It's not like he's in wolf mode, you know, where you can track him down." She tapped her head. "Brains, Buffy. You have to use 'em or you lose 'em. Which is something I'm not sure has ever occurred to you."

Willow's scared, she reminded herself. But it was still a mean thing to say.

But I deserve it, she reminded herself. *I more than way deserve it.*

"By the way, Mrs. Gibson's house has been purchased for below market value by someone named H. Ombra," Willow went on. "If you care."

"I noticed the For Sale sign was gone," Buffy offered, her voice unsteady. "I was patrolling over there last night. Extra," she added. "Searching."

"If you're so proud of yourself for all this extra patrolling, how come you haven't found that Acuff girl, either?"

"Hey." Buffy frowned at her. "I know you're wigged, and I'm really sorry, Willow. I—"

"You're the Slayer. You can take it," Willow shot back, raising her chin.

Buffy cocked her head. "Are you okay? I mean . . ."

Willow's mouth twisted into a sneer. "What are you talking about? There's nothing wrong with *me.* You're the screwup."

"Willow." Buffy dropped her hands. *"Please."*

Willow glared at her. "Everyone who hangs with you dies, have you noticed that? Sooner or later. I guess it was just Oz's turn."

Deliberately she turned her back on Buffy and clicked on the screen with her mouse. There was a long silence, during which she went through several more maneuvers with her computer. Windows popped up and collapsed with startling speed.

Wounded, Buffy turned to go, but took her time gathering her bag. Willow—the Willow she knew and loved—would not let her leave like this.

But this Willow muttered, "Shut the door on your way out."

Buffy swallowed hard and left with as much dignity as she could muster. In the hallway, she shut the door and leaned against it, listening, praying Willow would have a change of heart and call her back in. But there was nothing, just the click of Willow's mouse and the tapping of her keyboard.

The next morning, Buffy tried to cheer up, and cleaned up the kitchen for her mom, who was rushing around like a maniac stuffing food in her mouth and kvetching about something at the gallery. A broken window or a lock or something.

Buffy even got to school early for a training session with Giles. Inside her Slayer's bag was a CD he would prize, and she was determined to work out to it rather than the stuff he said made his brain dribble out his ears. Four Star Mary, now *there* was an awesome group. But the Bay City Rollers was what would make Giles dance with glee.

"Heya," she said, sailing into the library. "Lookee here, Porter. I've got—"

She was drawn up short by the crash of something breaking in his office. Without a second's hesitation, she sprinted for the door and was about to open it when he appeared in the doorway.

"Hello, Buffy," he said shortly, looking less than thrilled to see her.

"Hi. What happened?" she asked, craning her neck to see past him. "Drop something?"

"Just a teacup. I'll see to it." He raised his brows. "What can I do for you?"

She wrinkled her nose at him. "Giles, wow, you *are* getting old." She did a little chop-socky dance. "Training, remember?"

He sighed. "I'm sorry. I don't have the time this morning."

Without another word, he went back into his office and shut the door, leaving Buffy to gape after him.

"I brought the Bay City Rollers," she called a little hopefully. "And I've got Shaun Cassidy and the Partridge Family on order. Giles?"

"Yes," he said, and at first she thought he was speaking to her. But then he went on. "Yes, I'll hold."

She hesitated.

He said, "David."

I probably shouldn't listen, she told herself, then inched more closely to the door. First Willow was the anti-Willow, and now Giles was Jerk Man. *And yet, this phone call may hold the key.*

"Oh, my God, I'm so terribly sorry," Giles said. "Is there . . . are you in a lot of pain? Dash it. No, I can't. I've got this bloody bimbo I have to take care of. No, no, I'm rather like her guardian. Yes, she's got a mum, but she's a dithering idiot. Well, what do you expect, here in California?"

Buffy was goggle-eyed. She told herself it had to be an act, something he was putting on for the benefit of this David, whoever he was. But if it was, he should get an award at the next Watchers' Follies.

"A transplant?" Giles said. "Good Lord."

She moved away. No act there. She was a bloody bimbo and her mother was a dithering idiot.

Her face prickled as she crossed the library. She felt completely numb. Had she landed on another planet without realizing it? Crossed over into another dimension?

Just as she was about to push open the library doors, she heard the sound of something else crashing to the floor.

"Red alert," she grumbled, "Giles has PMS."

"But it was worse than that," Buffy said to Cordelia as they sat together on the quad at lunch. Buffy had bought a burger and fries, and to Cordelia, the burger smelled like dog food. She thought she was going to throw up. "He called me a bloody bimbo."

Cordelia rubbed her temples. Her head was throbbing so badly she could barely concentrate on what Buffy was saying. Okay, truth, she couldn't concentrate on it at all. The world was blurring and her vision was going all kind of like a kaleidoscope. Whatever Buffy's trauma was, it couldn't be as bad as this.

Migraine, she thought hideously. Her mother was plagued with them. Cordelia had kind of hoped that she herself was immune to them. Like varicose veins, and wrinkles. The thought that she might be starting to get them at the ripe old age of seventeen was too horrible to contemplate.

"And he said my mom was a dithering idiot."

"Maybe he was trying to impress someone," Cordelia ventured, not at all sure what was going on.

"*Excuse* me?" Buffy said. "Like who, the British Society for the Advancement of Rudeness?"

"What?" Cordelia touched her forehead and groaned. "I feel awful. I can't talk about this right now." She gestured at her nonfat yogurt and her apple. "I can't even eat. I feel kind of nauseous."

There was a pause. "Do you think you might be possessed?" Buffy asked.

Cordelia lowered her hand to her lap. "I swear, Buffy, you are not making any sense." She lurched to her feet, not an easy thing to do when you were wearing a very short plaid skirt and your head was pounding, but she managed. "Can you drive me home? No, of course you can't. You can't even pass your driver's test."

"Hey," Buffy said angrily. "You know I haven't even taken it. My God, what is wrong with you people?"

Cordelia squinted at her. The pain was screaming out of control. "And they call *me* insensitive."

She groaned again and started to trudge across the quad. Maybe the nurse would give her something. Probably not, since that would be dispensing medicine and they might get sued for it. And Sunnydale High was in for a ton of lawsuits, you could bet that was for sure. What was one headache compared to three dead students and a whole bunch of severely injured ones?

"Thanks for this special moment," Buffy called after her.

"Talk about possessed," Cordelia muttered to herself.

Jordan paced angrily as he observed the Sunnydale Art Gallery from across the street. Who was to know they'd have a great burglar alarm system? He'd waited for the night the security guard came late, then he'd broken that window and zzzzzing! that sucker had screamed bloody murder.

The Queen and her boyfriend—Julian was his name—were getting tired of waiting. They weren't talking about him joining the family anymore. But she was still wearing diamonds, and they did all kinds of awesome stuff like dissolving pearls in wine and drinking them. Jordan knew they were his one-way ticket out of Sunnydale for good.

About that time, he felt someone staring at him. You walk long enough on the wrong side of the law, you get a sixth sense about that kind of thing.

He whirled around, thought he saw a small, thin face staring at him from the darkness of an alley. Couldn't quite place it, but it looked familiar.

He gazed at the alley for a while. Nothing moved. He saw no face.

Just getting paranoid, he thought.

He turned his attention back to the gallery.

Decided to just go for it.

He walked across the street and pushed open the door. A little bell tinkled.

A nice-looking woman, about forty, with curly blond hair, looked up from unloading a crate of chipped clay pots and smiled at him.

"May I help you?" she asked.

"You got urns?" he replied.

Afternoon, when the shadows loom long over the chalkboard horizon.

Xander didn't know how he had gotten through this day. He was edgy, and his mood was not improved by the way he'd wasted his lunch hour driving Cordelia home. She had babbled on about a brain tumor all the way home; he had no idea what she was talking about or why she had bestowed upon him the designation of her driver. All she had done to acknowledge his presence was to say "Huh?" when he called out "You're welcome, Queen C" as he drove out of sight.

Now Xander sat across from Buffy in government, and she was not looking in the pink, either. The room was sparsely populated, with Cordy and Willow both out sick, and Oz missing. That only spurred their teacher, the unfortunately but aptly named Ms. Broadman, to make class so deadly dull that the rest of the class would think twice about showing tomorrow.

It was driving Xander nuts, and he needed three looks from Buffy, two clearings of her throat, and a partridge in a pear tree to stop drumming his fingers on his desk.

Then, blessedly, finally, the bell was just about to ring, and they could get the hell out of there.

"Now, about your tests," Ms. Broadman said. "I have some concerns, and I'd like to see the following students after class." She glanced down. "Grace Wilcox, Sarah Beck, Mallory Morel, Buffy Summers, and Xander Harris."

The bell pealed, and the rest of the class fled. Grace, Mallory, and Sarah, who usually sat in a cluster in the back and passed notes all period, hunched over nervously. Xander turned and glanced questioningly at Buffy, who shrugged.

"Since I'm involved, it can only mean one thing: we are the F-bees, and there are too many of us for the hive to feed," Buffy said.

"Thus proving that I needn't waste my time with fruitless studying, ever again," Xander said happily, although in truth, he was extremely bummed. *God, I must be a moron.* "I read those chapters so much I practically memorized them. And yet."

"And yet," Buffy said, sighing. "I, for one, did not study at all. I looked for Oz. And listened to my mom complain about the gallery."

Xander cocked his head. "Business is slow? Statues are ugly?"

Buffy shrugged. "Actually, 'half-listened' is a better term. Since it didn't involve staking a bad guy or looking for a good one, I sort of bypassed the direct feed and went for bandwidth. Summing up, she was very pissed off, but not at me." She lowered her voice. "That was all any Slayer or teenage daughter needed to know."

"Indeed," Xander said authoritatively. He started drumming his fingers on the desk. Let Broadman glare. This class period was over and he was on his own time.

After a minute or so, which stretched out into infinity, Ms. Broadman picked up a thin pile of papers and came around to the other side of her desk.

Xander felt a little sorry for her. All that stuff about a pretty face on a *zaftig* body was true. Lovely eyes, had Ms. Broadman. Nice hair, too.

But whoa, camel, attractiveness demerits for the chewed-on look: she tapped the top of the stack with short, bitten nails and bloody cuticles. This was a new habit, and it grossed Xander out big time. Cordelia, too. They had actually discussed it without sniping at each other too much. And mutually decided that someone that tightly wound needed some help.

On the other hand, maybe with all these headaches, Cordy herself needed to slow down. Or something.

Drum, drum, drum, went his fingers. *Maybe I should try out for the Dingoes as a percussionist.*

"All right." Like a doctor studying a medical chart, Ms. Broadman glanced down at the top piece of paper, lifted it, and skimmed the next page.

Xander blinked. He knew his own handwriting, and he knew a big red "A" when he saw one. Astonished, he looked over at Buffy, who was grinning back at him and giving him a thumbs-up.

"No way," he blurted.

"Way, Xand." Buffy looked very proud of him.

"Mr. Harris, I wish to show you your test paper," Ms. Broadman said, giving him her attention. She handed him the stapled pages. Sure enough, the A remained. It wasn't just some silly mirage.

"Wow." Xander blinked. "This is amazing."

Ms. Broadman inclined her head. "My thought, as well. I was extremely pleased. Until I read Julie Masterson's paper."

That was apparently the next test on the stack, which she lifted with a flourish and also handed to Xander. Julie had received an A as well.

Xander glanced at it, then at his. He waited.

Buffy waited.

The three girls in the back stayed quiet.

"Look at the first section of your test paper," Ms. Broadman suggested.

It was multiple choice.

"Read your answers."

"Um, A, B, A, A, B, C, D." Whoops, the C and D were both marked as wrong.

"Now please read Ms. Masterson's answers."

He skimmed them silently. They were exactly the same. Xander shrugged.

"A coincidence."

"Now read your first essay question, on how a bill is passed."

"Okay." He skimmed that, too. He raised his brows at Ms. Broadman. "I read the book this time. It's practically like that word for word, and—"

"No. It's not," Ms. Broadman said. "At first, I thought that as well, but I checked the book. Close, but not close enough. Much closer to Ms. Masterson's answer, in fact." She sniffed as if something smelled worse than a reanimated zombie cat. "Now, I direct your attention to the fifth question."

She made him go through the same rigmarole. His test, Julie's.

"No," Xander insisted. "It was the book."

"I think not," she said crisply, plucking the papers away from him and walking around her desk. She picked up a red pencil, flashed him a look of contempt, crossed out his A, and made another mark. She showed him the test.

An F.

"This is more in keeping, don't you think?"

"I didn't cheat off her," Xander insisted, his stomach clenching. "I don't even know her." Then, realizing how that sounded, he added loudly, "I don't cheat in class."

"No. Just outside of class." She gestured to Willow's empty seat. "Off your friends."

"Willow doesn't cheat," Xander said, his blood pressure rising. He felt hot. And sick. "She's tutored me, yes."

Ms. Broadman sneered at him. "And done your homework for you."

"And she's not here to defend herself or Xander," Buffy said.

Xander threw Buffy a grateful look. "Yeah," he said.

"The F stands," Ms. Broadman said.

Xander's mouth dropped. He couldn't believe it. The one time he tried his very hardest; the one time he succeeded beyond his wildest dreams. The unfairness of it was too much. He flared with fury, leaped out of his chair, and grabbed for his paper.

Ms. Broadman yanked it out of his reach and held it above her head with a funny little smile.

"That's my property," Xander said. Now he was livid. She was *enjoying* this. "You . . ." The word was on his tongue, and it wasn't witch.

"Xander, chill," Buffy said quietly.

He whirled around. "Back off, Buffy," he flung at her. She jerked, wide-eyed. He turned back to Ms. Broadman, narrowing his eyes at her. "Give me that paper, *now*, or I—"

She ripped the paper in two.

He stared at the pieces. His mouth worked but no words came out. He couldn't remember ever being this angry. He balled his fists; her brows raised as if to say, *Just try it*.

Without another word, Xander stormed from the room. He slammed the classroom door as hard as he could.

She will pay for this.

Oh, man, will she pay.

Chapter 4

GILES SENT BUFFY A NOTE DURING HER LAST-PERIOD class, which she had spent listening to everyone talk about Xander Harris's wigout in government. Written on an official pass request form, he requested that she come to the library immediately after school. Teachers and other faculty types could do things like that without arousing any suspicion.

Like talking to Giles right now was anywhere on her top ten. Not eager, she ducked into the rest room first and splashed some cold water on her face, then bent outside at the drinking fountain. She kept looking for Xander, wondering about the fallout, worrying about her friend. And friend he was, for which she was grateful. She didn't seem to have quite as many as she had once assumed.

She swung through the double doors to find Giles at the study table, surrounded not by towers of books about demonic possession, as she had hoped, but with his elbow on a plain manila folder. He didn't even look up when she walked over to him, even though her boots were making plenty of noise.

"Yeah," she said coldly.

"Good." His voice was distant. She was hurt; she had assumed—okay, hoped—that he wanted to apologize, and now she waited for it, making no show of hiding her anger.

But when he kept scribbling, she put her hand on the desk and said, "You asked to see me. You have seen. Are we done?"

"Sorry." Then he looked up and pushed up his glasses in his Giles way and pinched the bridge of his nose in his Giles way, and she wanted to cry or sit down or break something, preferably one of his bone china teacups. Because he talked like Giles, and he acted like Giles, but he couldn't be Giles, not if he thought she was a bloody bimbo.

"Very sorry," he added. Then he lifted his elbow off the folder and said, "I have something to show you." He hesitated, and his voice was soft. "You may want to sit down."

"On the other hand, I may not," she snapped. She realized she was being childish, but she couldn't help herself. She flipped the folder open. Then she saw, and she sank into the nearest chair.

Buffy had seen a lot of autopsy photos in her years as a Slayer. She had seen a lot of dead bodies, too. Mangled, decomposing bodies, putrefied corpses, the remains of demons so revolting that now, in the library, she couldn't make herself remember what they looked like.

But this was the worst.

"Oh, God," she whispered.

"They're looking for Mark Dellasandro."

"Why?" she croaked. "He couldn't have done this." Nothing human could have done this.

"Because a ring of his was found embedded in the . . ." He pointed. She saw the glint of metal.

He flipped to the next photo. This one showed the face.

It was Lindsey Acuff.

The room spun.

Giles inclined his head. "I'm sorry, Buffy. I know you were trying very hard to find her."

"Oh, God, *God,*" she whispered.

"This was not your fault," he said firmly.

The gentle tone of his voice startled her. It also gave her fresh hope that for some strange reason, he had been forced to say the cruel things he had said about her and her mom on the phone to England.

She glanced sideways at him. His lips were pursed together as he turned the stack of photos facedown and picked up the first of a number of what she recognized to be police reports.

"I want Willow to hack into the computer, see if there's anything missing from the autopsy report," he began. "As is often the case here in Sunnydale."

"Okay," Buffy said. "Listen, Giles, everyone's been very . . . different lately. Including, um, you."

She flushed when he frowned at her, but she wasn't about to pull punches now. The bar had been raised, if not in numbers of deaths, then in the sheer savagery of them.

She turned in her chair to gesture to the book cage, where he kept his collection of the really good stuff— leatherbound volumes on folklore and legend, ency- clopedias of demons, monster guides, that kind of thing. Also, where they locked Oz up when he turned into the star of *Teen Wolf Three: The Willow Years.*

"I'm starting to think maybe possession." She ducked her head. "Those dreams, seeing my double with the evil heart . . . that sounds like possession, doesn't it?

"So, the books," she continued eagerly, realizing she had his attention. "And the autopsy research, sure. But I think you'd better ask Willow to do it. She's not really listening much to me these days, she's cranky also. And we could ask Xand—"

"I beg your pardon?" he said finally. "Did I hear correctly? You think I'm possessed?" His eyes narrowed and his features grew hard.

Uh-oh.

"Giles, think about it," she said, squirming mentally, if not physically. "You, um, you said to your friend David that I—"

"You listened in on a private conversation?"

"See?" she cut in. "You're really pissed off at me, and you, well I do piss you off a lot, but not like this, Giles."

"I can't believe it." He whipped off his glasses and stared at her. "I know you're an unmannered girl, and I try to make allowances for it. After all, your home life has been unstable and, one must admit, you've had to spend more time learning which kind of cutlery to use to fillet a demon, not a salmon. But this is beyond the pale, Buffy. This really caps it."

"No, listen. Listen to yourself." She got out of her chair and held out her hands. "Giles, we have dead people all over Sunnydale. Parents, students, and now this little girl. That's what's important, not how rude I am and whatever you said about salmon.

"Look, I'm sorry I overheard you. You don't know how sorry," she added. "But we need to focus."

He raised his chin. "How dare you tell me how to act." He turned away from her. "I think you'd better go."

"But Giles, how you're acting is bizarre," she insisted. "And if you were yourself, you would know that."

There was a silence.

"Fine." She threw up her hands in despair. "Terrific."

She stomped out of the library and started walking home.

About halfway down the block at the beginning of Waverly Park, Xander caught up with her.

"Hey, Buffy," he said, jostling her. "What's the haps, gal toy? You look how I feel."

"Xander." She blinked at him and stopped walking. Facing him, she searched his face. "You're cheerful."

"Relax." He wrinkled his nose. "It's only temporary." Then he cocked his head and gave her a questioning look. "What's up? Because you are not cheerful."

"It's just that . . ." She thought a moment. "No. Never mind." She smiled and squared her shoulders. "Observe my cheerfulness."

"Oh." He smiled brightly. "I see. You've developed multiple personalities and you're trying to give everyone a chance to act out." He closed his eyes. "I'd like to speak to the slightly less perky one, known as Buffy."

"Buffy here," she said, as perkily as possible.

"Okay." He stared hard into her eyes. "Tell me

what the hell is going on. Because I think you know, Buffy. And I want to help."

She considered. Xander had had a flare up, but he appeared to still be Xander. She decided to level.

"Here it is. I think people are getting possessed," she said. "No one's acting like themselves."

He dropped the act. His shoulder slumped a little and he looked older. It startled her to realize he had a five o'clock shadow, just like a grown-up. Over the years, Xander had been busily turning into a man.

"Yeah, I'll say."

Yes. "So you've noticed it too?" she asked him.

He folded her arm around his. They started walking side by side. "Sure. Possessed by terror. Talk about everybody being somewhere else. Buffy, think about it. Some guy takes out his parents, then blows away half the kids on the quad. It makes for a major group wiggins. People are jittery, to say the least. So maybe the rest of us are just very, very tense."

"Tense?"

"Remember my working definition: 'Stress is when you wake up screaming and you realize you haven't fallen asleep yet.' Some people get awfully tired of murder, you know? They're just wacky that way."

She nodded slowly. "Giles just showed me some very gross autopsy pictures. Another very bad death."

"In Sunnydale. How new," Xander said. "And the winner is?"

She took a breath. "That girl I was looking for. Lindsey Acuff."

Xander was clearly shocked. "Oh, my God. She was just a little kid."

"It was horrible. It's like Jack the Ripper came to town."

"Well, I hope he stalks Broadman. And I hope he eats her liver," Xander muttered.

Buffy shook her head. "Xander, if you had seen these pictures, you wouldn't even say that." At his bruised expression, she said, "I know she was completely unfair to you. And yeah, she was enjoying lording it over you. I think you should take it up with the school board, since we already know Snyder won't back you. Rat-headed little gnome," she added bitterly.

"Oh, I'll take it up with *her*." Xander's mouth twisted. "And I'm serious, Buffy. I wish someone would take her out."

"Xander."

They walked a few more steps, during which all cheerfulness ceased and Xander looked like he wanted to bite the chain-link fence.

"You're just . . . also tense," she said quietly.

"All I've got to say is, she'd better watch her back." The muscles in Xander's arm were bunched up. Very contracted. Very battle-ready.

"Take it easy, okay?" she asked. "For me?"

Xander patted her hand. "For you, Buffy dear, the moon."

The moon.

Oz had lost track of time. He looked up, even though he could see nothing. The cage in which he was imprisoned—for cage it was, of chain link—was in a cold, wet room that smelled of mold and alcohol. It was a strange combination, and he couldn't place it. He knew nothing about where he was, who had captured him, or what they wanted.

He only knew that someone had faked that car accident. When he had slammed into the overturned vehicle, his seat belt had saved him, but given him a very nasty jolt. He passed out. For how long, he had no idea.

When he came to, he was in another van, this one speeding, and he had on a blindfold. His overdeveloped sense of smell detected a very heavy perfume odor, and as he sniffed, a woman laughed in his ear. Sharp nails ran down his neck and across his right collarbone.

The scent of blood—his—had touched the air.

"So. You're finally awake," she'd whispered. "What glorious fun we'll have."

"Um, I **need** to tell you I'm committed to somebody," he said. "So I'm not much into the dating scene."

Several other people had laughed at his remark. There had been cruelty in the sound, and anticipation, and Oz pretty much wished he had been paying better attention to the road instead of stewing about Devon and searching for the perfect background track for his own personal angst.

Not to mention that my insurance rates are going to go up.

"Moonchild, when is your transformation due?" she had asked him.

"Excuse me?" he'd tried. The hard punch to his jaw told him they already knew all about his werewolf gig. So no sense pretending otherwise.

"When is it?" she demanded.

Would they kill him before? During? After? A dozen scenarios ran through his mind.

"When is it?" she said again, bellowing in his ear.

"Excuse me, I'm a little disoriented. What day is this?"

"Friday," she'd replied.

"I've got eight days to go," he informed her.

"Oh, good. Then we can train you." She kissed him then, running her tongue down the side of his face and breathing hot, moist air in his ear. He hoped she wouldn't be offended by the fact that it wasn't doing much for him.

Sitting blindfolded in a speeding van in fear for his life tended to take all the fun out of being hit on.

"Train?" he echoed uncertainly.

"Yeah. We need to housebreak you," a man said in a very cultured British accent.

And that's all anyone had ever told him about what was going on. So far.

He knew a few things: that he was in a metal cage, much like the one in the school library. That he might be underground. It smelled earthy and dank, like the town crypts and tunnels. He also knew his captors had plans for him, and that they were very eager to set them into motion.

His world became a strange routine of dozing and waking for the arrival of food, which was some kind of gruel heavy on the carbos—brown rice or something. And pills, which at first he hid, until someone shined a flashlight on his face and said, "They're just vitamins. Take them." Then they had waited for him to put the pills in his mouth.

He had obeyed, straining to make out the features of the person behind the flashlight. But after the hours—days?—in darkness, the brightness of the beam made him squint. The identity of the figure remained a mystery, although it sounded like a young guy, maybe someone his age.

It was difficult to keep them hidden inside his upper and lower lips while he ate, but he managed. After flashlight guy left with the bowl, he spit them into his hand and crawled around his cage, trying to find a place to hide them. Eventually he'd located some dirt and rubble, and starting sticking them in there.

But now someone was coming. It was perfume woman. He heard the squeak of a door and turned to the sound, hoping that at least a crack of light would reveal his surroundings.

No luck.

She was wearing hard-soled shoes; by the click on the concrete, probably heels.

As she drew near, he tensed.

"Oz," she whispered, and he grimaced. She knew his name. He shouldn't be surprised. After all, she knew he was a werewolf. Knew he was going to be driving on Route 17.

Which no doubt meant that she knew he had a friend named Buffy, who was a Vampire Slayer.

"Oz, don't be coy," she continued, a slight edge to her voice. "I know you're awake." Then she laughed, and ice water poured down Oz's spine. It was a crazy laugh. Perfume woman was two tacos short of a combination plate.

So not good news for someone in his position.

He was about to speak when more footfalls joined perfume woman's.

"Maybe he's dead," the other voice murmured. It was the flashlight guy again. Oz frowned, trying to figure out who it was.

"Don't be stupid, Jordan. Why would he die?"

Perfume woman said angrily. "We feed him and water him regularly. Although we obviously don't bathe him." Her voice was laced with disgust. "In my day, the stock was treated much better than this."

The stock? Like livestock?

Oz did not like being the stock.

"Maybe being in captivity," the other voice—Jordan—*Jordan who?*—said. "Like a jungle animal."

"Grrrr," said perfume woman. She laughed again. Oz was not charmed.

He heard the jingle of keys, the scraping of metal on metal, and realized they were opening his cage. His heart started racing. This might be the only chance he got to escape. He had to take it, even if they punished him for it. He doubted they would kill him, at least not before they did whatever they had in store for him. And on the other hand, if what they had planned was something that made perfume woman laugh, maybe he was better off dead.

As quietly as he could, he got to his feet. Despite his current tour of duty in one Slayer's army, he hadn't mastered the art of planning escapes, and he was getting so amped he was having trouble thinking. He had to find a hole in their offensive line, get through, get out first, and, possibly, lock them in. Oh, and maybe he should knock them out.

What I wouldn't give for a Stratocaster right now. It would be a good bludgeoning tool.

"Turn on your flashlight," perfume woman said to her companion.

Yes, Oz thought, bouncing slightly on the balls of his feet.

The micro millisecond that he saw the beam, he lunged at the guy who was holding it, yanked it out of his hand, and slammed it into his face. Then he swung it around, wincing when he made contact with what had to be perfume woman's face. Someone grabbed for him; he ducked and ran through the open gate, then took the time to shut it after himself and put the pin in place. An opened padlock dangled from it. That must have been what the key was for.

He took off in a dead run, barely registering that he was in some kind of subterranean complex. There were stacks of cardboard boxes and wooden crates along the walls. Then he ducked into a tunnel carved from rock and hunched down, bulleting through as fast as he could go.

He was weak from being in the cage. *Next time I get captured—if there ever is a next time—I'll do like all the convicts do and exercise to stay in shape.*

"There he is!"

It was perfume woman, and not too far behind him. It would do no good to look over his shoulder unless he aimed the flashlight at her, and he figured there wasn't much he could do about anything she might be doing, anyway. The twisting tunnel had no other corridors; there were two ways to go, forward and backward. If he stopped running, she'd be on him. So even if she had a gun, all he could do was keep going.

As he ran, he stumbled, then realized the earthen floor beneath him was canting slightly downward. Pointing the flashlight downward, he saw a murky pool of water only seconds before he splashed into it. With a shout, he slipped down to his waist, then almost to his chest. He had the presence of mind to hold the flashlight over his head, but he realized he'd just given perfume women warning about what to expect.

He flicked off the flashlight and began to dog paddle across the pool. The cold water numbed him, and his sodden cords were like weights on his legs.

Something darted against his leg and he jerked, wanting like anything to turn the flashlight on. Instead, he swam harder.

"Okay. Pull him up," the woman shouted.

Before Oz had time to react, something enveloped him, tightened around him, and yanked him out of the water. It was a net.

Bright lights on poles flashed around him, blinding him. As he blinked and struggled, he heard the mad laughter of the woman, joined by several others.

"Not bad, for your first session," she said.

Oz shaded his eyes and squinted. "My first session?" he repeated.

"Of your training."

He saw her then, a tall figure, very muscular, with dark hair that curled and tumbled over her shoulders. She wore a dark robe that sparkled as she raised her hands and applauded him. She made a show of touching her jaw. He couldn't make out her features, but her voice was filled with amusement.

"Okay, put him back in his cage." She turned on her heel. The robe billowed around her.

Shivering, Oz clung to the ropes as slowly he was lowered toward the pool. Then a man carrying a board sauntered into Oz's line of sight. Bald, with scars extending from the center of his head down the sides, he was dressed in a sleeveless black leather jacket, black leather pants, kicker boots, and gloves. He set the end of the board at his end of the pool and let the board fall forward. It spanned the pool easily, slamming to the ground on the other side.

When the net was waist high, the man pulled a knife out of his leather pants and started cutting. His face was scarred, too, and one eye was missing.

"I'm Antonius," he said gruffly. "I'm your instructor."

"And I was hoping for the personal trainer of Brendan Fraser. Or perhaps the muscle stylings of Madonna."

Antonius grunted. "You got spunk, kid. Spunk's good. It'll help you last."

Last. Oz didn't like the notion of "lasting." It smacked of not lasting.

"I gather you've done some lasting in your day," Oz continued.

"Some." He shrugged. "Several centuries of it." Grimacing, he sawed at the net, then huffed, sheathed his knife, and grabbed a torch. He drew it across the net. The section nearest Oz sizzled and smoked. As Oz struggled, his wet clothes gave off steam and scalded his flesh. He cried out, struggling hard, managing to free himself only by grabbing the fiery sections and yanking them apart.

Shouting, he splashed back into the pool, plunging underwater. He stayed submerged, swimming as hard as he could, searching for one of the sides. This water had gotten in here somehow; maybe he could use the same pipe or hole to escape.

Whatever had darted against him before now slithered across the backs of his legs. Then it clamped hard around him and began to contract. Oz could no longer swim. He flipped over and grabbed at the creature, his fingertips making contact with a smooth, undulating mass approximately two feet wide. It was some kind of snake.

Some kind of snake with big, sharp fangs.

They sank into Oz's wrist and bit hard, nearly taking off his hand. Oz gasped in shock, inhaling water. His body contracted, struggling to expel what was so clearly not oxygen, but as there was no air to replace it, it was a useless effort.

Oz's eyes rolled back in his head. When the thing bit him again, he didn't react.

As he felt himself go flatline, he thought, *So much for lasting.*

In Sunnydale, tension became a living creature. It was a monster that searched for hosts and spun webs inside them, gluing their nerves into glommy masses of confusion and sewing their brains to the backs of their spines.

Like the water tension in a glass, where the liquid appeared to defy gravity, tension defied logic. Like the tremors preceding an earthquake, it neither created nor sought relief. The beast, tension, could shake cars apart. It could rip the soul right out of a person.

Tension grew, multiplied, and divided.

It mutated.

It spread.

It killed.

Willow sat in the glare of her computer. She had to type one-handed, but she could still manage it. She had been shot once in the side and once in her left upper arm. Her head hurt.

Her heart hurt.

She kept wondering if she had had some kind of bad dream, or if she had actually been so awful to Buffy. It seemed impossible, yet the words, the memories, lingered.

Willow reached for her chamomile tea and sipped. Then she pushed back from her computer and stood. Stretched, and winced as the stitches pulled.

She went outside and smelled the night-blooming jasmine in her yard. The Santa Ana winds had finally died down, and she was a little chilly in her sweater and corduroy overalls as she walked to the driveway and down to the sidewalk. It hurt a lot. She wasn't supposed to go out yet.

She was halfway to Hammersmith Park when she realized she was actually going to Buffy's house. To apologize.

That made her smile, and she picked up her pace, even though she was already tired. *It isn't too smart to be alone in Sunnydale at night, especially when you've recently been shot.*

The moon was hidden by clouds, but every night, it grew rounder. In two days, Oz would transform. She swallowed hard against her fears.

She crossed the street and looked up to Buffy's bedroom.

Silhouetted against the light, Buffy was sitting against Angel. Then she leaned her head against his shoulder and he stroked her back. They kissed. The kiss grew very passionate.

Willow clenched her fists. Oz was missing, by now presumed dead, and she was up there making out with her vampire boyfriend?

She was so furious she started to shake. She turned on her heel and stalked back home.

As soon as she shut the French door to her bedroom, her mother knocked on the other door.

"Willow? Do you need anything?"

"Go to hell," Willow muttered.

"What, honey? I can't hear you."

Willow sat in the darkness and seethed.

"You're losing it, Buffy," Angel said. "What's up?"

"Me?" She ran her hands through her hair. "All my friends are acting like total jerks and *I'm* losing it?"

He nodded.

She sighed. "I . . ." *I let them down, because I was with you,* she thought. "I didn't . . ."

She shook her head. "I'm fine."

He looked at her.

"Really."

Kept looking.

Helen stepped from the shadows below the home of the Slayer. She clenched her scarlet-coated fists. Tonight was a special night: they had sacrificed the eleventh human of the sacred number to satisfy the Dark Mother. Seven to go.

To commemorate the event, she had decided to go on a killing spree. A private bloodbath all her own. But now, by pure accident, she saw *this*.

A century of longing for Angelus, dreaming of him, lusting and planning to get to him, and he was in the arms of a Slayer.

She bit through her own lower lip. Tasted her own blood. She shook from head to toe. As always, betrayal stalked her. *Why did I expect anything different from him?*

She stared at him, her eyelids flickering as she remembered his caresses. What terrible thing had happened to him?

In three nights, we will kill the Slayer. Meter will protect us forever, and make us her dark gods on earth. And then, he and I will hunt together, as we once did.

She stood watching, miserable, wretched, quaking with fury.

Standing a short distance away, hidden by another tree, Julian dug his fingers into the bark and tore out huge chunks of wood as he watched Helen moon over Angelus.

She will not betray me a second time.
She will die first.

Chapter 5

DOWN IN THE BAT CAVE, JORDAN THOUGHT FROM HIS vantage point behind a large rock. A nervous wave of giddiness swept over him. He had been sent by Willy to see how the renters were doing, but how they were doing was not something Jordan might be able to explain to anyone.

Swathed in black from head to toe, Helen sat before a marble dressing table. It was covered with skulls topped with red candles. The wax as it melted looked like blood. In the distance, water trickled. Bats squeaked. Farther away, muffled sounds of construction intruded upon the stillness.

She was staring into a mirror, putting on makeup.

"How beautiful am I today?" she whispered to the mirror, uncapping a tube of lipstick. She sensuously ran it along her lips, blotted them together, and leaned toward the glass. From his vantage point, Jordan could not see her reflection. Which was fine. Because if he couldn't see her, she couldn't see him.

"Grace, how beautiful am I?" she asked, reaching for one of the skulls. She faced it toward the mirror as if allowing it to see. "He still loves me. I know he does."

She turned the skull around toward herself, took up what looked like a jeweled ice pick, and made stabbing motions at the empty eye sockets.

"He watched me kill you," she whispered. "It was . . . transcendent."

Then she brought the skull to her mouth and kissed the death's-head grin. She set it down.

"And he watched me kill *you*," she cooed. "Slowly. It took almost a week."

She laughed and wrenched the candle off the top of the skull. Turning it upside down, she jammed it into the empty cavity, carefully passing the flame all over the interior.

"Slayers last so long."

She seemed to lose interest in the skull. Setting it on her lap, she checked her lipstick in the mirror. Then she reached her hands forward and cupped another skull, which she lovingly lifted above her head.

"Demetrius," she whispered. "I never stopped loving you."

The skull raised high, she plucked another one up and brought it up to face the other.

"My darling," she moaned. "Oh, Diana . . ."

She began to moan, making a low, agonized sound that froze Jordan's blood. *This is one weird chick.*

The moan became a wail as she clutched the two skulls to her chest and rocked back and forth.

"Angelus, Angelus," she keened. "Angelus, come to me. Love me."

Footsteps sounded in the dark passageway. Jordan

flinched, terrified, but he couldn't help craning his neck to see who it was.

Julian, the blond Englishman, swept in. He was dressed in a long robe covered with a kind of rectangle of purple, and a sort of backwards headband of gold leaves in his hair. He carried the same two goblets as when Jordan had first met them.

"Julian," she cried, whirling around with the skulls in her hands. "Don't lock me up! Don't do it!"

She started shaking and sobbing. The blond man pulled her to a standing position. The skull in her lap tumbled to the ground with a thunk.

"Helen, why would I?" he asked in a silky singsong voice. "Have you done something wrong?"

"No. No," she said quickly. She was trembling.

Talk about looking guilty.

"The Watchers Council has forgotten about you," Julian went on. "No one seeks you out. By the time they realize what's going on, we'll be gods, and they won't be able to touch us."

"We need the ashes," Helen said. "We have so little time."

"We have killed eleven," Julian said, satisfied, as he took a sip. "We need seven more." He handed her a goblet. "The Slayer has six followers. I include her Watcher."

"Ah." She stared down at the goblet, obviously afraid to drink from it.

"We'll get her through them. And then we'll take her heart. Beating as we pull it from her chest." He lifted the goblet, then poured the contents on the floor—looking so very much like blood.

Uh, this is not what I signed up for, Jordan thought, wigging.

Then suddenly the dark cave flashed with light. Jordan ducked behind the rock. His heart was pounding.

"Oh, Meter, dark goddess, mother of all that is dead, our protectress," Julian called. His voice got slurry and dreamy. He sounded high.

"Mother of all that is dead, mother of dark gods," he added.

Jordan positioned himself so that he could peer into the mirror on her dressing table. He couldn't see the two people, but he did see an enormous statue of a woman with a stone table in front of it. The statue was a woman, sort of, only with her features very distorted. Her eyes were narrow and savage, and her mouth was pulled back in a grimace, her teeth sharp and pointed. She was standing on a pile of bones and skulls.

"We will bring you the ashes of your son," Julian whispered, "and the heart of the gods' champion on earth."

"We swear this," Helen added.

Jordan shook. *I can't see them. Where the hell are they?*

He crept around to the other side of the rock, knowing it was stupid, but he just couldn't help himself. *Must be those self-destructive tendencies the social workers were always talking about.*

Julian was carving her arm with a wicked-evil knife. It was bleeding badly and he was catching the blood in one of the goblets. She was gasping but clearly into it.

Whoa. Intense.

"To our mother, who reigns over the gods and goddesses of darkness," Julian said, raising the cup.

He climbed onto the statue, poured the cup into the stone mouth. The eyes appeared to widen in delight.

"Our victims suffered," the Englishman assured the goddess. "We have killed many, and we will kill more. And on your special night, we will feed you the heart of a Slayer. And we will give you the ashes of your child, Caligula. And you will live again on earth, and raise us up."

"Raise us up," the Queen intoned.

"And we shall be as gods," Julian whispered. "And no one will be able to stop us."

From his hiding place, Jordan watched and thought, *Holy moly.*

The rich really are different.

Eight days had passed since Oz had gone missing. Tonight was the first night of his werewolf phase.

Buffy had failed.

She was due to meet Xander at the Bronze at eight. She had asked Angel to show, too, in hopes that the three of them could put their heads together and see what they came up with.

Then the phone rang as she was dressing.

Giles said, in his old Giles voice, "Buffy, something's come up. A vigilante group has gone after Mark Dellasandro. Apparently he was spotted in the vicinity of the reservoir."

Buffy was half-dressed in a long gray skirt and a T-slip top, the right shoe of a pair of black heels in one hand, the left shoe of some chunky platforms in the other.

"I think you should go there. Protect him. They're screaming for his blood."

She dropped the unwanted shoe. "Giles," she said

mournfully, "we have police here in Sunnydale. And I'm Bronze-bound."

There was silence. Then Giles said, in an even, flat voice, "Oh, I do beg your pardon. I had no idea you were off to have fun while a boy is being hunted like an animal and Oz is still missing. Give my regards to Angel, won't you? When you join him on the dance floor."

"Hey," she shouted. "Not fair!"

"Is it? I do apologize, Buffy. For ever thinking you were anything *but* a bimbo."

"Giles!"

She was shouting at the dial tone. She started to speed-dial his number, then threw the cordless onto her bed. She changed into more slayage-friendly clothes—good old sweats, a jacket, how charming—and picked up her bag.

It was only nine P.M., but the Bronze was packed. People half-danced, half-groused to Dead Buttercups, a band whose previous claim to fame was that they played Wednesday nights at the Bronze. Hump night—Wednesday—was not a primo spot, but it was certainly better than Monday or Tuesday. It was kind of a B minus on the bell curve of the week. Same with Dead Buttercups—okay band, nothing special. Not even an A for effort.

The espresso machine was practically smoking, it was being worked so hard. The people who could drink alcohol were chugging shooters and expensive imported beer. Claire Bellamy and Nick Daniels, the manager and assistant manager of the Bronze, should have been happy. But they were pissy and bossy and unfairly kicking kids out for no good reason than that they felt like it.

The Bronze was no different than the rest of Sunnydale. High-voltage tension was like a disease, very contagious, and spreading.

"A mass hysteria. Like when people actually thought the Spice Girls were cool," Xander suggested. "Only, I never did."

"Huh," Willow said. Her bandaged arm was in a sling and her chest still hurt her a lot. "I know you took their CD cover into the bath—"

"Will, head out of the gutter," Xander chided, feeling himself flush. "I most certainly did not."

Xander let his gaze wander to the entrance to the Bronze. If Willow knew he had suggested she show so that she and Buffy could make up, she'd probably crush his spine, the mood she was in.

Of course, he was not in a much better mood.

In fact, he wanted to punch someone—anyone—out. Preferably Broadman, who had not backed down in a week, and was not allowing him in her classroom, which was going to get him expelled. Xander had stopped in today to talk to the vice-principal, Mr. Osborne. The VP had suggested he move up the chain of command. Which meant Snyder. Which meant, why bother?

So Xander had gone back to Broadman this afternoon, and she had not budged.

"You must realize that your actions result in consequences," she'd said to him.

Xander had glared at her. "You, too."

She raised one eyebrow, like that strange woman with all the makeup on *Drew Carey,* and said, with no small amount of taunting, "Mr. Harris, are you threatening me?"

"I'll ask you the same question," he'd replied. "Why are you doing this to me? What pleasure can it possibly give you?"

"I've never liked you," she said. "Your brother was a screwup and you're just like him. As far as I'm concerned, the sooner you Harrises are out of the school system, the better."

"Oh, and you're going to help speed things up." Xander took a step toward her, and she smiled.

"I should warn you, I know how to take care of myself."

"Yeah, *broad man,* that figures. No one else would want to."

Xander was sorry he'd said that as soon as it came out. It was the kind of stupid, juvenile thing that was sure to end up in some report that she made, some kind of "WARNING, PROBLEM STUDENT ARMED AND DANGEROUS, SHOOT TO KILL" label to add to the labels that were already plastered all over his permanent record: "CHRONIC UNDER-ACHIEVER, THINKS HE'S A COMEDIAN, OFTEN TRUANT, FREQUENTLY TARDY." And so on, and so on, and so on.

He expected some kind of snotty reply, but instead, Ms. Broadman made a fist and slammed it down on her desk. She hit the end of a pencil, which went flying à la David Letterman, and ended up clattering in front of the doorway.

And in the doorway, Vice-Principal Osborne stood, observing the entire thing.

"You know, Mr. Harris," Mr. Osborne said, "I was actually coming here to appeal to Ms. Broadman and ask her to give you a second chance. But now I want to kick your butt, you smarmy little cretin."

"What?" Xander stared at the man, who, he had thought, was actually a fairly civilized human being. He dressed friendly, in Dockers and sweaters, a sort of throwback to Principal Flutie, who had thought school was about sharing your feelings and developing self-esteem, and who had been eaten by some kids at school possessed by hyenas.

Maybe this was all part two of that creature feature.

Xander blurted, "Stop. We're all under some kind of influence."

"Really." Ms. Broadman pulled back her lips in a nightmare smile. "I'll have to add that to the report. What exactly are you on, Xander?"

"No, I don't mean it like that," he said anxiously. Then he realized that, just like always, justice was not going to be served at Sunnydale High. Pre-Slayer, it had been just as bad, only without monsters and demons. Of a supernatural sort. That he had known about.

"I'm not on anything." He looked at the VP. "I don't want to kick butts." He pointed at his teacher. His hand was shaking. "What she's doing to me is wrong."

"Oh, I think she's got the right idea," the man said, coming at Xander. "If it entails doing you bodily harm."

Mrs. Broadman grabbed his arms from behind just as the man made a fist.

"Hey!" Xander shouted. Then he pulled a Slayer maneuver, dropping to his knees and contracting into a ball. Ms. Broadman flopped over his shoulders and collided with Osborne, who had been just about to punch Xander in the stomach.

Xander pushed himself away from the tangle and darted around the sprawling grown-ups, slamming the door shut after him. He ran down the hall, imagining all the awful things he could do to both of them. Thing was, they were pretty awful. Gut-wrenchingly gross, in fact.

Yoikes. Buffy's right, he thought, as he lost his balance and fell on his butt. *We're all getting possessed.*

Some tall red-haired guy had called out, "Way to go, Harris."

Xander had bitten back a furious retort, held on as his brain unreeled a plan to slit the throat of the red-haired guy. Or torture him as slowly as possible.

Buffy was so very right. By what or who they were getting possessed, he didn't know. But he did know he wasn't himself.

Not himself by a long shot.

Now, four hours later, as he stood beside Willow at the Bronze, he realized his best ol' buddy was talking to him. Or at him.

"She's always been so selfish," she was mumbling. "Oh, sure, she acts all sad and tragic to get our sympathy, but she doesn't care about us. She just got us to like her so we'd help her. She doesn't even care if we die, except there'll be fewer of us to help her out."

Xander blinked. "Willow?"

Willow frowned up at him. "She hasn't been looking for Oz at all. She just makes out with Angel. She's risking sending us all to Hell by being with him, but she doesn't care."

"Willow, listen, I've got it," Xander said suddenly, finally riffing off something Buffy had said. "Jack the Ripper, yes, only it's like that Classic Trek episode." He took her by the shoulders and gazed hard into her eyes. "Some kind of evil entity is inside us, making us all kind of, well, bitchy at least."

"I'm not bitchy," Willow snapped. "I'm fine."

"No, Rosenberg," he said. "Uh-uh. You most certainly are not."

"What would you know about it?" she said. Then she reached out and shoved him. "You've dated the Wicked Witch of the West."

"Willow." His temper rose. "Willow, take it easy." His hand made a fist. Willow saw it and sneered at him.

"You'll never hit me. You're not man enough."

Xander felt his anger grow "Willow, stop. Just stop."

She narrowed her eyes at him. *"Wimp. Loser."*

That did it. Before he realized what was happening, he threw back his hand and slapped her.

"Oh, my God," he whispered as she blinked in astonishment. "Willow, I'm sorry. Will—"

"You will pay," she bit off, turning her back. Then she yelled, "Hey! Who wants to make twenty bucks easy? I need someone to kick Xander Harris's butt."

Angel stood just inside the main entrance of the Bronze and shook his head. *This place is a pressure cooker.*

In the alley, he had stopped no fewer than three fights. Not so much because he was a nice guy, but because the alley was too narrow to go around them.

In the corner of the Bronze by the coffee machine, two girls were screaming at each other. The thrash of the band was covering their words, but if looks could kill, they'd both be history. To Angel's immediate left, a skirmish had broken out on the dance floor, and the assistant manager looked to be on the verge of joining in instead of stopping it.

There was something going on, and it was more than a group bad mood. Angel didn't know what it was, but he did know he had to help put a stop to it. But the answer wasn't stomping on a few loose sparks such as some back-alley brawls. Someone had to find the fire and completely extinguish it.

"Hey. Dead Boy." Xander tapped him on the shoulder.

"Xander," Angel said tiredly. Xander knew how much the nickname bothered him, and used it at every opportunity. Sure, Xander liked to riff off people with his sharp wit—proving what Angel would have assumed was obvious to everybody, but apparently wasn't, that Xander had keen native intelligence.

But in Angel's case, there was a whole lot of hostility accompanying the barbs Xander aimed his way. At first, it had been caused by Xander's pure, unadulterated jealousy as Buffy fell in love with Angel. Then, after Angel had lost his soul and tried to take them all out, Xander alone had opposed the idea of trying to reverse the curse and restore him.

"Where's your squeeze? Your babe? Your honey?" Xander asked snidely.

"Sorry?" Angel asked, frowning. The guy was out of control. His forehead was beaded in sweat and he was pale and trembling. His eyes were darting back and forth, the pupils mere pinpricks. "Xander, are you on something?"

Xander rammed his right fist into his left palm. "Why does everybody keep *asking* me that? Man, that frosts me!"

"Easy," Angel said, holding out his hands. "You just seem . . . a little on edge."

Xander clenched his jaw. "Maybe that's because your trashy little girlfriend was supposed to meet us here over an hour ago.

"Stood us both up. Willow's right."

He jerked his head backward. Angel followed the direction. Willow sat on a stool, a pile of shredded Styrofoam cups in front of her. As Angel watched, she picked up another one and punched holes in it with her fingertips.

"Willow's right?" Angel repeated carefully.

"Yeah. Buffy doesn't really care about us. We're just some stupid Slayer groupies she keeps around in case of emergency. We're pawns she'd sacrifice in a second if it kept her alive for two."

"Xander, that's not true, and you know it," Angel said, cocking his head and studying the guy who had risked his life time and time again for Buffy. And for whom Buffy had nearly died at least a dozen times. "You two . . . all of you. You're special to her."

"Mmm-hmm, right." Now Xander began ramming his fist into his palm again. "So special she lets *you* hang around, even though it might cost you your soul.

"Face it, *Angelus*. She's just using you, too."

Angel was taken aback by the hatred in Xander's tone. He knew they all still had a problem with him, Xander especially, because Xander loved Buffy, as he, Angel, did.

Angel had a complicated past, to say the least. An Irish wastrel changed in 1753 by his sire, Darla, he had become the vampire Angelus, the One with the Angelic Face, and the terror of all Europe. He killed his own family. He drove a beautiful, innocent girl named Drusilla mad by killing everyone she loved as well, then changed her into a vampire when she hid from him in a convent.

Then he had killed a Kalderash Gypsy girl, and her clan had exacted a cruel revenge: they gave him back his soul. As soon as their curse took effect, Angel, still a vampire, remembered every terrible thing he had done as Angelus. Every cruelty he had committed. Every innocent he had slaughtered. The vampires he had created, and loosed upon the world.

And then, not knowing the rest of the curse, he had allowed himself to fall in love with Buffy. On the night of her seventeenth birthday, she had given herself to him with love, in a sweet, blissful moment free of torment—a moment when he did not suffer, did not feel he would be forever unlovable. Because of that moment, his soul had been taken from him once more.

And if he ever knew that joy again, he would lose his soul again.

"Xander," he said quietly, "did you call her house?"

"No answer. Left a message."

"Has it occurred to you that Buffy might not have shown because she's in trouble?"

"Ya think?" Xander retorted, pretending to consider. He tapped his chin. "Naw. She probably just forgot."

"Xander." Angel sighed. "Listen to yourself. Something's going on."

"What do *you* want?" Willow demanded, coming up to the two of them.

"Willow." Angel looked from her to Xander and back again. Her features were set and hard. She looked almost evil. If he didn't know better, he would think she had been cursed, her soul removed, a demon inhabiting her body.

On the other hand, he didn't know better.

Without a word, he turned.

"Hey, Dead Boy, where you going?" Xander called after him. "Stay and have a pint of O-positive with us. We're *dying* to spend some quality time with you."

Angel crossed to the pay phone by the bathrooms.

"Hey! I'm talking to you!" Xander bellowed. "Turn around when I'm talking to you!"

Not himself, Angel reminded himself, dialing Buffy's house.

No answer.

Angel hung up and looked around the room, not at all happy with what he saw.

As before, Jordan pushed against the lower left window of the Sunnydale Art Gallery. As before, it didn't budge, so he wrapped his jacket around his gloved fist and punched it.

This time, no alarm went off.

He nodded. Willy had done good, locating someone to disconnect the system. Jordan was only sorry he hadn't gone to the cheeseball before. It had taken a while for it to occur to him.

Thing was, he was forgetful lately. In fact, he was having these blackouts. Hours—chunks of them—were missing from his memory. He woke up with dirt on his clothes. Okay, and blood. The ring Brian Dellasandro had given him in partial payment for the "potion" was gone, too. Now that he knew his very dangerous and very psycho new friends were into all kinds of drugs, he figured they'd been giving him something. Figured he was in big trouble.

Figured the only way to save his own life was to do exactly what they wanted until he could clear out.

He crept into the art gallery and walked right over to the case where the attractive blond woman had shown him the "Greco-Roman Urn," as she had called it. It was the only one in the place, so he figured it had to be the one. About six inches tall, it was shaped kind of like a Chianti wine bottle, only made of brownish-red pottery, with curved black handles on either side and black figures on it. The figures were not so nice—demons chowing down on people, animals devouring each other. Just the kind of thing to float Helen and Julian's boat.

There was a heavily sealed stopper on top, some kind of disk covered with what might be wax. The woman had explained that they'd been afraid to open the urn for fear it might break. No problemo. He didn't want to break it, either.

He took a couple shiny necklaces and knocked some stuff over, so it wouldn't be obvious what the thief had been after. With one more quick glance around in case there was something else worth stealing, he tiptoed back across the room and climbed out the window.

He was just about to saunter casually over to his car when Mark Dellasandro ran up to him.

"This is for Brian!" the kid shouted. Then he hit him with a crowbar.

Jordan Smyth—with a Y—went down for the count.

* * *

The werewolf threw back its head and howled as Julian checked its paw. It was chained to the floor. The water serpent had bitten it hard, but Julian's healing skills had once again proved excellent.

"Can he fight?" Helen asked. "Or should we kill him now?"

"He can fight," Julian answered. "He'll die a glorious death."

Chapter 6

Jordan was so afraid he thought he was going to throw up. Beside him, Willy the Snitch didn't look much better off.

They were in the underground cave-rooms beneath the Alibi, facing the music. Helen and Julian were extremely pissed off. At Jordan. *So* not something he wanted to happen.

After he came to outside the art gallery, his first thought was to get the hell out of Sunnydale. But a black van was parked at the curb and some very creepy guys were walking up to him. They asked for the urn. He told them what had happened. And they'd loaded him in the van, where Willy was already sweating.

Then they'd come here, driving through a Sunnydale Jordan did not recognize. Massive amounts of road rage. People fighting in the middle of the street. *It has to have something to do with these guys and their Dark Mother,* he'd thought.

"You let someone steal the Urn of Caligula," Julian hissed at him. "Right out from under you."

"It was a kid named Mark Dellasandro," he said. "I saw him."

"And why would he do that?" Julian grabbed Jordan by the hair, exposing his neck. Then he changed into something that made Jordan wet his pants, literally. A monster. A demon, with gold eyes and long, sharp teeth.

He hissed again and lowered fangs to Jordan's neck, letting them prick Jordan's skin.

Jordan couldn't even scream.

"What have you been up to?" the creature said in a low dangerous voice.

"Nothing," Jordan said. "Honest."

"Find it. Bring it back."

The monster let go of him. Then he casually walked over to a lumpy blanket on the floor. He pulled back the blanket. It was a young girl, bound and gagged.

"If you don't, this will happen to you," the creature said softly.

As he watched, Jordan found he could scream after all.

He just didn't think he would ever be able to stop.

The Sunnydale Reservoir was actually an ancient lake, formed from the collapsed cone of a volcano. The Spanish explorers called it Lago del Infierno, or Lake of Hell, and claimed that when they first set eyes upon it, it was burning, with flames shooting "tens of miles into the sky, as if to scorch the wings of the angels themselves."

Through the centuries, there had been numerous sightings not only of "Sunni," the sea monster that was supposed to inhabit it, but of scores of other demons and monsters. Giles had a theory that the lake and its volcanic ancestor were the remnants of an earlier Hellmouth and that somehow, this portal into Hell itself had been closed or deactivated and the new one opened. He spent the occasional hour researching Lago del Infierno in hopes of closing the existing Hellmouth in the same way.

In the valley below, there were tangerine and avocado groves, and grazing lands for cows and sheep. The farmers who owned the groves, cows, and sheep complained that the dam built on the southern rim of the lake was unsafe. In fact, a number of sizable cracks had been patched in the concrete in the fifties, and could be seen from Route 17, which was a distance away.

But nothing ever came of their complaints. The dam stood.

What nobody seemed to know was that the dam leaked. In fact, water trickled through gashes at the base of the dam at a fairly good clip. It should have been measurable. It probably was. And the proper authorities bought off, no doubt. Or threatened into silence . . .

Mark Dellasandro, cowering in the manzanita bushes that were flourishing in the runoff at the base, knew he should tell someone about the leaks. They were pretty bad. If the dam burst, the valley would be flooded. People would die.

But he couldn't tell anybody. There were people all over the reservoir calling his name, searching for him, promising that when they found him, they were going to make him pay for a murder he hadn't committed.

Tears ran down his cheeks as he huddled, completely alone, totally without friends. Brian had always looked out for him, taken care of him. You had a brother like that, you had gold. And now Brian was in a coma, and their parents were dead, and oh, God, this had to be a nightmare. It couldn't be real. He was going to wake up and discover it had all been a terrible dream.

Only it is real, he told himself. *And no one is going to bail you out. These people want to kill you.*

Maybe they should *kill you.*

Maybe you deserve it . . .

"I think I see him!" someone shouted, and Mark cringed, trying to make himself smaller among the scratchy bushes.

"Brian, help," he whispered. "Someone, anyone, help."

Then the skies opened up and it began to rain. Clouds rushed in over the moon, cloaking Mark in blessed darkness.

The rain fell in heavy, cold sheets. Mark couldn't even see his hands clasped around his knees. He allowed himself one deep, ragged sigh. For the moment, he was safe.

He pulled out the little pottery bottle and examined it.

Buffy finally got to the reservoir just as the rain started. The place was swarming with big, burly, off-duty police officers and Sunnydale High football players. So many big guys to catch one little guy. Buffy pitied Mark Dellasandro. Unless he had done what he was accused of.

Then she pitied his soul.

She knew what Hell was like.

"You, there, girl!" someone yelled at her. A yellow flashlight beam strobed through the rain and a chubby man in a raincoat stenciled *Bitterman* said, "Raincoats and weapons are being issued in the shed."

Weapons?

Buffy said, "Thanks. Where's the shed?"

"Back the way you came," the voice said.

That she doubted, since she had snuck like Rambo down the hillside, staring down at the reservoir before she had approached. But she nodded at the man named Bitterman and pretended to head off in a new direction.

Instead, she darted into the closest building to get out of the rain while she tried to figure out what to do next.

It was the bathroom. There were some splatters on the concrete around the base of the stainless steel sink. In the dim light, they looked like brown paint.

Or dried blood, Buffy thought, bending down.

"Look! There he is!" someone shouted outside.

Uh-oh. Buffy straightened and dashed back outside.

The crowd was stampeding toward the dam. Buffy was caught up in the crowd. There must have been two hundred people, cold, white-blue lightning lighting up the eagerness on their faces.

Bloodlust, Buffy thought with a shiver. She had seen it on the faces of demons and vampires; once raised, they would do anything to slake it. She had seen vampires so thirsty they had impaled themselves trying to get to her. Starving demons who must have known, somehow, that attacking a Slayer was not the ticket to long life, but who couldn't help themselves as they charged her.

Now she had seen it on the faces of human beings. It made monsters of them all.

A man rammed into her from the side, raised his brows, and said to her, "I've got a rope. We find that kid, he's dead."

"We should call the police," Buffy insisted.

He grinned at her. "Honey, I *am* the police. I'm a detective with the Sunnydale Police Department. We're all here."

The whole town's gone crazy, Buffy thought. *It's finally happened. And there's nothing I can do about it.*

"Then you know about being innocent until proven guilty," Buffy insisted.

He winked at her. "That's one for the civics books."

It was almost ten, according to the clock on the wall over the Bronze's pool table. Angel stood.

"I'm going to look for Buffy," he said.

He was at the exit to the Bronze when the manager, Nick Daniels, said to his assistant, Claire Bellamy, "Jack just called. Mark Dellasandro's been spotted at the reservoir. There's a lynch mob after him."

Angel smiled grimly. He knew exactly where Buffy was.

He hurried into the night, his black duster trailing behind him like the wings of a giant, ebony bat.

"Wow," Cordelia breathed, as she walked into the Bronze. She stood at the doorway, surveying the scene, and froze in utter shock.

On the stage, the band was destroying their instruments. There were at least half a dozen fights going on, and the air was filled with the crash of breaking glass. The floor was littered with smashed coffee cups, and dotted with blood.

About ten feet away from her, there was a guy on the floor. Someone was straddling him with one fist raised.

It was Xander.

She grabbed his fist and held it. "What are you doing?" she demanded, then looked down at the guy on the floor. It was Luke Engstrom, the Razorbacks' place kicker. "Oh, my God, Xander, don't hurt him! We need him for the playoffs."

Xander whirled around and said, "Hey, let go of me." His face stayed hard, angry, cruel.

"I'll teach you to mess with my teammate," someone yelled, then barreled toward Xander. It was Chess Wiater, one of Sunnydale High's running backs.

Then Wiater slammed into Cordelia and sent her sprawling.

For a few moments she saw red dots. And then she saw stars.

"Hey," Xander protested, as shadows moved around him. The room spun as the rage inside him wound down like a worn-out battery. He smelled something spicy. Flowery.

"Relax. I'm an off-duty nurse," said a woman's deep, throaty voice next to his ear. "I'll take care of you. You need immediate medical attention. Inhale again."

"Cordelia," he managed, as the scent filled his nose once more.

"Taken care of," she assured him.

* * *

It wasn't exactly a crowd that gathered. Willow wasn't even certain that gathering had much to do with it; more like the craziness that was overtaking the Bronze was swallowing them up.

But she was more than up to the task. The nearness of so many sweating bodies irritated her and she elbowed her way through them, giving anybody who didn't move fast enough a sharp jab.

Then she ran into a hard chest, and something spilled on her, a red-colored drink that smelled like a garden. "Hey," she growled, and looked up.

The owner was one of the most incredible-looking guys she had ever seen. He was at least as old as Angel—well, as Angel in people years, not vampire years—but where Angel was tall, dark, and handsome, this man was honey blond, with a trim beard that was not exactly a goatee, and his eyes were a very interesting green. He was grinning down at her in a pleasant, easy way.

"I beg your pardon," he said. He had a British accent like Giles. He wore a black leather jacket, leather pants, and a white T-shirt.

"Hey," she said, flustered, and as she stared up at him, then glanced down at the blossom of red on her sweater, her bad mood seemed to dissipate. She blinked, feeling refreshed, as if she had just awakened from a nice, long nap.

"Your friend appears to have been hurt," he said, moving aside to reveal Xander sprawled out on the floor. His eyes were closed.

"Xander!" she cried, diving to his side.

"I'm a trained medical professional," the man offered. "I can take care of him."

Willow shook her head. "Um, sorry, but, well,

Xander is no stranger to the hospital." She twisted her hands and looked around for a familiar face.

"I can treat him."

"No," Willow said, crinkling her forehead and putting on her resolve face.

The man raised an eyebrow. "You're a feisty little thing, aren't you? I'm most impressed. You'll do well."

"Something wrong?" Nick Daniels stood beside Willow and faced the man.

"I'm just trying to help. That young man launched himself at this young man." He pointed to Chess Wiater, who was sitting crosslegged on the floor and groaning.

"Damn kids," Daniels muttered. He turned to Willow. "Go tell Claire to call the police. I'll see what's going on here."

Willow hesitated. She didn't want to leave Xander. On the other hand, she didn't want Nick to take his protective presence away from Xander.

Then Xander groaned and rolled over. Willow moved away from both men.

"Will," he groaned, then inhaled sharply. "You smell really weird."

"Gee, thanks." She touched his forehead. "Are you okay?"

"I just need to make the Tweety Birds stop flying around my head."

"Let me help you up." She put her hand under his elbow.

"Ooh." Xander cupped the back of his head. "Gee, d'you think if I sue Wiater, I'll have enough money for college?" He looked around. "Where's Cordelia?"

Willow blinked. "She was with you?"

"Uh-huh. Just walked in." He looked at the other kids, some of whom were melting away from the scene now that the excitement was over. "Any of you guys see Cordelia Chase?" Others still appeared to be anxious to create even more excitement, eager to trash the place.

"She went with those people." A girl with braces and a long, dark braid down her back pointed toward the exit.

"'Those people'?" Xander echoed, looking at the entrance.

"The blond man. And a dark-haired woman," the girl said.

Xander looked at Willow. Her lips parted. "That English guy. He said he was a doctor." She frowned. "No, he didn't say that. He said he was a trained professional."

"We're going," Xander announced, taking her hand.

She chewed her lower lip as she let him lead her out the door. "And he said I'd do well."

Together they ran out the front door, just in time to see a black van speed away like a shiny predator beneath the streetlights.

"Hey!" Xander shouted, waving at the car. He tugged the arm of the nearest bystander, a short, runty guy he'd seen before, in detention. "Was there a girl, she's a really beauti—"

"Watch who you're punching, jerk!" the short guy yelled, and punched Xander in the stomach.

Xander doubled over and retched. Willow held his shoulders and stared after the car. She was trying to memorize the license plate.

But there was no license plate.

"Buffy," Xander said. "We have to get to Buffy asap."

Cordelia smelled flowers all around her. Part of her muzzily imagined she was having a wonderful dream. Flowers, and candlelight. Lots of candlelight. And straw.

Wet, stinky straw.

That she was lying on.

She realized then that her eyes were open, and she was staring at a lovely silver candelabra flickering with long, white tapers. She lay sprawled on her stomach on lumpy, damp straw.

As she blinked, a shadow crossed into her field of vision and stared down at her. Cordelia ticked her gaze upward. It was a vampire. She was a woman, dressed in flowing black, with long, shiny black hair.

"Ah, you're back."

"Back," Cordelia echoed, horribly confused. Her head was throbbing and her mouth was dry.

"Back among the living. For now," she told Cordelia. Her laughter was rich and she smelled of a very strong, spicy perfume.

"What do you want? Where am I?" She tried to sit up, but her head hurt too badly.

"You're in our court," the vampire announced.

Then, with a wave of her hand, she made a sweeping gesture and took a step to the side.

Cordelia's mouth dropped open. She and the woman vampire were in some kind of circular arena. There was a waist-high stone wall surrounding the area, all carved and elaborate. But she didn't have time to look at that, not right now.

Because beyond the wall, in semicircles of stone

bleachers, vampires and demons sat and watched her. Some were dressed like they were going to a toga party, while others wore clothes from other time periods—velvets and laces and even a few really hideous disco outfits. There was a demonic creature, mostly sores and fangs, in a brown leisure suit. Other monsters were completely naked, and while she had seen a lot of very gross creatures, most of them were even grosser.

There must have been at least fifty of them, and when they saw her looking up at them, they cheered.

"I win!" someone called out. "Two hours and twelve minutes!"

The others groaned. A couple of them fished wallets out of their clothes and began to count out bills. Money started trading hands all over the arena. Cordelia was dumbfounded.

"They bet on how long you would be unconscious," the vampire told her. "They bet on everything. It passes the time." She chuckled. "They get bored so easily. They require constant entertainment. But it keeps them from scheming too much.

"That was something we learned in the glory that was Rome."

Standing at the top of the rings of seats was an extremely attractive blond man. He was dressed in a black leather jacket, black pants, and a white T-shirt.

"He was at the Bronze," Cordelia murmured.

"Yes, we both were," the vampire told her. She leaned over Cordelia and ran a sharp fingernail down her cheek. "Pity. You're so lovely."

"Don't touch me," Cordelia shot at her, but inside she was shaking, *Pity? Why is it a pity?*

"Where's Xander?" she demanded.

"He got away," the vampire told her sorrowfully. Then she smiled. "But don't worry. We'll get him." She looked up at the blond man. "Won't we, Julian?"

"Yes, of course," the man answered.

Cordelia looked up at him and caught her breath. He was in full vamp face. Which might mean he was planning to feed.

Which might explain why it's such a pity that I'm so lovely.

"Listen, you guys, you'd better let me go," Cordelia said, her voice catching. "I'm a friend of the Slayer, you know what a Slayer is?"

A creature covered with yellow scales and some kind of reddish-brown calluses covered its enormous mouth with one of its claws and guffawed. Some of the other monsters and vampires stopped handing each other money long enough to laugh. One applauded. Something that looked like two worms tied together turned and looked up at the vampire named Julian.

"Oh, we know very well what a Slayer is," he answered. "And we're delighted that another of her friends has joined us."

"Another," Cordelia said slowly. Uneasily.

Julian raised his hands and clapped them as if he were summoning a servant.

To the far right, there was a crashing sound, and then a howl. Cordelia jerked and covered her mouth, staring wide-eyed in the direction. Most of the others craned their necks, obviously eager to catch a glimpse of what was going on.

Then a metal door swung slowly open, and a towering, slathering werewolf charged into the arena.

Chapter 7

Buffy MANAGED TO PUSH HER WAY THROUGH THE crowd at the reservoir. She was cold, filthy, wet, and in a very bad mood as she caught hold of some manzanita bushes and kept herself upright as she half-slid, half-ran to the southern side of the dam. She flicked on her flashlight, to discover a set of concrete steps angled down and around the side, barred by a padlocked gate.

With one quick upswing of her hand, Buffy snapped the padlock. She pulled open the gate and hunkered down on the other side, deftly shutting it behind her. She flicked off her flashlight. No one else seemed to have realized this quick route to the base of the dam was here. Though she was, for the moment, hidden in darkness, the next flash of lighting might reveal her or the stairs.

She had no idea if Mark Dellasandro really was down there, but she knew she had to get to Mark first, or he'd be a dead man.

A dead boy, she corrected herself. *He's just a kid.*

She reached the base of the stairs. Stretching before her was a sort of catwalk that didn't take her all the way down to the very bottom of the dam. There was only one way to go down that far, which was to jump off the catwalk.

She landed hard but she didn't take time to see if she was injured. Instead, she crouched low and began to crabwalk along. Water was pouring on her; she held up a hand to the rain and realized it was coming from another source. She felt for her flashlight. She'd lost it in the jump.

She glanced over her left shoulder. The next lightning flash revealed leaks in the dam. She caught her breath at the size of them.

She kept moving, and finally dared to call softly, "Mark? It's a friend. Please. Trust me. I'm here to help you."

She thought she heard a rustle in the bushes, but with the yelling above her and the hard rain, she couldn't be sure.

"Look over here! Stairs!" someone shouted.

Buffy sighed. Soon they'd all be down here.

"Mark," she said desperately. "Show yourself. It's your only chance."

She heard a whimper, and dove directly into a stand of manzanita. The branches whipped her face and the backs of her hands.

But she touched human skin on the other side, and grabbed hard before he had a chance to change his mind and dart away.

"No," he said, terrified.

"I'm Buffy," she replied, crashing painfully through the bushes. "Buffy Summers. I'm going to help you."

Above her, moving with the crowd, Angel faded into the shadows and started a tortuous race down into the valley by hanging on to bushes and sliding in the mud, avoiding the stairs and the deranged people who clambered down them.

Hold on, Buffy, he thought anxiously. Which she would do.

She was the Slayer.

Xander and Willow sat knee-to-knee in the semi while the trucker told them about his run from Boston to St. Louis, then out to Bishop and now down to Sunnydale. Like everybody else, they'd heard about the mob up at the reservoir. It sounded like a good place to find Buffy, so they'd hitched a ride. Both Xander and Willow had hesitated when the truck had pulled over, but beggars couldn't be too choosy.

So far, the man had talked and talked while the two of them pretended to listen. They were trying to scan the landscape, but the rain was coming down so hard it was a futile effort.

"Weird place, Sunnydale. You ever seen marsh gas? You got your marsh gas here in Sunnydale. Also, your close encounters." He looked hard at Xander. "You know what I'm talking about, son?"

Xander swallowed, hoping this wasn't some kind of prison secret code for anything to do with him and Mr. Sixteen Wheeler. He said carefully, "Like Scully and Mulder?"

"We were them for Halloween one year," Willow told the man.

"X-Files." The man nodded. "It's all true." He added a stick of gum to the enormous wad in his mouth. He had at least five sticks in there that Xander knew of. "I've driven from one side of America to the other. No other place as weird as Sunnydale." He picked up his megapack of Juicyfruit. "Gum?"

"Thanks," Willow said, taking a stick. She offered one to Xander.

"Trying to quit," he said. He put his hand on Willow's arm and whispered, "Are you noticing what I'm noticing? That even though we're really in a mess, we're not so wound up about it? Like we were in the Bronze?"

"Yeah. And other times."

The bright lights on the truck's instrument panel caught the red highlights in her hair just so. Will, his Will. How could he ever have been short with her? Cruel to her?

"I think it's what Buffy said. I think we were possessed," Xander added. "And somehow we've gotten depossessed."

He put his hand on hers. "I'm sorry, Willow."

She gave his hand a squeeze. "Me, too, Xander."

"Okay, so friends again." *Or whatever it is we are anymore.*

"And, speaking of weird stuff," Xander said, raising his voice to include the trucker in the conversation, "what have you seen weird lately? Here, I mean. In Sunnydale?" He scratched his cheek. "Like, ah, weird black vans without license plates? Or—"

Static pffted the conversation. The trucker picked up a set of earphones complete with a curved mike— kind of a rock star look for him—and said, "Yeah, Big J, c'mon?"

He cocked his head, listening.

"That's a big ten-four."

After a few more sentences, the trucker hung up. He turned to Willow and Xander and said, "You guys had some murders recently?"

"We always have murders," Willow blurted, then quickly said, "Yes. There was a guy who killed his parents and also some kids at school. And then more people were found dead, and—"

"We don't want to bore the nice man," Xander interrupted.

"So you're joining the crowd at the reservoir."

"Um, possibly," Xander said carefully. "And you?"

The man clenched his teeth and shook his head with obvious regret. "Boy, I got me a shotgun in the back needs some use, but I've got a schedule to meet. I'm hauling carcasses and even though I've got refrigeration, they've got these dates stamped on them six ways to Sunday."

"Carcasses," Willow murmured faintly.

"Cattle." He made a face. "I tell you what. I'm halfway to being a vegetarian after I saw them load 'em up." He shivered. "Got all these sides of beef in there swaying like hula dancers." Wiping his mouth, he added, "Do you want to know what they do with the heads?"

"No," Willow and Xander said in unison.

"The reservoir," Xander pressed, hoping, wanting, and very much needing to return to the subject at hand.

The trucker gave Xander and Willow the once-over. "Couple of kids like you, you might want to steer clear anyway. If I remember my militia days, it's going to be pretty rough stuff up there."

"Oh, we're into rough stuff," Xander assured him. Then he swallowed and said, "Um, but with lots of people." He flushed. He was sure that sounded even better than *Meet me in the showers, prison boy.*

They drove for about one more minute before the trucker abruptly lurched over to the side. Willow's hip smacked into Xander's and he grabbed her thigh to try to steady her. Wild romance-novel tingles shot up her leg and she tried to clear her throat without making any noise. After all, this was Xander, not Oz.

Oz. Tonight was the first night of his transformation.

She clenched her fists against her legs. She just knew that the people who had taken Cordelia were the same people who had taken him. At least, that was her hope. She could describe the British man to Giles— or the police, if they would do any good—and the black van was a lead, if not a very strong one. But it was something. So far, for Oz, there had been nothing.

"Sorry about that," the trucker said, as the semi rolled to a standstill. "I almost missed that turnoff." He hunched over his steering wheel and pointed through the windshield again. "That's the road up to the reservoir. We can go on up."

"Oh, thanks," Willow breathed. "That's really nice of you."

The man unrolled his window and turned his head, hawked out his wad of gum.

When he turned it back, his face was a hideous, demonic mask of brilliant red. Horns sprouted from his head. His eyes were a glowing, unearthly crimson. He pulled back his lips and Willow saw the longest, sharpest teeth this side of Hell. Fire dribbled from his mouth as he cackled and reached for her.

"Think nothin' of it," he said.

Willow screamed. Xander grabbed her just as the demon yanked on her arm and prepared to bury his fangs in it.

"You're the ones called Xander and Willow," he said, running an obscenely long tongue over his fangs as they fumbled for the door handle. "You're friends of the Slayer, who has been sighted at the reservoir. Julian told me to bring you alive, that's all. He didn't say *intact.*"

"No, no!" Xander yelled, hitting the monster as it slathered over Willow's arm. "Stop!"

Then the driver's-side door burst open and the monster was yanked from the cab. Willow was pulled along with him until his grip slackened and she hung half in, half out of the truck.

Lightning flashed, and Willow saw the demon and another figure in silhouette.

It was Buffy.

Xander was about to drag Willow back into the cab when she stopped him.

"Xander, look!"

He did. The two were racing away through the storm, Buffy in the lead, the monster in pursuit.

"Oh, thank you, thank you, Buff," Xander whispered. Then he helped Willow up to a sitting position and said, "I'm going out there to help her, Willow. You figure out how to drive this thing. We'll do something resourceful with it. Like drive away really fast."

"What? But I . . ." She stared down at the gear

shifts and pedals. She was inches too short. "Xander, I'll go help her. You can drive."

But he was already out of the cab.

She pressed on the gas. The truck vroomed and lurched. Died.

"Manual. Right," she murmured. "I can do manual."

Then the passenger door opened again and she let out a yell. It was a mud monster. It was the creature from the black reservoir.

It was a kid.

"My name is Mark," he said, and in another time and place, it would be comical how he blinked through the mud, kind of Three Stooges. "Buffy told me to get in here."

"Yeah, okay," Willow said. She took a breath and asked hopefully, "Would you happen to know anything about trucks?"

To her intense amazement, he nodded. "Me and Brian, our uncle owns a trucking business. I know all about big rigs." He gestured to her. "Let me get behind the wheel and we can drive all the way to Mexico, if you want."

Buffy saw Xander sneaking around the truck and motioning to her. She knew he was preparing for a surprise attack, and she also knew it would be a far, far better thing for him to keep his distance.

So she shouted, "Xander, keep back! I can handle it!"

That was enough distraction from self-survival for the demon to backhand her. She flew through the air from the force of the blow as if she'd been shot from a cannon and backslid into the mud.

"Breaker, breaker," Xander bellowed, waving his hands and jumping up and down. He shook his butt at the demon, who turned and watched him, snorting flames. "C'mon, Big Red. Chew me up and spit me out. I double-dare you."

Buffy shut her eyes in frustration at his idiotic show of courage, but she couldn't help a rush of gratitude as she scrambled to put distance between her and the demon. It was possible Xander's little dance had just saved her life.

"C'mon, baby, light my fire," Xander persisted. "C'mon, baby—"

"Enough!" the demon bellowed, vomiting flame in Xander's direction. Xander dove out of the way, sliding through to home.

Then the red guy whirled back around and tore after Buffy, shooting out more fire, so close and so hot she felt blisters on her cheeks. She fled, not liking showing her back. Mostly because she liked having one.

As she escaped to the firmer footing of the highway blacktop, she was not a happy girl. This guy was major bad news. True, she had expected a little something, based upon the screams she'd heard coming from the truck. Then, when she'd seen what was happening to Willow, she figured it was maybe luck or a miracle that of all the off-ramps on all the highways cutting through this icky little town, she and Mark had chosen this one to get back onto the highway. In fact, they had thought they had successfully flagged down a ride from a black van when the truck pulled over to the side.

Now, it was pretty obvious to her the demon hadn't seen either one of them. Probably because he had been too busy treating Willow's arm like a piece of corn on the cob. And as for the van, it must have sped away.

She turned and faced flamethrower boy, completely unarmed, and wondered what the hell she was going to do to protect herself and the others.

Xander watched helplessly as the demon closed in on Buffy. There had to be something he could do. After all they had been through, he was not about to lose his number one Slayin' vixen to some gun-totin' demon trucker with a Juicyfruit monkey on his back. But he'd been pretty much pushed out of the fight, hadn't he?

"Hold on, Buffy," he said to himself, so not the hero of hour. "While I watch like some bimbo in a nightgown and a matching pair of feathered high heels."

Then he brightened. What had the demon told them?

I got me a shotgun needs some use.

And was that true?

One way to find out.

"I'm baack," he said to Willow, opening the little door behind the passenger door. He was surprised to see her in the passenger seat, more surprised to see some nerdy kid next to her behind the wheel. "Cover for me, or something."

"He can drive," Willow said eagerly.

Xander nodded at the kid, not knowing who he was, not caring, especially if he really could drive, and wasn't just trying to impress Willow, and poked around in the crawl space behind the seats. There wasn't much there, just a few, oh, God, bones.

"And a shotgun," Xander said triumphantly, grabbing it up. He started scooting back out and said to Willow, "So. You guys are figuring out the driving part?"

Her hair bobbed with her happy nod. "Yes. Figured. We can move this puppy any time you want."

"Okay. I'm going to draw his fire, so to speak." He looked at Willow. "I'll try to wound him but whatever happens, I most definitely want you to run him over." His gaze ticked toward the kid. "Can you do that?"

The boy was hollow-eyed. "What's going on? What is that thing?"

"He can do it," Willow promised, putting her hand over the boy's hand.

"I'm gone," Xander told her, and jumped back out of the truck.

He ran around to the other side and headed for the end zone. The demon was practically on top of Buffy, and she was dodging huge belches of fire. Steam rose into the rain wherever the gouts of flame hit anything solid.

Xander spread his legs for balance, aimed, and fired.

To his euphoria, the demon's head shot up and flames volcanoed into the storm. It whirled around and blasted more fire. This time Xander didn't move, didn't flinch. When flames landed mere inches in front of his body, he shot at it again.

Another direct hit. It staggered backward.

Then Buffy darted up behind it, jumped into the air, and double-kicked it in the small of the back. It arched slightly from the impact, and Xander shot it again.

It spread out its arms and made a half circle, which

Buffy avoided by dropping to her knees. Then she drove straight for its shins, obviously attempting to topple the creature.

Somehow she'd miscalculated, though, and the demon's response was to lean down and pick her up under her armpits. She kicked, hard, then double-kicked, and flipped up and out of its arms.

Xander gestured to Willow to follow him, and he began running toward the monster.

In the back of his mind, he remembered saying very cruel things about Buffy this very night. Believing them. But right now, he would die for her.

"You ugly, gross thing!" he shouted at the demon. The roar of the truck as it began to move might have drowned him out, or maybe the boom of thunder overhead, but something else drew the creature's attention. Its eyes widened in terror and Xander wondered what it was about the scenario that was flipping it out: truck, gun, boy wonder.

Just in case it was him, Xander kept running toward it, wondering how the heck they did stuff like this on TV, just ran around like fools shooting things without having to stand still to take aim.

"You're disgusting!" Xander shouted again. To his amazement, the demon kind of hunched over, like it was scared or shy or apologizing or something.

So Xander kept running.

The truck's air horn blared behind him, blasting his eardrums. He jumped, looked over his shoulder, and hauled out of the way.

The truck was bearing down on the demon.

"No! My queen!" it cried. Then it opened its mouth and spewed flame at the truck.

While Xander watched in horror, the entire front of

the truck burst into flame. Then it rammed into the demon, sending it flying, and ran right over it.

The flaming truck kept going straight onto the highway. Xander raced after it, shouting Willow's name, dropping the shotgun and moving as fast as he ever had.

The driver's-side door opened. Someone tumbled out. One someone. Only one.

The truck blew. The ground shook from the explosion as the truck went up, bursting with awesome force. Huge chunks of half-molten metal flew in all directions, arcing through the rain and screeching back toward the ground like bombs.

"Willow!" Xander screamed. "Buffy!"

"Hello, Slayer," said the figure in black, backlit by the explosion.

It had been standing on top of the truck when the big rig had begun to roll toward the demon. After the demon had set the truck on fire, the figure had darted to the back of the vehicle and leaped off, landing on its feet with an easy grace. It was hooded and robed.

It was the figure from her dreams.

"Hold on a sec, okay?" Buffy said, her finger raised as she turned toward the fire storm to see if everyone got out. The stench of burning rubber and an odor of cooking meat—*oh, God*—filled the air.

The figure advanced and put its hands to its hood. Threw it back.

She was a vampire. Just a vampire.

Buffy was disappointed. After all this time, and all those nightmares, she'd been expecting something much more dramatic. Vampires she could slay in her sleep. So to speak. Okay, with her eyes closed. With one hand tied behind her back.

Buffy motioned with her hand. "Five seconds, okay? Hold on. We'll fight. I just need to check—"

"Oz," the vampire said. "He's alive."

She unclasped her robe and let it drop to the ground. She was very cut, with muscles on her muscles, and she was dressed in some kind of weird body armor, complete with a Xena-style bra.

"Wow. Where'd you get that?" Buffy asked in admiration, even though it took every bit of her focus not to race for the truck. One of the advantages of all her training with Giles was a developed ability to concentrate, which, unfortunately, still had not extended to studying. "Do they take charge cards?"

The vampire walked stealthily toward her, positioning her hands in a fighter's stance. She was awesome. "Mock all you want."

"No mocking," Buffy assured her. "Honest. I'm really impressed. See, I don't have a costume. Not even a cape. I could go for a new look."

"Your grave clothes will be your new look." The vampire narrowed her eyes. "Do you have any idea how many Slayers I've killed?"

Buffy shrugged. "Do you have any idea how many vampires I've killed? Cuz I don't. I lost count. I'm the McDonald's of slaying. Over three billion slain. Something like that."

The vampire raised an eyebrow. "Boasting is unseemly."

"So is biting people on the neck and sucking out all their blood," Buffy retorted. "But that doesn't seem to stop you people."

"No. It doesn't stop me," the vampire said, spreading her mouth as she morphed into vamp mode. "It impels me."

"I've gotta get a thesaurus," Buffy muttered.

"I will fight you for the lives of your friends."

Buffy took that in. "Okay."

The vamp narrowed her golden eyes and cocked her head. "This isn't the forum I had in mind."

"Picky, picky," Buffy said. "It works for me."

Then she took the offensive, running at the vampire as she felt at her waist for a stake. *Uh-oh.*

She was fresh out. What a stupid miscalculation.

Well, there was nothing to be done about it now. She flung herself at the vampire, shifting her trajectory just as she sprung when the vampire feinted to the left, then darted to the right. Buffy's right heel caught her hip, and her left landed hard in the center of the vampire's right side of ribs. The vampire grunted and slammed onto her back.

Buffy landed on both feet, and before the vampire had a chance to get up, she landed on top of her, straddling her, while her gaze darted left, right for something to impale her with. The firelight from the burning truck cast flickering orange light over the ground, but Buffy kept coming up empty. She thought about Xander's gun, and wondered where it had landed.

It really is just like the dream, she thought, as she pummeled the creature. With the fire blazing nearby, and the figure beneath her, which she was punching out for all she was worth . . .

She was gaining the upper hand, and felt a renewed surge of power with the knowledge. Okay, cool outfit and wicked-scary dreams, but a vampire was just a vampire, after all, and she hadn't been exaggerating too much about how many she'd dusted . . .

Then she heard someone shouting, "Buffy!" and she was confused. Because it sounded like Angel.

She glanced up. The female vampire took advantage of her distraction to undercut Buffy's chin, whipping back her head. Another human being would probably have suffered a broken neck. It was Buffy's luck—and misfortune—to be the Slayer; despite a rush of pain and dizziness, she quickly recovered her momentum and punched her attacker in the face again.

"Angel?" she called.

Beneath her, the female vampire shouted, "Don't kill him!"

Buffy frowned at her. " 'Don't kill him'?"

The vampire caught Buffy's fist with both her hands and yanked her hard to the right, pulling Buffy off her body and throwing her into mud. Buffy scrambled in the thick ooze for a toehold as the vampire dodged away from her.

By the time Buffy managed to get to her knees, the vampire was running toward the burning truck.

Buffy gasped. Directly in front of the fiery vehicle, at least six vampires had hold of Angel. He was struggling to free himself; as Buffy slipped and slid, and finally got to her feet, he managed to shake at least one off and had another in a choke hold.

Then a slim figure ran toward him, followed by a taller, beefier version of a humanoid. Willow and Xander.

They're alive.

Xander was carrying something stick-shaped, and as Buffy darted toward the group, making her way as fast as she could, he rammed the stick through the back of one of Angel's attackers. The thing exploded—vampire, good—but the one next to him whirled on Xander and grabbed the stick out of his hands.

Xander was hurled into Willow, and they both went down. One of the vamps sprang toward them. The female who had fought with Buffy reached the fracas and shouted something in a language Buffy didn't understand. The other figure turned away from Buffy's two friends.

Then the female reached Angel, moving with an eerie sort of theatrical rhythm as she advanced on him and at the same time took the stick from the other vampire. In the pulsing fire glow, while three of the others held Angel, she became a silhouette as she aimed the stick directly at his unbeating heart.

Buffy screamed, "No!" and ran, calling on everything inside herself to reach them in time.

Chapter 8

THE RAIN WAS POUNDING ON THE ROOF OF GILES'S apartment building. Every dish in his kitchen lay demolished on the floor. Every glass, shattered. A half-opened bottle of single malt Scotch wafted odiferous, telltale fumes.

Thank God he had come to his senses before he had reached his record collection, the destruction of which had, indeed, crossed his mind. If he had truly been possessed of a mind at the time.

There had been many moments in Giles's life when he had lost his temper. A few, when he had lost his mind. But this had been like nothing else. He had never felt such complete rage.

He had no idea how it had come upon him, except that he had been told of David's death by David's aunt, Lady Anne, and realized that not only had he missed the opportunity to say good-bye to an old friend, but that he would have to miss the funeral as well. That had sent him over the edge. He had even less of an idea regarding how the completely overwhelming rage had left him.

He thought back to his own behavior these past days. Abominable. What had he been thinking? Had he actually told Buffy he thought she was a bimbo? What on earth had possessed him?

"*Possession*. Aye, there's the rub," he muttered. He cradled his hand in his chin. He was very tired, and enormously embarrassed. His kitchen was a disaster and should be cleaned up immediately.

Instead, he went straightaway to his bookshelves and began searching out all the titles which contained the word "possession." He had quite a number in his home library, and he was certain there were even more in the library at school.

He stacked them on the coffee table in front of his sofa and began to read. In due course, he discovered that there were a thousand theories about how one could become possessed; everything from angry spirits to bad peyote was cataloged in one volume or another.

The rain clattered on. He was about halfway through the stack when he finally admitted defeat. There wasn't enough to go on, and he blamed himself for that. Buffy had been trying to talk about this for weeks, and he had not been listening. Maybe a regular person could blame that on possession, but not a Watcher. He had higher standards to live by. He had a Slayer to protect.

With a sigh, he picked up the phone and called Buffy's home. An apology was in order. That, and a brainstorming session. He had been most remiss in his duties. He prayed he would never be so again.

The phone was answered on the first ring.

"Yes." The tone was harsh, angry. The voice belonged to Buffy's mother.

"Joyce. Ah, Ms. Summers," Giles amended, when she didn't respond to his use of her first name. "Giles here. Is Buffy—"

"She's not here. And if you find her, you can tell her thanks a lot for not leaving a note. *Again.* What does she think this is, a pit stop?"

"I'm so sorry." He cocked his head. "Is everything all right there?"

"Here? Oh, everything's just terrific." She bit off each word. "Some jerk broke into the gallery and stole a very valuable ancient Roman artifact. Which, we have since discovered, we are liable for. And of course it was underinsured."

"Oh, my. I'm so dreadfully sorry indeed. If there's anything I might do—"

"There's not," she cut in rudely. "But if you see that daughter of mine, tell her to come home. I'm sick and tired of worrying about her. The least she could do is call."

"Yes, of course I shall. And might I suggest—"

She hung up.

He was not offended in the least. He knew she was not herself. He sincerely hoped she did not trash her kitchen. Or, if she did, that she had adequately insured her prized possessions.

And he also hoped that she, like he, ran across the antidote for whatever gripped them in this nasty temper, and cured her of it as soon as possible. For Buffy's sake, if not her own.

And so, back to the books.

About half an hour later, he looked up and thought, *Ancient Roman artifact?*

Slipping and sliding through the mud, Buffy shouted, "Stop!"

And to her pure and total surprise and relief, the beautiful, dark-haired vampire paused from staking Angel and smiled at her. She raised her brows as the rain washed down her pale face and pooled around her feet. There was no reflection in the moonlit water.

"Why should I stop, Slayer?" she asked. Now Buffy detected an accent. What kind, she didn't know. It wasn't Transylvanian, or whatever passed for it in the movies. Definitely not Californian. Or British. "He's a vampire."

"This is my territory," Buffy tossed off. "I don't want to hurt my rep."

The vampire smiled. "He's your property. Your lover." She whipped her head toward Angel, keeping the stake pressed against his chest. "Is that not so, Angelus? You have turned your back on your kind for one of them?"

"Now you're really pissing me off," Buffy said, smoothing her sopping hair out of her face. "'Cause you sound like Darla."

"His sire," the vampire filled in. Buffy was surprised she knew about Darla, but maybe not so much. Angel was a celeb in vampire circles. "Tell me, Angelus, how is she?"

"Dead," Angel said. "I killed her."

The beautiful vampire actually registered shock. It took her a few seconds to compose herself.

And in those few seconds, with a quick nod at

Angel and another at Xander and Willow, Buffy rushed her, grabbing her wrist and thrusting her backward. Angel's captors immediately rushed to her defense, giving him a chance to use their momentum against them as he ran forward, dodging to the right side of Buffy. He managed a good, strong side kick to the large one on his right, at the same time that he yanked the stake out of another female vampire's hand and dusted her.

Then he was a blur to Buffy as he started putting the other vamps through the paces. Buffy concentrated on the female, giving her everything she had and then some—blow after blow, a hail of kicks and punches. Most of them landed, but few seemed to do any real damage. Same deal with Buffy herself.

"We're evenly matched," the vampire announced, panting. Her eyes glowed golden through the wet night. "This is thrilling."

"Yeah. Color me thrilled, too," Buffy said, grunting as the vampire smacked her in the face. "I'm just rolling in thrilled."

To her left was the explosive sound of a kill, followed by Xander and Willow cheering in unison. Buffy smiled briefly, proud of her drenched but stylin' Slayerettes. But a quick glance told her they were outnumbered and in trouble. She renewed her concentration and threw every ounce of energy she had into her assault. If she could take out the queen bee, she would have free rein among the drones.

Lightning flashed; thunder rumbled. Vaguely she heard the hum of a car engine, followed by the squeal of brakes close behind her. Buffy gathered up the woman vampire and rolled to the left. The front bumper of a black van—the van she had seen before—narrowly missed Buffy's head. Then someone kicked her hard in the small of the back.

"Hey," she growled, letting go of the vampire with one hand as she reached around and grabbed the kicker's ankle.

"Thanks, Buffy," Angel said, and as Buffy looked back and up, the vampire whose ankle she'd grabbed exploded into dust as Angel impaled it.

"Another time, Slayer," the dark vampire announced, snaking out of Buffy's grasp. She leaped to her feet and headed for the van.

The windshield was tinted; Buffy could not see the driver, who must have opened the passenger side for the vampire, who jumped in.

The vehicle squealed away, to a chorus of protests from the abandoned vampires who were fighting Angel, Xander, and Willow. Buffy quickly joined in, and in outside of a minute, two of the three remaining bad guys were dust.

The third was another demon, a blue, rubbery thing covered with a very smelly coating of what felt like fat. It was difficult to hold on to, but Buffy managed to keep its arms behind its back as Angel threatened it with a piece of red-hot chrome from the truck, which he held with the folded material of his duster.

Xander and Willow looked on with not such happy faces, and Buffy figured she knew why: in the past, they each had seen what Angel had done to creatures he wanted information from. Including Giles, back when Angel had become evil again.

"Why is she here?" Angel demanded, thrusting the chrome at the demon. "What does she want?"

"She'd kill me if I told you," the demon murmured.

"Oh, that is so cliché," Xander said. "I suppose next thing you'll tell is you're both with the CIA."

"Angel, I think the big question of the day is, who is she?" Buffy suggested, tightening her grasp as the demon renewed its struggle.

Angel looked hard at Buffy. "I know who she is."

"Oh." *Care to share?* Buffy wanted to ask, but she decided to wait until they got whatever they could out of lard boy. No sense letting the enemy in on your debriefing.

"Okay. Answer one from column A, then. Let's start with why you guys are out here on such a miserable night." Buffy gave the guy a shake. Willow swallowed hard and slipped her arm through Xander's.

The demon grunted. Its almond-shaped eyes were focused on the hot metal; after a time, it said, "She told us she wanted you, Slayer."

Buffy sighed. "And Cordelia says I'm not popular."

"Do you know where our friends are?" Willow piped up. "Dark-haired girl. Really cute guy." She glanced upward at the moon. "Whoops. Not a guy."

"And the girl is very beautiful," Xander added loyally. "Probably also crabby."

The demon shrugged. "I know not."

"You know not? Did you learn English off some tapes in your car?" Buffy said. "Angel, burn him."

"No!" the demon shouted, as Angel waved the steaming chrome at him.

"Look, Crisco, we have questions. We need answers. You killed an innocent little boy tonight." Buffy gave herself the luxury of a moment to mourn poor Mark Dellasandro, although she felt not a bit of guilt that she was glad Willow was the one who got out alive.

"I'm sure it's not the first innocent little boy he's killed," Angel said, morphing into vamp face. He pressed the metal against the demon's arm. Its shriek was unearthly. Its entire body began to smoke and shudder, and then to soften and melt. A big piece broke off and plopped into the mud, where it sizzled.

"Yuck," Buffy said, grimacing. "Um, someone else want to hold this guy?" She smiled hopefully at Xander. "Feeling left out?"

"Nope." Beside him, Willow weakly shook her head.

"Tell us something. Anything," Buffy ordered. "I have a feeling the next time Angel puts that hot metal against you, somebody will be scooping you up in a bucket."

"I can say nothing. He will kill me."

Xander raised a hand. "Ah, excuse me, friend? Way I see it, Angel's going to beat him to it."

"No." The demon threw back its head. "My body matters not. Julian will kill my soul. He will feed it to Meter."

"You've got a soul?" Buffy wrinkled her brow and frowned at Angel, who frowned back and moved his shoulders. "How does all this work, anyway? Who's got souls and who doesn't?"

"Who's on first?" Xander piped up, but at a look from Buffy, he shrugged and said, "Settling back into silent mode here."

The demon's mouth parted slowly and the lower half kind of dribbled down its chin. *Eew.*

"Thee hath amathed great power, thee and her king."

Angel said, "I thought Helen got away from Julian."

Buffy threw him a look. *Helen? Julian?*

"Got away?" It was the demon's turn to look puzzled. "From Julian? But thee adoreth him."

"That's not what I heard," Angel persisted. Buffy felt a flare of what might pass for jealousy in more normal girls, who had real boyfriends who were also normal. She decided to call it intense curiosity and left it at that.

"Then thomeone hath been telling you taleth, vampire."

The rest of the demon's mouth slid off its face. An eye followed. Then the other one.

"Thufferin' thuccotash," Xander murmured in awe.

Willow made a retching sound and turned away. Xander held her shoulders and said, "Easy, Will."

Buffy let go of the demon as it collapsed into a puddle in the mud. She said to Angel, "If you'll barf, I'll barf." Then she frowned. "Are you capable of barfing?"

"There are some things a guy likes to keep private," Angel said with a faint smile.

"Yeah, like his taste in porno," Xander said, turning back around. When Angel and Buffy both stared at him, he shrugged and said, "Not that I, ah, indulge. Who needs to, when your ex-girlfriend dresses like a hooker?"

Willow scowled at him. "It's only funny if she's here, Xander. Otherwise, you just sound . . . catty."

His brows shot up. "Catty? Me? When have I ever been . . . oh, my God," he said, his gaze traveling past Buffy and toward the destroyed truck. "Buffy."

He pointed. In the glare of the fire, a small figure

stumbled toward them. It had to be Mark Della-sandro.

Buffy took off after him, followed by the others. When he saw her, he opened his arms, then dropped them to his sides. He folded, landing on his knees, and hung his head.

By the time she got to him, he was sobbing uncontrollably. Somewhat uncertainly, Buffy embraced him; her throat tightened as he clung to her, weeping. She had heard grief like this before. She knew she would hear it again.

But for this boy, this was fresh grief, raw and cutting and soul-deep. He had been through so much.

He was going to go through so much more.

After a few minutes, Buffy gently but firmly pulled away and squatted in front of him.

"You're all right," she assured him. Then she couldn't help but add, "For now."

"They're going to kill me," he whispered. "Everyone's gone crazy, just like my . . . my . . . bro . . ." He closed his eyes. Tears streamed down his face.

"He's right, Buffy," Xander said. "Everyone's checking into the asylum." He cleared his throat. "Willow and I signed ourselves out tonight, but I don't know why. Maybe we'll get crazy again." Shrugging, he put out his hand to Angel. "Hey man, truth, you know I'm not your number one fan. But what I said tonight—"

"It's forgotten," Angel said quickly. A look passed between the two, and Buffy knew it wasn't forgotten.

Willow stayed quiet, and Buffy was sorry about that. She squared her shoulders. "Okay, the chick. What's going on? Who is Helen?"

"It's a long story. One I don't want to tell twice, and I think Giles should hear it." He gestured to the boy. "Maybe we could ask Giles to hide him?"

"I'm not sure that's a good idea," Buffy admitted sadly. "Giles is one with the body of nut cases."

"Possessed," Willow translated.

"Mucho possessed," Buffy said. "He called me a . . ." She pursed her lips. *No reason to go there.* "There are some things a girl likes to keep private, too, I guess."

She sighed. "Let's stick out our thumbs," she said. "I'm absolutely certain someone will want to pick up five people covered with mud."

When Giles opened the door, he smiled at Buffy and said in a rush, "Thank heavens you're all right. Call your mother."

"Got it." She crossed to the phone and picked it up. Her number was programmed in; she punched 1 and bobbed to music only she could hear.

"Mom?" she said brightly. "Hi, I'm sorry—"

Her eyes went wide. Then her face became shadowed, and she glanced over at Xander and rolled her eyes.

Xander felt for Buffy. It was hard enough to be a Slayerette—okay, easier for him since his parents didn't keep up with his comings and goings—but it was definitely harder to be the one wearing Slayer shoes when it came to those big parental issues. Xander had assumed that once Mrs. Summers knew about Buffy's special calling, she'd let up. Give up trying to treat Buffy like a normal teenage girl and get on board the slayage train.

It had not happened that way. Somebody with a life

as complicated as Buffy's needed a lot of support. Xander tried not to judge, but it was sad that her mother only seemed to add more pressure.

"This is Mark Dellasandro," Willow said to Giles.

"Hello, Mark." Giles's expression didn't change at all, but Xander knew him well enough to read his body language. The presence of this boy was a good thing, as far as Giles was concerned. "Would you like some tea?"

"Yes, please," Mark said. He was shivering. Everybody was covered in mud and slime, but from what he'd told Willow, he had been exposed to the elements for many more hours than the rest of them.

"And a shower," Willow called. "And maybe some toast. I'll help you."

"Oh, that's all right," Giles said, but Willow was intent on being a helper. She trailed after him.

She looked with alarm at Giles, who stood in the center of the most thoroughly trashed kitchen Willow had ever seen. He said to her, "I'm all right now, Willow," and then he stepped across the shards of white china and clear glass, and reached into the cabinet to the right side of the stove. He brought out a dark blue cup embossed with a gold Egyptian ankh.

She closed her eyes and murmured the daily spell of protection that she had begun saying every morning:

"By the light and the heart of the earth,
"I forbid all evil spirits my bedstead and couch;
"I forbid you my house and my home;
"I forbid you my flesh and blood and body and
  soul.

*"I irrevocably forbid you entrance to my mind
and my thoughts;*

"My fears and my strengths;

*"Until you have traveled over every single hill and
vale;*

"Forged every stream and river;

"Counted all the grains of sand on all the shores;

"And every star in the sky.

"I forbid you."

Then she looked at him and said, "Do you have a couple more teacups? That are, um, not broken? And some actual tea?"

His answer was an appreciative nod. "You fill the kettle, would you?" he asked. Then he turned to the alcove opening between the kitchen and the living room, where the others were standing awkwardly and said, "Xander, show Mark where the shower is."

"Thanks," Xander said. "We'll figure it out. However, we will be showering separately." He clapped Mark on the shoulder. "Come on."

The two went upstairs.

As Giles put loose black tea in a tea ball, Willow filled the kettle with water from the tap. Giles said, "I've got bottled water," then touched his forehead. "Oh, I forgot to get some at the market. I've been using the tap all week. Hideous stuff."

"Better in England?" Willow asked.

"Not really." He smiled at her. Then, as the guys trooped upstairs, he lowered his voice and said, "How much does Mark know?"

"Not much. He doesn't even know Buffy is the Slayer." She swallowed hard. "He didn't see the

Crisco demon decompose into the mud but he did see the fire-breathing trucker one."

"Good Lord. You ran into demons?"

"And this big shot vampire. Her name is Helen. She knows Angel."

Giles stared at her. The look on his face made her hair stand on end.

Giles was terrified.

"Helen?" he said, his voice a ghost in the ruined kitchen.

Behind them, Angel said, "The Betrayed One."

They turned. Angel stood in the doorway, his duster off, his shirt a tatter of ribbons. There was a bloody mark on his chest directly over his heart. Where the vampire had pushed the stake in, just so far. Another jab, and she would have dusted Angel.

"Helen. Oh, my God." Giles ran both his hands through his hair. "We thought she was dead."

Angel said, flatly, "So did I."

There was a long silence. Then Willow said, "What's the Betrayed One?"

"My mom is still possessed," Buffy called from the living room. She was replacing the phone on the charger. "Or else she's going through menopause. Y'know, it would be nice sometime if the first words out of her mouth weren't, 'Why didn't you call?' She knows what my nights are like. Maybe I should buy her a police scanner. Or I could wear a camera. Slayercam. It's a thought."

Giles gazed from Willow and Angel to Buffy. He looked stricken. Vaguely, he said to Willow, "Please finish making the tea," and walked from the kitchen into the living room.

* * *

Giles found himself thinking of the night Jenny had died. He had walked into this very room—through the front door, of course—found the wine he had assumed she had brought, and the inviting note. The votive candles, one on each stair, leading to his bedroom. He had loosened his tie as he'd climbed the stairs, his heart soaring with the sweeping opera music on the stereo. This was to be their night of desire fulfilled. The sweet culmination of their longing for one another.

Bliss. Crescendo.

Instead, a dead woman lay in his bed, staring at him with perhaps a hint of reproach: *Why didn't you stop him?*

Why didn't you save me?

"Oh, dear God, Buffy," he said, sitting down. He folded his hands between his knees and bent his head. He did not want to speak of death. He had had enough of it.

"Giles, what? What's wrong?"

She's so young. So new to the world. Why does the universe have to keep throwing deadly monsters her way?

"Buffy, I don't know how to tell you this," he said honestly. "The vampire you encountered. Helen."

"Yeah. Some trampy babe," Buffy said. She made a face. "So not my date for the prom."

"Buffy, sit down." He gestured at the couch.

"Giles, I'm mud girl," she protested. "I'll stand."

"Buffy, please," Giles said urgently. "Listen to me. Helen is one of the most vicious creatures who has ever walked the earth. Centuries ago, the Watchers Council expunged all reference to her from the Slayer's Handbook. They made it a punishable offense to so much as utter her name. And anyone who spoke of her to a Slayer would instantly be cast out and shunned for the rest of his or her life."

"Wow, are you guys Watchers or Amish people?" Buffy asked.

"They believed that learning of her existence would so demoralize a Slayer that she would give up all hope of living out a normal life. You see, Helen made it her special mission to kill Slayers." He cleared his throat. "One after another."

"Really, Giles, whatever they told you about her, it's not true. I kicked her butt." Buffy looked smug. "Did I not, Angel?"

"Buffy, listen to him," Angel said, coming into the room. "When I knew her, there was a Slayer in England at the time. Her name was Grace. Helen was relentless. She ran that girl to ground like a bloodhound after a fox, and she ripped her to shreds." His face was grave, his eyes dark and hooded. "Literally. And she loved every minute of it. She reveled in it."

He hesitated. "There were others."

"And you were there," Buffy said softly.

"Yes, I was."

"Well." She worked to regroup, and Giles gave her the moment. He was grateful to Angel for coming to his aid. Buffy must be convinced that Helen was a terrible menace. But a part of Giles reflected bitterly that at the moment of that young Slayer's wretched death, the demon-filled Angelus had probably danced on her grave.

"There were no more sightings of her," Giles continued. "She no longer . . . challenged Slayers. And so, the Council assumed that she had died."

"Well," Buffy said, more heartily. "I'm sorry, only

not, because if that was the big bad Helen, you guys don't need to worry about her anymore. She's slowed with the years."

Angel held out his palms. "You didn't defeat her, Buffy. She quit the field."

"Ran." Buffy fluttered her lashes at the vampire. "Skeedaddled. What's that stuffy stuff about discretion and valor? Or was it more like, 'run away and live to fight another day'? Anyway, she definitely booked."

The teakettle shrieked. Giles jerked, hard. Willow called, "Sorry," from the kitchen and started banging around.

"We must research this," Giles said to Angel, who nodded. "Buffy's mother said something about a stolen Roman artifact. Perhaps Helen's found a way to cast spells on people, or instill violence in them in some way."

"Ethan Rayne prayed to Janus," Angel pointed out. "The two-faced god."

"Yes," Giles mused. "I'll try to track that down." He clapped his hands to his knees. "We've not a moment to lose."

"Wait. I'm not following," Buffy protested. "Neither one of you has impressed me with why we're panicking over the arrival of a vampire who wears bras made out of stainless steel. I could use a little more backstory here."

Giles looked at her. At Buffy Summers, his Slayer. At a young woman who was his friend. He did not want to tell her what she needed to know. And as he often did, he found it incredibly ironic that the Watchers Council had admonished him in his capacity as Watcher several times for "transference." In other words, for feeling his fate was tied up with hers.

He found their objections to his caring about her as much as he did entirely bizarre. The Slayer was required to put her life on the line until such time as she had no life left. How could one *not* care?

"Giles," Buffy prodded. "Please hit return so we can wrap around to the next line."

He took a breath. "It's as simple as this, Buffy. Helen is at least nineteen hundred and seventy years old. From A.D. 41 until 1801, when she disappeared from our annals, she killed every single Slayer she came up against.

"Dozens and dozens, Buffy," Giles concluded.

"Hundreds," Angel darkly corrected him.

Buffy's smile faded. She looked at the two of them, searching their faces. Then she licked her lips, swallowed, and squared her shoulders.

"Maybe so," she said, "but none of them was *me.*"

Bravo, Giles thought, moved. He managed a nod.

"My thinking, exactly, Buffy. Which is why we must get to work." He rose and turned away to hide his expression. What he had not told her was that every Slayer who had died at Helen's hands had suffered a gruesome, brutal death. The vampire queen was as evil and sadistic as the times which had spawned her—the hideous reign of the mad Roman emperor Caligula. The man's name was synonymous with cruelty, torture, and madness. Helen had learned well from him.

Far too well.

Giles cleared his throat and said, as calmly as he could, "Willow, do you need help with the tea things?"

"Oh, no, not really," she said brightly. Then she

saw his face and stammered, "That is, yes. Lots of help. I totally need lots and lots of help."

Giles pushed up his glasses and went into the kitchen. His hands were shaking.

I must not let her down, he thought. *I must arm her with everything I can.*

This is one battle she may actually lose, and I cannot let that happen.

In the underground caves, Helen sat at her dressing table. A skull was placed on a pedestal before the mirror, candles flickering in a circle around it. It had been adorned with makeup—the white bones shaded a healthy brown, the cheeks crimson, the rictus grin a slash of scarlet. The eye sockets were circled with black and blue.

Tears streamed down Helen's face as she mixed her potion, muttering to herself, "I'll torture her for a century. I'll torture her until her arms and legs fall off. My one love. My one true love." She stopped and stared down at it. "Angelus. My Angelus. That bitch. That Slayer bitch."

Then she heard footsteps, recognizing them as Julian's. Panicking a little, she looked in the mirror. Of course, there was no reflection of him. Just as there was none of her.

"What are you doing, my love?"

"Preparing the potion for the arena," she replied steadily. *Though of course, it is for him. After I kill the Slayer, Angelus will realize that he loves me. Julian must be gotten rid of.*

"Why the tears?"

She shook her head. "I didn't get the Slayer. If we fail . . ."

"We won't. Don't be so impatient."

Closing her eyes, she thought of the centuries he had kept her walled up. The agony. The loneliness.

To make the world forget her, he had claimed. To stop the Slayers from coming after her.

"Just for a little while, love," he had told her. But he'd loved having her all to himself. It had been just like the old days, before the change, when he would come visit her in her cell.

"Yes, I'm impatient," she said now.

He kissed her again. Then he leaned around her and kissed the decorated skull.

"Night, Diana, dear," he said, patting it on the head. He touched Helen's shoulder. "Come to bed, my love."

"In a minute, Julian, my darling." She patted his cheek.

Once he had left the chamber, she turned the skull upside down and extracted a bottle from it. Being very careful not to let any of it splash on her, she opened it and poured it into the potion.

There.

It's done.

Whatever happened next was in the hands of the Dark Mother.

Chapter 9

The Roman Empire, A.D. 39

FAR FROM THE SEVEN HILLS OF ROME, HELEN, A DARK-haired girl of fifteen, huddled behind the shed where her father kept the wine barrels, and bit into her hand to keep from screaming.

Standing among the vines, the grapes glistening in the moonlight like fat, black blood drops, Diana, Helen's best friend in all the world, stood in a fighter's stance. Rushing toward her was a fiend from a nightmare. It wore the appearance of a man contorted into an evil mask of long, sharp teeth and glowing, golden eyes.

"At last, Slayer, I've found you," it said. "My master will be delighted when I bring him your head."

"Do you think so?" she asked, tossing back her shining blond hair as she ran backward. "And if you come back empty-handed, will he take your head?"

"An unnecessary question," the fiend snarled.

"Diana," Helen whispered, too terrified to move. She had never seen a thing such as this; never dreamed such creatures actually existed—although, of course, she had heard the rumors about the emperor's demonic court in distant Rome.

"Prepare yourself, Slayer," the monster continued. "This night, you die."

Helen could only watch as the monster lunged at Diana, only catch her breath when Diana slammed both fists square into its face. It howled and grabbed at her. She squatted and curled into a ball, flipping backward like a Minoan bull dancer, then grabbed an overhanging branch of the olive tree and shoved both her feet into the monster's chest.

Still it came for her, reaching for her ankles. She pulled her legs up and scrambled onto the branch. The creature wrapped its hands around the branch and yanked with all its might.

The limb cracked. Helen finally found her voice and cried, "Diana!"

To her amazement, both Diana and her unworldly foe stared in her direction with an identical expression of surprise and dismay. They looked like lovers caught in guilty pleasure.

And then the fiend yanked on the branch again.

"Come down, or I'll rip her heart out," it said to Diana.

"You'll never reach her," Diana countered.

Then the branch broke off, and Diana tumbled to the ground. She leaped to her feet, then stumbled, obviously hurt.

"Helen, run!" she screamed. She took a step forward, then lurched sideways, flailing for support on a vine-covered trellis.

The monster wavered for a moment, then raced toward the shed.

Helen jumped to her feet, realizing as she did so that the creature had not actually seen her until that moment. She had given herself away.

She couldn't look away from the creature, couldn't breathe, couldn't move. In mere seconds, she would be dead.

"Oh, Minerva, merciful goddess," she whispered, wobbling as the world shrank into a pinprick of light, and in that light the monster raged. "Take me to heaven with you now. Or turn me into a tree, or a rock."

She smelled it before it touched her. Its fetid odor was of the grave. Its eyes glowed. Its fangs flashed like knives.

Its nails raked her shoulder. It grabbed her and threw her onto her back, straddling her. Then it loomed over her and opened its mouth.

Its fangs touched her neck, pierced the skin.

A strange, haunting shriek volleyed in her ears. The creature's weight abruptly lessened, then it was gone. As she stared, a cloud of dust rained down on her.

Behind the dust stood Diana, a portion of the olive branch in her fist like a spear.

"Are you all right?" she asked, bending down with her hand outstretched.

Terrified, Helen pulled away from her. Then she buried her face in her hands and said, "Divine One, I am not worthy to look upon you."

There was silence. She finally looked up, to see Diana staring at her.

"You saw more than you should have," Diana said finally. "I'm very sorry for that."

Helen swallowed hard. "And now, you must . . . you must kill me?"

Diana shook her head. "No, of course not. But I must beg you never to speak of it."

"Of course." Now she took Diana's hand and got up from the ground, anticipating at any moment to be struck by Jove's lightning for touching an Immortal.

"Let's walk in the vineyard," Diana suggested.

To Helen's surprise, Diana was still limping. She used the branch as a walking stick, helping herself along, until finally she grunted in frustration and rested beside the large boulder they had often played on as children.

After a time, Diana said, "It's actually a relief, your knowing."

Helen replied unhappily, "But won't the gods strike me dead?"

Diana blinked. "Why would they?"

"Because I know that one of them walks among us."

"Oh." Diana closed her eyes and smiled faintly, even sadly. "Of course. That's how it would seem to you." She opened her eyes. "I'm not a goddess."

"You are the goddess of the hunt, herself. The one true Diana," Helen insisted.

Diana shook her head. "That I share her name is an honor I don't deserve. I'm something different, Helen, but I am human, the same as you." She took a breath. "I'm called a Slayer."

"A slayer of demons," Helen said.

"Exactly." She tapped the base of the boulder with the end of the branch, then moved her foot slowly, in a little circle. She grimaced, and Helen was assured that she was not completely divine after all.

"I was born to this," Diana continued. "I was chosen by the Fates. I don't know how, or why, really.

I only know that I have a sacred obligation to fight evil." She looked very grave, and in that moment, very young. She was a year older than Helen—sixteen—which was not that young at all. They had friends long married, and Diana herself was betrothed to Demetrius, son of the vineyard owner to the west.

"How do you know?" Helen asked. "Did the Oracle speak to you?"

"No." She tapped the boulder. "I don't know if I should tell you anything more."

Helen was abashed. She thought best friends shared everything.

As if she could read her mind, Diana put her hand on Helen's shoulder and said, "I only recently learned of this. Truly. And my first question to my Watcher— after I'd recovered from the shock—was if I could tell you."

Helen burst into tears. "And that demon? Where did it come from? What did it want?" When Diana pulled away slightly, Helen cried harder. "It almost took my life. You have to tell me what it was."

Diana dangled the stick and looked down at the earth, as if it were a pool and she could see herself. "It was a creature called a vampire. It was a demon inhabiting the body of a dead man."

"It stank like a dead man."

Diana chuckled. "Yes. They generally do." She regarded her friend. "The vampires and other evil creatures know when a Slayer is nearby, and they seek me out. I don't know how they know. I only know we are mortal enemies, they and I, and I must fight them until there are no more of them, or until I die."

Helen was stunned. "How many of them are there?"

"They're legion," Diana replied, sounding tired and sad. "They've been on this earth since the Giants walked, and they can make more of their kind. The truth is, dear friend, that they will outlast me."

As Helen began to protest, Diana raised her hand. "Perhaps the gods can change my destiny. I don't know. My Watcher says it's never happened, though."

Helen tried to take it all in. It was too much. She didn't understand any of it. No part of her wanted to believe it.

"What's a Watcher?" Mark Dellasandro asked from the stairway of Giles's apartment.

Angel, Buffy, and Giles looked sharply up. The boy was drowning in Giles's gray sweatpants and an ancient, dark blue Oxford sweatshirt he'd forgotten he had.

Behind Mark, Xander made a moue of apology for the interruption.

"Nothing you need concern yourself with," Giles said politely, standing. "You must be starving. Willow's made some tea, and I'm sure there are things for sandwiches." He looked across the kitchen alcove at Willow, who had stood transfixed throughout Giles's narrative about Helen.

Now she blinked and said, "Oh, yes, things. Sandwiches. Things." She bustled over to the refrigerator and opened the door.

Buffy muttered, "Whistler said a Brit's fridge is like a nun."

"I beg your pardon?" Giles asked.

But just then the boy came all the way down the stairs into the room.

"What happened to those girls?" he asked.

"Oh, it's just a play we're working on for school," Buffy tossed off. "Diana and Helen. We're big into Greek tragedies, huh, Xander? He and Willow and I did a scene from *Oedipus Rex* for the school talent show in sophomore year." She shrugged. "Well, we tried to. Instead, there was a guy with a guillotine."

She looked at the others, who along with Giles, were silently urging her to cease and desist. "It's a long story."

The boy frowned at her but said nothing. His eyelids flickered as though they must weigh twenty stone apiece.

"Sit down," Giles said gently to him. "I'll get you a cup of tea."

Giles went into the kitchen. Willow was hunched over, pawing through the leftover bits of some recent restaurant meals, and Giles thought he heard her sniffling.

"Willow?" he asked quietly.

She looked from the refrigerator. Her face was red and her eyes quite puffy. She wiped her face with the arm of her sweater and resumed her search for sandwich makings.

"I'm still mad at her," she whispered miserably. "I thought once I got unpossessed, I wouldn't be. But she hasn't found Oz." She bit her fingernail. "I keep thinking she hasn't tried hard enough. What does that say about me?"

"That you care for him very much," Giles said compassionately. "That people are much more complex than at first it would seem. Else, how can we love and hate someone at the same time?"

She considered that. "But I *know* she's been looking. I *know* she's been trying."

"The head knows," he replied. "The heart does not." He felt for a moment the enormity of his own loss. Jenny, sweet Jenny. Yes, if he admitted it, there had been times when he had actually hated Buffy for giving Angel such happiness that he had become a demon, then hated her for not killing him. Missing someone so much . . . loving them, and never having them again . . . Sometimes it was too much to bear. He understood Willow's heart, even if she did not.

"It's hard to deal with lack of concrete results, when a loved one is in jeopardy. Believe me, I understand."

He gave her a wry smile. "How many times have you seen me lose my temper with her? Yet you know I never stop caring about her. And yet, upon occasion, my concern for her far outweighs my affection for her."

That seemed to comfort Willow. Her mouth shifted as she put a hand on the refrigerator. "Sandwich things," she said bravely. "The adventure continues."

He flashed her a smile. "Good show. I'll give you a hand. I believe there's some cucumber and butter."

She blinked at him. "And?"

He pursed his lips. "That makes a nice sandwich."

"In England, maybe. Here, well, I was thinking maybe some roast beef? Swiss cheese?"

"Quite. Neither of which you will find in the crisper."

"Oh." She blinked. "Well, cucumbers. They're . . . crunchy . . . and green," she ventured.

Feeling a pang for the lost days of Britain, he left the

kitchen, walked into the living room, and picked up the portable. Punched in a number he knew by heart. Put the phone to his ear.

"Sunnydale Pizza," a voice said on the other end.

"Yes, hullo. I should like to order two large pizzas for delivery," he began.

"Mr. Giles," the voice said. "Hey, man, how ya doing? The usual?"

Xander put on Giles's James Dean denim jacket— *Whoa, where had this little number come from, Carnaby Street? Certainly not the Men's Warehouse*—and walked out onto the street.

The street that was a bit noisy and crowded for this time of night. People were milling around on the sidewalks, spilling out into the road; a car came by and half-swerved toward a clump of men, who chased after it like dogs.

Xander was wigged, but he kept it to himself as he strolled on by the various groups. He had thought to calm himself down and talk himself into maybe some optimism about where Cordy was and what was happening to her. A phone call to her house had revealed that her parents had no clue as to where she was, without revealing that he was the loser formerly known as boyfriend.

Someone threw a beer bottle against the chain-link fence on Xander's right. There was another, more distant crash of glass. Car brakes squealed.

Catty-corner on the next block, two men began shouting at each other. The taller one threw a punch at the other one and a crowd formed with the speed of a lit match.

Then he heard someone say, "I just saw the little

bastard with my own eyes. Some kids went with him into that condo complex down the street."

Someone else said, "I've got a gun."

The first someone replied, "Good. We'll go door to door if we have to, but Mark Dellasandro's dead before sunrise."

As casually as he could, Xander hung a lazy U and began to walk back toward Giles's house.

"That's one of them!" the first someone yelled. "That kid with the dark hair. Hey, kid!"

"Uh-oh," Xander muttered.

He broke into a run.

Cordelia looked up from the floor of her cell at the dark-haired vampire and said, "What? Are you nuts?"

The dark vampire was holding out a spear and a shield. A very dirty and crusty spear and shield, like might be found in the Sunnydale Museum, where the broken pottery and half-rotted baskets did not so much live as lie around gasping.

She shrugged and said, "If you want to face your friend defenseless, be my guest."

She put the spear and the shield on the floor and turned to go. Cordelia raised out a hand.

"Wait!" she cried.

The vampire turned, her brows raised.

"Please," Cordelia huffed. "Please wait."

The vampire smiled. "That's better. See? You can be trained. We were beginning to doubt it."

Cordelia wordlessly glanced down at the whip marks on her own shoulder and counted to ten. Now that her terrible headache was gone, she could think more clearly. Sure, she was scared, but she was also

Queen C. It was taking a lot out of her not to tell this bitch exactly what she thought about her. But that was not tact. That was self-preservation.

"What do you want?" the vampire asked, leaning against the metal cage and crossing her arms and legs.

"I want to know why you're doing this," Cordelia said bluntly. " 'Cause it's kind of, um, like, a little on the edge? As in, majorly insane?"

The vampire threw back her head and laughed. "Julian!" she cried. "Do you hear that?"

"Indeed."

From the shadows just beyond the cage, Julian, the very scary but hunky blond vampire, took two steps forward. He was with some slimy guy. Cordelia squinted, then glared at the proprietor of Willy's Alibi Room.

"Willy," she said, "you, you . . . *creep.*"

"Hey." He shrugged. "The price was right."

"Like, your life," Cordelia said.

He made a gesture as in *Whatcha gonna do?*

"We pay him rent on these lovely accommodations," Julian said. "This is a set of secret rooms beneath his bar, did you know that, dear girl? There was a period in your history when liquor was illegal."

"There was?" Cordelia asked, surprised. "I thought that was, um, marijuana."

"Oh, God, the American education," he said, sighing and rolling his eyes. "It was called Prohibition, and it took place during the thirties. This was where the illegal drink of that time was funneled into Sunnydale. This little town was notorious for its moonshine."

He laughed. "As it is now. Moonshine. A pun. You see, your friend wears the coat of Romulus."

Cordelia sat back on her heels. "Y'know, I really don't understand any of this," she said dully. "And I subscribe to *W* and I used to watch 'House of Style' until Cindy Crawford stopped doing it. But I've never heard of a designer named Romulus."

At this Julian doubled over. He laughed until tears welled in his eyes.

Then he turned to the vampire woman and said, "Helen, I must turn her. She's far too delightful simply to drink."

"Turn her, and I'll stake you both myself," the dark-haired woman said.

Julian gazed at Cordelia and thrust out his lower lip.

"Pity," he said mournfully. His face hardened and he turned into the demon she knew he really was behind the Brad-Pitt looks.

Who is so out, she thought savagely. *Everybody knows that.*

"Pick up the spear and the shield," he said, eyes glowing, fangs glistening, "or I'll drain you now."

"Julian, say please," the dark-haired vampire said. "We must set a good example."

"Both of you can go to hell," Cordelia muttered under her breath. If she had anything to do with it, they'd be there shortly.

She picked up the spear and shield. Sure, she'd learn how to use these things. As soon as possible.

But not for the reason they think.

She hid her face. Okay, she wasn't the Slayer, but she was a friend of the Slayer. Okay, maybe not so much a friend as someone who put up with the Slayer. She'd seen Buffy in a battle or three hundred. She could make some moves of her own.

And then I'll take these two down, and I'll, like, wound Oz or something so he won't kill me, and we'll get out of here.

"Are you crying, lovely one?" Julian asked softly.

"Huh, me? No way," Cordelia said, wiping her face with the hand that held the spear.

Then she turned and saw Jordan Smyth. Jordan, who she had tried to help get straight and stay in school. Jordan, who had confessed to a major crush on her.

"Cordelia," he murmured, shocked.

Chapter 10

Xander raced into Giles's apartment and slammed the door. Heads swiveled toward him, and Angel, in a pair of clean, tight jeans and an Oxford sweatshirt, stopped on the stairway from the loft.

"I was, recognized," he said, gasping a bit.

Buffy, like Mark, was rolling in sweat clothes. She said, "By who? Autograph hounds?"

"They saw us come in here with Mark," Xander explained. "I can't give you names and astrological signs, but they're on their way here."

"We have to leave," Giles said. "We can get to my car."

Buffy took Mark's hand. It was thin. His face was long and pinched. "We'll take you to another place, okay? You'll be safe."

"They're going to find me sooner or later," he said tiredly.

"No. They. Are. Not." She shook his wrist.

"C'mon, be strong for me. I want to protect you, but there's only so much of me."

She threw a look at Willow, another at Xander. They were depending on her to find Oz and Cordy. She felt guilty sitting here. She should be out. She should be doing something.

I have so let them down. I've let everybody down.

She said, "Mark, listen to me. I need your help. I really do."

The boy did not look up to the job. Buffy put her hands on his shoulders and bent down. He was small for his age. She wondered if the other boys teased him at school.

He buried his face in his hands. Buffy was sorry. Very, very sorry. But this was no time for him to lose it. She had to get him out of there.

Firmly, she put her hands around both wrists and began to half-pull, half-drag him out of the apartment as she looked at the others.

"Giles, if I were you," she said, "I'd grab anything I really treasured. When they can't find Mark, there's a really good chance they'll take their frustrations out on anything and anybody."

Giles looked around. Nodded. "You're quite right, of course."

"Oh," Willow moaned. "We're never going to get to rescue Oz."

"Or to eat," Xander added, then stirred himself. "Or to save Cordy, I meant. First priority. Oz. Eating would be, let's see, third." He glanced guiltily at Willow. "Not that saving Oz is second in priority to saving Cordelia. No way. I mean—"

Buffy watched Giles go up the stairs to his loft

bedroom. She said to Xander and Willow, "You guys ready to roll?"

"Sure," Willow said.

Buffy looked at her best friend and wondered why she should be surprised that Willow's eyes were swollen and her face was blotchy. It was obvious she'd been crying in the kitchen.

When Willow saw her looking, she snapped, "Just leave me alone, Buffy, all right? I know you have plenty to worry about without worrying about me."

"Will," Buffy said, wounded. "What's wrong?"

"Oh, nothing. Just that you have plenty of time to give Angel kissage and not nearly enough to look for my boyfriend. So thanks a lot."

Buffy was overcome with shame. Willow didn't even know that Buffy had been at Angel's when she had been shot. If she had, she would probably never forgive her.

Which would be right. Because it was unforgivable.

Footsteps clattered on the walk. Then the door shook with a thunderous knocking on the other side.

"Open up or we'll break the door down!" a man yelled.

"Plan B," Buffy said, nodding to Angel, Giles, and the others. Mark put his hands in the baggy pockets and hunched over. Willow picked up an umbrella, and Xander took up a fighter's stance.

"Oh," Giles groaned.

"I'll get you out of here safely," Buffy said.

The door shook as something was rammed against it. Buffy gestured for everyone to take up positions on either side just as it crashed open. Buffy jumped in front of everyone else and said, "Hang a U, and there won't be any trouble."

Six men crowded around the entrance to the apartment. Standing slightly in front of them loomed a very large, very hairy man wearing a baseball cap that read *Wilkins for Re-Election*. He was wearing a dark blue down jacket and a very baggy pair of khaki pants.

"Outta my way," he bellowed at Buffy, shoving her. "All we want is the kid."

Buffy flared, grabbed the man's hand, and flipped him over her shoulder. It was only luck that landed him on Giles's couch.

"Excuse me?" she demanded.

The next man to barrel through the door pulled out a gun and pointed it straight at Buffy.

"Where is the little bastard?" he demanded.

Buffy turned around. Giles and Mark were nowhere to be seen. *Good.*

"I'm warning you. I'll use this," the man said.

Buffy glanced at Angel. He could take the guy out, of that Buffy was fairly certain. Bullets couldn't kill vampires. But they could really tear them up.

The man aimed the weapon directly at her face. His mouth pulled back into a wild, feral grimace and he held the gun with both hands.

"Killer. Killer. Killer." His voice rose to a fever pitch, loud and out of control.

"Killer," a red-haired guy murmured behind the man.

"Killer," another man whispered dangerously.

"Phasers on overload," Xander shouted over the din.

Buffy replied, "Got it."

Then they were a blur, vampire, Slayer, Willow, and Xander, as Angel pushed the man's hands toward the ceiling and Xander yanked him off his feet. As he went down, his gun discharged; a bullet shot into the ceiling and lodged there. He didn't have a chance to fire a second one as Buffy pried it loose from his grip and stuck it in her belt. She didn't like guns. She didn't need guns.

The rest of the crowd came at them, then, not four more men, as she had expected, but more like a dozen. They streamed in from either side of the door.

"It's showtime," Buffy said, as at least five big, angry men rushed her. She jumped into the air and gave the first in line a hard side kick. He stumbled backward, knocking into the others at least hard enough so each one lost his balance. In the millisecond she had, she whirled around and clocked the guy on the couch, who had been showing signs of stirring.

As she turned back, she glanced in Angel's direction. He was holding his own against another four. One of them was wielding a baseball bat, which he aimed directly at Angel's head. As it arced downward, Angel caught it and yanked it out of the man's grasp. He blocked the man's angry punch with it; the assailant howled in pain and lurched out of range.

Another man executed some very slick karate moves, then whirled around in classic kick-boxing style to deliver a sharp jab to Buffy's chin. Her head whipped back; she let herself go with it and grabbed the arm of the sofa like a pole vaulter. She slammed back into the man on the couch, who groaned and went down for the count for the third round. Another time, another place, it might have been funny.

But this was here, and now.

"Think about it!" Willow shouted, as she rammed

the umbrella point into the man's chest. "Think about what you're doing."

But they were beyond thinking; their faces were twisted into masks of rage. They looked like animals. *Or demons,* she thought. *Anything but human beings.*

"Get out of here!" Buffy shouted at Willow. "Make sure they're okay."

Angel battered two men at the same time, then ducked as they swung at him and hit each other. Buffy found time to flash a smile, until the two realized what they had done and pretty much went berserk. They brutally clawed at each other, going for each other's eyes, grabbing and pulling and biting like rabid dogs. Angel hefted the bat and whacked it against the back of the younger man's head, obviously holding back, and watched him go down in a crumpled heap. The other launched himself at Angel, but he took a giant step backward and blocked him with the bat, using it like a short quarterstaff.

Then something crashed, and something else cracked. Buffy grimaced and landed a sharp uppercut on the heavyset man who had stepped up to the plate.

"You break it, you buy it!" she shouted. "And the guy who lives here is rich!"

Something came crashing down from the loft, narrowly missing Buffy's head as it careened to the floor. It was his lunar globe, recently purchased to help Oz with his werewolf deal. It was a shattered mess on the floor that crackled like bacon as the men stepped over it.

"Okay, that does it," Buffy said. She took the man's confiscated gun out of her belt, squinted, raised the gun over her head, and pulled the trigger.

"That's *enough,*" she bellowed. "Stop!"

No one stopped. No one even registered the gunshot.

So, round twenty-two.

About ten minutes later, Angel and Buffy stood alone among the damage. People were lying among scattered books and an overturned chair.

"I didn't kill anyone, did I?" she asked anxiously as she pressed her palm over the hitch in her side and took some deep breaths.

"No." Angel tapped his boot against the side of a man sprawled facedown on the floor. "They're all still breathing."

"Willow?" she called. "Giles?"

There was no answer.

"They must have gotten away," Angel said. "Good."

She nodded in agreement. "You know what I'm wondering? Why the police never showed."

Angel took that in. "Busy elsewhere?"

"Or wacko, also." She smoothed back her hair. "It's got to have something to do with your girlfriend," she said. Her cheeks warmed at the obvious tone of jealousy jaywalking across the road of her sentence.

But Angel's attention was focused elsewhere. From beneath a pile of books, he lifted up a pottery container with two curved handles. There were black demons dancing across the face, and it was stoppered with what looked like wax.

"It's something from her time," he said. "This is something of Helen's."

They looked at each other, and Buffy hefted the object in her hand.

She said, "I'm thinking answers."

They left together.

Outside Rome, A.D. 39

Demetrius was as tall as Apollo. His dark curls tumbled to the nape of his neck. His chest was broad, his hips narrow, and as he sat sipping a goblet of new wine, Helen wanted him more than anything she knew.

More than anything, except for the friendship of Diana, who was betrothed to him.

"I don't understand her," he said, looking defeated. "I know Diana loves me. But there's so much of her hidden away from me." He half-looked at Helen, then turned away. "I've begun to wonder if she loves another."

Her heart was racing and perspiration trickled down her chest. It was a glorious, sunny day, scented with wine and honey. As they sat on the boulder by the olive tree, their hips touching, Helen blazed as if any second she would burst into flames.

"Diana loves you more than life itself," she said again.

He took her hand and toyed with it, not as a lover, but as a childhood friend. "Then why does she cloak her heart from mine?"

"She . . . has responsibilities," Helen said awkwardly, staring at their intertwined hands. At the warm brown the sun had licked onto his flesh; the muscles and veins of his fingers and the back of his hand.

"Oh, Demetrius," she said in a rush. She turned her head. If it meant her life, she would lift his hand to her lips, and kiss it . . .

"Helen?" he whispered, as the tears streamed down her face and her mouth found the center of his palm.

He was clearly surprised, obviously shocked. Roman women were mere extensions of their households, like furniture, like cutlery. But Helen had a soul. She had a heart.

Unlike Diana, she was free to love him.

"Demetrius, I want you," she said miserably.

He drew in his breath. "I am betrothed."

How cruelly he said it, with what harshness. Helen wilted, humiliated beyond endurance. She drew away, pulling her hand away from his and scooting off the rock.

He jumped off and moved to assist her, his right hand gripping her waist, his left, her hip. She wanted to move against him, but she curled away, abjectly humiliated.

"I'm so sorry," she murmured. "Don't tell Diana."

"Helen, please tell me," he pressed. "Why doesn't she allow herself to freely love me?"

"She . . ." She closed her eyes against the tide of her emotion: did she recognize her betrayal, or even then, did she try to convince herself that it was out of concern for him?

As the sun set, and the moon rose, he sat in stunned silence as she poured out the story she had sworn never to tell another living person. She broke her word, as deliberately as one might.

"I can't thank you enough," he whispered, taking up both her hands and kissing them fervently. "You are like the goddess Juno, as merciful as you are beautiful."

She soared the heavens, she descended the depths. She had betrayed her closest friend.

She had found a way into the heart of the man she worshiped.

He said, "I need time to think on this." He smiled in a strange, stricken way at her. "The breaking of a betrothal is not an easy business."

"Indeed," she said unhappily. She was reeling. She had done it.

He left her there, walking away. She hugged her knees to her chest. Her first impulse was to run to Diana, but of course she could not do that. She had changed their relationship forever.

No. Diana did that, she reminded herself. *Diana changed it.*

Her heart searched itself, seeking forgiveness.

Far away, in Rome, Caligula the Emperor sat arrayed in splendid robes and jewels, quite at home among the shrieks of pain and madness in the torture chambers beneath the Games arena.

A gladiator had been bound to an altar before him, and behind that stood an immense statue of Meter, Caligula's dark mother. From her eyes blazed fire, and her mouth dripped with the poison Caligula had concocted, in secret, and administered to his victim. After studying its effects, the emperor would sacrifice him. And eventually, when the stars were right, he would bring Meter forth, into the world.

With his golden cane, he moved the living man's viscera, frowning with impatience as the man screamed in agony.

"Oh, *please,*" the emperor muttered, then lifted the cane out of the steaming mass and leaned his chin on it. "Julian, do you see anything?"

The vampire leaned over the bound victim, and Caligula waited, breathless. It was the custom of this time and place to read fortunes in the organs of animals, birds, and corpses. Only in the merciless court of the emperor did one seek destiny in the flesh of living human beings.

Though the night was chilly, it was hot in the dungeon, where torture fires blazed. The stench of death was thick, and the shrieks of other captives ruined Julian's concentration. He shrugged and yawned. It was near sunrise, and he was weary.

"It augurs well, my lord," Julian told the emperor.

Caligula thrust forward his lower lip. "You always say that," he pouted. " 'It augurs well.' What on earth does that mean?"

Julian knew Caligula was seeking reassurance, demanding compliments. The emperor was as needy as he was insane. "That you are blessed, and Fortuna walks beside you," the vampire asserted.

"Bah." Caligula shifted his weight.

"Is it not so?" Julian asked.

The truth was, he was sick of Caligula and his madness. Of his childish, unending demands for reassurance that he and he alone was master. Julian could snap his neck in an instant. Had, in fact, been promised much if and when he accomplished the deed. . . .

"My lord," said a guard, visibly out of breath. He was half-chasing, half-escorting a youth crowned with a glorious head of dark, curly hair. Julian grinned to himself. The spindly, bald emperor needed this boy, but Caligula detested him for his every attractive attribute. Which the lad, Demetrius, possessed in abundance.

Demetrius fell to his knees and said in a rush,

"Great Caesar, I greet you." He inclined his head. "Noble Julian, I bring you both excellent news. I have confirmed it. My betrothed, Diana, is the Slayer."

"Ah." Caligula thrust his tongue between his lips and sat back in his chair. "So. All that work of wooing her was worth it."

Demetrius nodded. "Not unpleasant work, I might add. Her strength is matched by her passion."

"Who told you she was the Slayer?" Julian asked suspiciously.

"Her best friend. Helen." He hesitated. "She loves me."

Julian smiled. As the saying went, *With friends like that, who needed enemies?*

"You have done well," Julian said. "What is your boon?"

Demetrius looked up at him with fierce hunger. "As you already know, my lord. To become like you."

Julian's eyes ticked to Caligula, who shook his head. The vampire flared with anger. Such as Demetrius would be a tremendous asset to his demon court.

Caligula threw away so many treasures.

"Done," Julian said, smiling at the emperor. He sank his fangs into the young boy's throat and drank. The blood was rich, the heart strong and youthful.

When he was finished, he dropped the husk to the mosaic floor of the dungeon. "He will not rise," he added, as he wiped his mouth.

Behind him, Caligula's captive moaned with terror and pain. The emperor leaned forward, his body tensing with eagerness.

"Tell me, slave," he said in a low, gentle voice, "what does it feel like to be disemboweled? Tell me, or he will do the same to you."

"Please," the man groaned. "Kill me now."

Losing interest—and because he was no man's trained dog—Julian turned away, his cape flapping behind him.

"Where are you going?" Caligula demanded.

"To rest. And then I shall leave, to capture the Slayer," Julian replied simply.

His boots echoed in the cavernous dungeon. His shadow leaped upon the blood-drenched walls.

His fists clenched.

His eyes glowed.

But I shall never give her to you, he thought, seething.

Chapter 11

JORDAN RAN.

After seeing Cordelia down in the secret rooms where the psychos from hell liked to talk about carving people up, Jordan finally lost his nerve. He made some excuse about having to go upstairs to talk to Willy. Then he got the hell out of the Alibi and stole a motorcycle. He drove like a maniac, with no idea where to go, where to hide. After a few minutes, he realized he shouldn't have split. His only hope for saving himself now was getting back the urn, and he had no clue where Mark Dellasandro was.

Then he saw the black van.

They were onto him, after him, and they were bearing down on him. He went into a blind panic, trying to dodge them, not paying any attention to where he was going.

I'm going to die, going to die, going to die, he thought.

He jumped off the motorcycle seconds before they

rammed it, rolled, and stumbled to his feet. Lurching, he dragged his right foot behind himself.

Then he realized he was standing in front of Mrs. Gibson's house.

They had run him to ground.

"Help!" he screamed. He ran as fast as he could, some deep-seated instinct for self-preservation overtaking him. His heart was triphammering and his foot hurt so badly he thought it might just tear off his leg.

He ran around the back and through the kitchen. It stank to high heaven inside the house. His stomach curdled and he fell to his knees on the linoleum and retched.

He ran into the living room and peered out of the Venetian blinds. There was the van, and about six of them were getting out.

"Oh, my God," he whispered, sobbing.

"Jordan," she said behind him.

She was wearing her vamp face. The moonlight cast glints of midnight blue in her hair. Her eyes glowed golden.

"I'm done," he said. His voice wavered. "Totally. I'm out."

She chuckled low in her throat. It was unearthly. She said, "Julian bet me the lives of ten men that you would ultimately disappoint us."

She glided dangerously toward him, her long, black gown rustling like dead leaves. She wore a golden tiara of intertwined bats in her loose, flowing hair.

She clapped her hands. Two dark-scaled demons whose heads were crowned with spiny protrusions stepped from the shadows, trailed by the Queen's blond vampire lover.

"Take him."

The blond vampire put his arm around the waist of the dark queen and licked her cheek. Together, they turned and looked at Jordan, and laughed.

As Jordan was dragged away, he said desperately, "Please, don't do this to me! You don't have to do this to me!"

She raised an eyebrow. "And yet."

Cordelia screamed as the black-and-blue body of Jordan Smyth was thrown into her cage and the door slammed and locked. Then she ran to him and turned him over.

Most of his teeth had been knocked out.

"Oh, my God," she whispered. "Jordan?"

His skin was freezing cold. She thought he might be dead.

He opened one eye, and groaned. "Cordelia. Sorry," he whispered.

She touched his forehead. His head was bleeding in several places. "What's this all about? Why are they doing this? What's going on?"

"Not now," he muttered.

"They're going to kill us," she said urgently. "You've *got* to tell me what's going on."

Just then, a half-dozen vampires swirled into view, carrying torches and laughing among themselves. One of them, a burly man with black scars on his cheeks, capered over to the cage.

"We're going to get the rest of your friends," he said to Cordelia.

"Why?" she asked.

He laughed and ran back to the group.

"Why?" she shouted after them.

"Sorry," Jordan whispered.

"Sorry, my butt!" Despite his injuries, Cordelia grabbed the collar of his shirt and shook him. "Jordan, they're going to kill us all. Including me!"

He sighed like he was too tired to even think of it.

"Listen," she began, "if you think I—"

"Keys. In my pocket."

Her eyes widened. "What?"

"They forgot. Keys to the cell."

She looked around at their prison. "This cell? And you were just going to lie there and moan?"

She fished around in his pockets. Her hand wrapped around a key on a satin ribbon. With a thrill of triumph, she pulled it out of his pocket and dangled it in front of his face. Silently he nodded.

Cordelia scrabbled over to the gate. No one was guarding her. Apparently they figured with her locked in, there was no need.

Hah, she thought as she slipped the key into the padlock and snapped it open.

She pushed open the gate. "Okay," she whispered. "C'mon, Jordan."

He shook his head. "I'll slow you down. Just go."

"Don't be a dumb jerk," she said harshly, glancing anxiously around. When he didn't move, she sighed and grabbed his arm. "Damn it, move!"

He sighed and half sat up. Cordelia looped her arms under his and tried to pull him to his feet. For a few seconds, he didn't move. Then he heaved himself up and stood.

"Good, good." Cordelia gestured for him to follow her and crept out of the cell.

Get out, she thought as she spied a spear propped

against the wall just below a flickering torch. Her heart pounded as she ran over and grabbed it up.

Jordan was slowly following.

"Okay. Which way is out?" she whispered.

He gestured toward the left. Cordelia nodded and dashed that way, craning her neck into the darkness. Which was better, to go down there blind or risk discovery by snagging the torch?

She decided to go under the cover of the blackness. Waved at Jordan to hurry it up.

He stared at her. She frowned and said, "Jordan, come *on.*"

Then she heard a very distinctive chuckle.

Turned.

Julian stood before her with his arms crossed over his chest.

Before she had time to think it through, she assumed a fighter's stance and jabbed the spear at him. He looked surprised and dodged it. With a fierce shout, she went on the offensive, rushing him, jabbing high, low, left, feinting right, and nearly catching him on the right forearm.

Then he growled savagely in his throat, like the monster he was, and his powerful left hand extended and grabbed the spear. Roaring, he broke it over his knee and flung the pieces across the cavern.

He came toward her, morphing into vamp mode. Cordelia broke into a sob and stumbled backward.

Behind her, Jordan said, "I—I did what you asked. Now you've got to let me go."

Julian transformed. He smiled at Cordelia. "Nice try. I'm pleased." Then his eyes narrowed with contempt as he looked past her to Jordan.

"I don't have to do anything," he replied, "that I don't want to do."

Sunnydale had gone completely mad.

All through the business district, throngs of people were breaking store windows and looting. They were setting cars on fire. They were fighting each other. People were running down the middle of the street, screaming and chasing each other.

The night echoed with gunshots.

In the Gilesmobile, Willow sat beside Giles and murmured warding incantations and binding spells over and over again. She was doing everything she could to keep the mobs from the car as Giles searched for a safe place to hide Mark Dellasandro. It seemed a hopeless task. They had each thought of, and rejected, Xander's, Willow's, and Buffy's houses, for much the same reason that they couldn't go back to Giles's apartment—vigilantes were roaming from place to place, searching for "the killer"—never mind that by now, others had died in all the bedlam and there were a number of killers running loose.

Willow said, "We've got to pump up the volume on how to stop this, Giles."

"Here, here," Xander said from the backseat. Then, "You okay, Mark?"

Giles had instructed Mark to lie down on the floor of the backseat. Willow knew he was afraid of what would happen if someone spotted Mark. They would probably all be pulled from the car, and torn limb from limb.

"Goddess Hecate, heed me," Willow murmured, rummaging in the bag between her tennis shoes. She'd pulled it from beneath her seat. It was a spare

spellcaster's satchel, which she'd given to Giles to keep in his car.

"Think of it like an extra set of flares," she'd told him. "For emergencies, if I don't have my regular bag with me."

A warm, large hand closed over her shoulder. She closed her eyes and put her hand over it. Xander. She could practically read his thoughts. They had been best friends for a long, long time.

They had loved each other for longer.

"We're gonna find them," Willow said, patting Xander's hand. "I have on my resolve face, and you know what that means."

"Yes, I do, Will," Xander said gently.

Then someone threw what at first looked like a beer bottle at Giles's car. It exploded against the windshield, spreading flames everywhere. As everyone inside the car screamed, Giles swerved around a man in a down jacket and a hunting cap, aiming a hunting rifle directly at them.

"What's happening?" Mark yelled from the floor.

"I'd say we've been spotted," Giles said.

Willow looked at Xander. He was white-faced. Leaning forward, he said as softly as he could, "Will, if they find this kid, they'll kill him." His eyes added, *And us.*

Then someone threw something else at the car, and the windshield shattered. The flames blew in, and Giles fought for control.

"And this would be about the time Buffy would show, if this was a TV program," Xander said. "Okay, Buff. Any second now. We're all trapped and powerless, just like you like us. So c'mon, Buffy, chica, honey, my one and only . . ."

Willow disappeared as she rummaged around out of view. She came up with two very large bottles.

"Holy water," she announced.

She shook it at the flames, but it wasn't doing much good.

"I'll slow down," Giles said.

"No!" Mark shouted, lifting up his head.

Giles was firm. "Just for a moment."

Xander looked through the rear window. The angry mob was trailing after, but Giles had put a lot of distance between the car and the bad guys.

On the floor, Mark was crying. Xander leaned down and patted him. "We'll make it, kid."

Giles peered through the smoky windshield. The fire was out. They passed the city limits; Xander wished that the fact of leaving Sunnydale made him feel better. *But evil doesn't care about street signs,* he thought. *Or traffic safety. It never yields the right of way.*

Giles said, "We're overdue for some good, hard research."

"Yeah, such as where to hide Mark. C'mon, buddy, you might as well sit up," Xander said, reaching down a hand.

The boy huddled on the floor. "No," he said. He sounded very flat, very wigged. Xander had seen this kind of thing before. They had all gone there on the dawn patrol, once or twice. Sometimes the ookalicious stuff was more than you could take, and you just checked out for a brief spell. Kind of like your own private vacation.

To the land of silent screams.

"Where to hide Mark," Giles echoed as they drove along. The night air blew in through the ruined windshield on Willow's side, making her hair stream away from her face. Xander thought she looked like a pretty figurehead on a sailing ship. Also, the little girl whose Barbie he had stolen.

Willow hesitated, then half-raised her hand, as if they were in class. "What about Angel's place?"

If Giles hadn't given her a look, Xander would have physically turned her head around so he could have.

"What, are you nuts?" Xander cried.

Giles said, "Willow, it would be a good suggestion if we were certain Angel would not be afflicted with the same sort of condition as we all have been."

"Yeah, we've already seen what Angel does when he's possessed," Xander cracked. "And it's not a pretty sight."

She bobbed her head. "It was just a thought. Maybe we can ask Angel to stay somewhere else." She shrugged. "But then, if he goes all crazy, he knows where Mark is. Not a good idea." She raised her brows. "Library?"

"I thought of that as well," Giles said, "but it's risky. We've had our share of close scrapes keeping Oz there. However, let's keep it on the list."

Willow was silent a moment. Xander put his hand back on her shoulder and gave her a squeeze. She nodded, as if she wanted to let him know she was okay.

"What about Mrs. Gibson's house?" Willow asked. "Just for the time being. It's been sold, but the new owner hasn't shown up yet. Everyone's gotten kind of bored with it. They don't sneak up on the porch anymore."

On the floor, Mark raised his head. "I know that house. It's haunted. I saw things moving in it."

"Yeah, I know," Xander said gently. "We all see things that go bump in the night."

"Wait a minute. When we see things that go bump in the night, that's because they're really bumping." Willow's eyes got big the way they did when her brain was processing minor factoids into tasty, cream-filled facts. "That house was sold to a H. Ombra. Didn't you say the Betrayed One's name is Helen?"

"Yes, indeed, I did." Giles looked at her. "Ombra is a variant of the Latinate for 'Shadow.' "

"And you saw things?" Xander said to Mark, who nodded.

"I really did," he assured Xander. "Shapes. I heard a woman laughing."

Giles looked at Xander in the rearview mirror. Xander blinked once and said, "Will? How many stakes you got in that bag?"

"Just a couple," she said, taking a breath. "But if we could find Buffy and—"

"Oh, bloody hell," Giles groaned.

Red and blue lights flashed in the mirror. Sure enough, a police car was signaling them to pull over.

"Giles, you maniac," Xander said. "Obviously, there was a speed trap back there. And you were going, oh, at least twenty-five."

"We can only hope they aren't possessed," Giles muttered. "Willow, open the glove box, please. I'll need my registration and proof of insurance."

"What you'll need," Xander muttered back, "is a gun."

"Oh, and do you have one handy?" Giles asked him.

Xander shrugged. "Nope. Not today."

Mark tugged on Xander's pants leg. Xander looked down.

Mark said, "I do." He looked embarrassed. "I took it from Mr. Giles's house."

"That's both good news and bad," Giles observed. "Since you have it, we face the possibility of actually having to use it."

As he rolled down his window, he added, "Please pass it forward, Mark."

Xander reached down for the gun as Mark reached up with his left hand. He grabbed the front of Xander's shirt and held him, and pointed the gun straight at Xander's face.

As he stared at the barrel, Xander's heart skipped a beat. Then it thought about leaping from his chest.

"What? Mark, give me the gun," Giles said.

At that moment, a voice called out, "Evening."

"It's the cop," Xander said to Mark. "So, what's the rest of your plan?"

Mark whispered, "To get out of here alive." His arm stayed steady and his eyes were focused. "No matter what."

Chapter 12

JOYCE SUMMERS WAS HOME WHEN BUFFY AND ANGEL arrived. She was in the kitchen, gulping down water like crazy, and wiping her forehead with a trembling hand.

"The whole town's rioting," she said, refilling her glass from the faucet. "Buffy, a drink? Angel, I don't suppose you drink much water."

"Actually, I can. Do," he amended.

Joyce turned around, saw the condition Buffy was in, and paled. She reached out a hand.

"Oh, my God," she said with a little cry. "What've you been doing?"

Then she must have noticed Giles's torn sweatshirt beneath Angel's filthy duster. It was ripped from his right shoulder across his chest to his hip. There were deep scratches in the flesh beneath it.

"Like you said," Buffy answered, shrugging. "The whole town's rioting. We had to fight our way from Giles's apartment to here."

"Let me get the first-aid kit," Joyce said, then took a deep breath.

"I'm fine," Buffy said. "Angel's fine. Sit down, Mom. You don't look too well."

Trembling, Joyce sat.

"Mom, we're looking for Giles. Has he checked in with you?"

Tears rolled down Joyce's cheeks. "I don't know. What do I look like, your secretary?"

Buffy blinked. "Mom?"

Joyce slammed down her fist. "I can't seem to control myself. It's just that . . . nothing is going right. The insurance company called to settle on our robbery. The stolen items weren't even covered! There was this . . . urn, I guess you'd call it . . . a piece of pottery from the reign of Caligula. It's over sixteen hundred years old. It was truly priceless."

Buffy stared at Angel, who stared back. Slowly she took the urn from her pocket.

"Is this it, Mom?"

"Oh." Joyce blinked. "Oh, thank God! Buffy, where did you find it?"

Buffy moved her shoulders. She was baffled. "In Giles's apartment."

She handed the urn to Joyce, who hefted it gently in her palm. "This is the one."

"We need to keep this," Buffy said. "We need to show it to Giles."

Joyce demurred. "It's evidence in a police matter."

"Mom, I was evidence in a police matter," Buffy drawled. "Please, you know the sitch. This is so very much beyond that."

Joyce exhaled, nodded. "Of course. You're right, dear. But when you're finished with it, please give it back. We can't afford to replace it. If we lose . . . or break it, the gallery will go under."

Buffy patted her arm. "Remember those eggs we had to take care of for health class at school? I'll be even more careful with it."

"Okay." Joyce managed a smile. Then she frowned. "But didn't you tell me those eggs turned us into zombies?"

Buffy held up the urn. "And I'm wondering if there's anything about this that's turning everyone into maniacs."

She put it back into her pocket and went off to check the answering machine.

Leaving Angel alone with Joyce.

They looked at each other. Joyce's blood pressure rose. She was always uncomfortable around the vampire these days.

Angel inclined his head. "How are you, Mrs. Summers?"

"You're staying away from her." It was not a question. It was an order.

His dark eyes were inscrutable, his face grim and set. "Yes, ma'am."

He was polite, she had to give him that. When he wasn't possessed. When he wasn't bragging to her about how he gone to bed with her seventeen-year-old daughter.

When he wasn't trying to kill them all.

Sudden hatred seethed through her. *Damn him.* Damn him for doing all the things he had done, and then being allowed to live. He should have died like a normal man over a hundred years ago. He should have died when Buffy killed him.

He should die now, she thought.

"Mrs. Summers, I . . ." he began, and sighing, turned away from her. He looked up at the ceiling.

She backed to the drawer with the steak knives. They had wooden handles.

Probably not long enough, she thought. *The broom, then.*

Very casually, she started for the broom closet.

Take him out. Kill him. Yes.

She opened the broom closet.

"Mrs. Summers," he continued, "I know you don't really like me arou—"

"Mom, did you know there's a message from the police on the phone machine?" Buffy asked as she came into the room. "They found some fingerprints at the gallery. They want to talk to you."

Joyce stared at her with her hand around the broom. She stood shaking from head to toe.

Buffy took a step forward. "Mom?"

Her anger shifted.

Rotten kid. She ruined my life. Ruined it. If she had stayed gone . . . if she was gone . . . yes . . .

"Buffy," she whispered, "run."

"Mom?" Buffy hurried toward her mother. "Mom, what's wrong?"

"I—I—" Joyce put her hands to her head. The broom clattered to the floor. "Buffy, get away from me."

Buffy put her hands over her mother's and made her look at her. Joyce fought to avert her gaze. She didn't want Buffy to see the hatred there. The loathing. *My life is a nightmare because of you.*

"I . . . I wish you were dead," Joyce croaked.

Tears stung her daughter's eyes. "No, you love me, Mom. I know you do. It's the . . ." Buffy trailed off. "Fight it."

"No. I hate you." Joyce narrowed her eyes. Her lips were trembling. "If I could kill you, I would."

Angel did not want to be a witness to this. It was too painful, too reminiscent of when he himself had said such terrible things to Buffy and everyone she loved. He only prayed Buffy realized that what Joyce was saying wasn't the hidden truth beneath an everyday facade of lies. Buffy's mother loved her above all living things.

"Mom, take it easy," Buffy said. Angel heard the hurt in her voice, and he clenched his hands because he could do nothing to ease it. Only stand there, and be there in case she turned to him for comfort.

Buffy looked over her shoulder at Angel. "We have to find Giles, or Helen, or both. We have to do something, Angel. This can't go on."

He nodded. "Then let's go find Giles," he said.

Buffy looked at him hard. "Or Helen."

He didn't answer, only walked to the front door to give Buffy some time alone with her mother. He wasn't positive that was the best thing to do, but it would have to do.

After a few minutes, Buffy joined him at the door with her Slayer's bag over her shoulder. The pain in her bearing cut him to the quick. She said, "You want to wash up before we go? I think I have one of my dad's old college sweatshirts in my drawer. It'd fit you. And you're obviously into the whole college logo thing."

"How'd it go?" Angel asked her.

Misery etched her face, making her look very, very tired. He wanted to lean her head on his shoulder and tell her everything was going to be all right. He wanted to make it all right.

"I was afraid to leave her alone. So, um . . ." She made a fist.

His eyes widened. "You knocked her out?"

Buffy blinked at him. "My own mother? No way." With the fist, she mimicked throwing back a drink. "I made her chugalug an entire glass of vodka."

From the kitchen, he heard Joyce giggle and call, "Okay, barkeep! Pour me another."

"Also, I handcuffed her to the chair." Buffy looked terribly uncomfortable. "She laughed and said something about Giles. That I didn't quite understand and never hope to."

"Oh, I don't know, Buffy. Handcuffs can be fun," he said before thinking. He rolled his eyes. "And I can't believe I just said that."

"If you had any class, you'd blush," she said.

"If I weren't a vampire, I would," he replied.

"Hey! I said, another round!" Joyce bellowed.

"At least she's happy." Buffy looked in the direction of the kitchen.

Angel couldn't help himself. Now he did put his arm around her shoulders as he opened the front door.

"She didn't mean those things, Buffy. Any more than Brian Dellasandro meant to kill those people."

Together they turned and looked out at the night. The moon was awash with pink. Above the treetops, red flared like searchlights across the dark sky.

"Sunnydale's on fire," Buffy said. "So to speak. Wouldn't it be nice if it burned to the ground?"

"It would only change things for a little while."

Buffy nodded. "The Hellmouth would still be here."

"The Hellmouth would still be here."

They headed out.

The police officer shook his head in disbelief as Giles continued his account of how he had come to be driving a smoking car. Naturally, he omitted the fact that he had been recognized as someone in league with Mark Dellasandro.

"Sunnydale's gone crazy. It's just like L.A. now, with all those riots. It's the killings. Got people all riled up."

"Indeed. If 'riled up' is the correct term to use," Giles said.

Xander cleared his throat.

Giles cleared his as well. "I've got to get these young people home. As you might imagine, their parents are quite worried about them."

"Yes, I might imagine that," the policeman said easily. He patted the car. "Hope you've got good insurance. My brother's an agent with Sunnydale Mutual, so if—"

"No," Xander said.

There were sounds of a scuffle, and then Giles heard Mark behind him, saying, "Freeze."

"Oh, no," Giles breathed, closing his eyes. He gripped the steering wheel.

"Take your gun out of your holster," Mark said.

"Now, son, take it easy," the cop replied, holding his hands in front of him. "I know it's been a bad night, but . . ."

"Mark," Giles began.

"No!" the boy cried. "Take your gun out. I know what you people are like. You shot my brother."

The police officer blinked at him. "Oh, my God," he said slowly. "You're Mark Dellasandro."

Giles heard Mark suck in his breath. Evidently the boy had just realized his mistake. They had been about to get away scot free, as the saying went. Now that he had pulled this stunt, they were in deep . . . trouble, as the other saying went.

"Give me the gun, Mark," the cop said gently. "It'll go easier for you."

"Take your gun out, or I'll kill you," Mark said unsteadily.

"No, boy, I don't believe you will," the man replied. "I truly don't."

"I will!"

Mark fired a shot. It went wide, but it was close enough to the mark. The policeman paled and unsnapped his holster.

"No, wait," Mark said. "Mr. Giles, you take his gun."

Giles said, "Mark—"

"If you don't, I'll shoot him."

Giles looked at the cop, who glared at Giles. "Aiding and abetting."

"I took them hostage," Mark piped up. "I told him I'd shoot this guy if he didn't drive me to Mexico."

It was the kind of story a fourteen-year-old would think up, based upon years of watching films about fugitives and murderers. Giles's heart went out to the lad, who was doing this only in fear for his life. Nothing more. But the cop might not know that. No one else did.

Giles said to Mark, "I'm getting out of the car, all right? To get his gun."

"My gun's against Xander's head," Mark said.

Giles heard Xander mutter, "Oh, thanks for using my name."

"Take his gun out of the holster and hold it with your thumb and pointer finger," Mark instructed Giles.

As Giles moved to comply, he knew he had to decide what to do. Aim the gun at Mark? Hand it to the policeman? Risk Xander's life? He truly didn't think Mark would shoot Xander. Not in his right mind. But could he trust that?

And the cop, could he trust him? What would happen to Mark if the man succumbed to rage while Mark was in his custody? Or if anyone else did?

He took the gun and held it as Mark had ordered him.

"Get his handcuffs," Mark said.

Again, Giles looked at the cop. The man swallowed.

"I've got a family," he whispered.

Giles hazarded a look over his shoulder. "Mark, I will not allow you to harm this man."

"I don't want to hurt anybody," Mark said brokenly. Then his voice hardened. "But I will, if I have to. Now, get his handcuffs."

Giles said under his breath, "The last time I did this, I'd had quite a lot of chocolate." Then seeing the cop's confused look, he said, "I'm so very sorry about this."

"Just don't let him hurt me, Mr. Giles."

Giles cuffed him quickly.

"Put him in his car," Mark told Giles.

Giles hesitated. That was probably not the best

idea. The man would probably be able to reach his radio with his mouth, something like that. Nevertheless, he did as he was told.

The man went willingly, slid in, and looked up at Giles. He whispered, "There's an extra key just under the dash."

Giles shook his head. "Sorry. I can't chance it."

The man shrugged. "Someone will come along."

"Indeed." Giles took a breath. "I am so sorry."

"You talk like you're responsible." His tone was suspicious.

"Mr. Giles, come on," Mark said.

The man bobbed his head. "He's closed the door behind himself. He'll be in jail before sunrise."

"He's only fourteen," Giles said.

The police officer's face grew hard. "He's a cold-blooded killer. If I'd realized he was in the car, I might have blown him away then and there. Saved the taxpayers some money."

Giles chilled at his words. He straightened and walked back to the car. Turned on the engine, and drove away.

As soon as they were out of sight, Xander handed him the gun.

"When did he stop holding it against your head?" Giles asked.

"As soon as you guys were out of sight," Xander replied.

"Well, I think you did the right thing," Giles said tersely.

In their search for Giles, Buffy and Angel ranged all over Sunnydale. So did crazy people. About a quarter of the business district was in flames. A group of men started shooting at the firefighters, so they drove away in their big red fire truck. They were halfway to the fire station when some kind of road rage overtook their driver, and he rammed a city bus.

"Where's the rest of the Justice League when you need them?" Buffy said as she and Angel raced through a flaming alley.

"The Bahamas, working on their tans."

"Thank God you have no interest in that," she said sincerely.

"No, but I find *this* interesting," Angel said, pointing straight ahead.

"Whoa." Buffy skidded to a stop and ducked behind a row of trash cans. Angel joined her.

At the opposite end of the alley, a trio of vampires stood in the firelight, pointing and laughing. And chomping down hard on Xander's nemesis, Ms. Broadman, as she struggled and screamed in their grasp.

The vampires wore Roman togas, just like she, Willow, and Xander had cooked up for their drama presentation for the talent show. Only, Buffy and the others had worn black leotards under theirs. These guys were half-naked, and fairly cut. And their togas looked a lot older, dirtier, and bloodier.

"No rest for the weary," Buffy said, pulling a stake out of her bag.

"Or the wicked." Angel took the stake, and she got out another for herself. She fitted another one into her belt.

Together, they darted in the shadows toward the vampires and their victim. Police sirens and ambulances screamed. Though Buffy kept her gaze firmly trained on her targets, her peripheral vision caught a man staggering down the street with a huge gash in his forehead. Across the street, a tree lining the sidewalk blazed, and the power line above it sparked like fireworks.

She gestured to Angel to take out the one on the left. He was the tallest. She would take on the two shorter ones.

He nodded.

As they crept nearer, her heartbeat picked up. One of her quarry was a dark-haired female. *Helen?*

No. Too short, Buffy thought, disappointed. Her grip tightened around the stake.

"Help me," Ms. Broadman moaned.

Buffy took that as their cue to move into attack mode. She pumped her legs and thrust her stake straight out from her chest. As she knew they would, the vampires heard the clatter of her and Angel's boots and turned, the shorter male still holding tight to Ms. Broadman.

"Stop, or she dies," he growled.

Buffy said, "So, she dies. She accused my friend of cheating and got him expelled."

Ms. Broadman's eyes widened. The vampire looked momentarily confused, and Buffy seized the moment: she rushed the female before she knew what was happening, and took her out. In two seconds, the vampire was dust.

"You will pay for that." The vampire holding Ms. Broadman flung her aside—*mission accomplished,* Buffy thought triumphantly—and came for Buffy.

Meanwhile, the taller vampire and Angel were circling one another, speaking in a foreign language that Buffy was fairly certain was not French. *Or else I'm doing worse in it than I thought.*

"Run, Ms. Broadman," Buffy said. "And let Xander back in school, okay?"

Without another word, the woman took off.

The vampire bared its fangs at Buffy, and hunkered down for a good long fight.

"Could it be that I have engaged the Slayer?" he asked, sounding really happy about it.

She hunkered back. Fight he wanted, fight he got. But she wasn't about to go more than a couple rounds with him.

"You want to get engaged? But I hardly know you. And, to my everlasting joy, I'm not going to get to know you."

She thrust the stake at him like a sword—Giles had had a fencing thing lately—he blocked it with his wrist and tried to loop it to the left, but she stepped back quickly and double-thrust.

"You fight in an alien manner," the vampire said.

"Alien? You can say that with a straight face, the way you're dressed?" Buffy asked.

Then she really went for him, hacking and slashing, never mind all the fancy footwork. He gave as good as he got, using his powerful arms and fists. He was made of steel; okay, not literally, but he had bulging muscles all over the place. And he knew how to use them, and she was not talking posing for Mr. Vampire America. Blood trickled down her face after he smacked her nose; she winced but kept up her momentum. With an opponent like this, she couldn't let down her guard, not even for a moment.

"Angel, how you doing?" she asked as she crossed her hands one over the other, then slammed the meat of them into the vampire's nose. Eye for an eye and all that.

Angel answered back in the not-French, then said, "We're insulting each other in Latin."

She headbutted the vampire, who groaned and staggered backward toward the street. Headbutted him again. He was on the sidewalk.

"Your grade, then?" She pushed the vampire, who tried to catch his balance by grabbing a mailbox, and missed it as he kept going.

Angel grunted. "The word for fatality, you know it?"

"I came, I saw, I dusted," Buffy offered. She double-kicked the vamp, finishing with a roundhouse.

The vampire fell off the curb and into the street just as a car roared down on it.

It smashed into him; he soared into the air. Buffy ran, following his trajectory like a fan at a Dodgers game. When he thudded to the blacktop, she lifted the stake up for a good downward arc.

The vampire exploded in a cloud of ash.

She looked left, right, saw that the car was gone, no one had noticed, and stood. Then she raced back to find Angel alone, a similar scattering of dust at his feet.

Buffy smoothed back her hair as Angel rearranged the tatters of the sweatshirt. She said, "Maybe we should have saved one. Made him talk."

"He talked," Angel assured her.

She eyed him. "Oh, like what?"

"Helen and her lover—that would be Julian—"

"—not you," she said, only half-teasing.

"They've come to Sunnydale to take over."

She yawned. "How original."

"They're behind the possession thing. They've got some kind of drug."

Her eyes widened. "A drug?"

He pointed to her pocket. "The vampires are drugging Sunnydale."

"And they always blame us kids for everything," Buffy said.

The arena was complete.

The construction workers, slaughtered.

Illuminated by torchlight, the combat field was ready. The rows of seats were cast in darkness. Standing in his spot, Julian watched Helen. She sat forward eagerly as the girl named Cordelia was dragged into the arena by two women vampires dressed in togas as Bacchae, priestesses of Bacchus, god of wine. The girl was wearing gladiatorial armor on her shapely frame and though her hands were tied, they clutched a child-sized sword. She was weak, being a daughter of the modern age, and so they made allowances.

In addition, they had picked an easy adversary for her: a hungry dog. A rather small one, actually. It was tied to a post, and as they pulled the girl along, it put back its ears and growled.

"Excuse me?" Cordelia—yelled. "You want me to hurt a dog? Have you people ever heard of the SPCA?"

The Bacchae untied Cordelia. She glared at them and glanced down at the sword. Julian's smile grew. She had such fire. Such spirit. And she truly was ravishing.

His personal definition of which was, "worthy of being ravished."

The Bacchae went to the post and awaited Helen's command to release the hound.

Cordelia stared at the dog. "Nice poochy," she ventured, coming toward it and holding out her hand.

It snapped its jaws at her. The girl screeched and backed away. The dog strained at the tether, leaping and barking.

"I am not doing this," Cordelia shouted to the darkness.

"Then you will die," Helen said.

"Now, now," Julian murmured, pushing away from the wall.

He walked down to Helen's throne and put his hand on her shoulder. Trailed downward. In the distant torchlight, her face transformed and she hissed at him with excitement. Then she changed into her human face and said, "If she will not fight the cur, she will die."

"No. Save her, dearest," he said. "She is far more valuable to us as bait for the Slayer. And as amusement in the Games we will present tomorrow night."

She pouted. "But I want to see her die *now.*"

Julian maintained his expression, but irritation rose within him. Her bloodlust required ever more exotic deaths and sacrifices to be satisfied. For some, that might prove alluring, but not for one as ambitious as Julian. It was a liability.

"No!" Cordelia shouted, as the Bacchae waited for the signal. She looked up in the same direction. "Come on, this is really stupid."

"I want her to die," Helen insisted.

"Oh, she will, my darling. Just not tonight." Julian bent down and kissed her. She exhaled, a child denied its treat.

He sauntered down the steps to the arena. Unceremoniously, he stepped over the wall.

He took the sword from the girl, who looked like she wanted to use it on him, walked over to the dog, and stabbed it through the heart.

It made no sound, not even a whimper. It simply keeled over dead.

The girl started sobbing.

When he turned around, she made herself stop. As he approached, she turned her head and closed her eyes.

Cupping her cheek with his hand, he murmured, "Was that so bad?"

Her mouth worked. Her stomach contracted. She was fighting not to vomit.

He gave her time.

After a few more seconds, she whipped her head toward him.

"If I throw a stick, will you leave?" she shot at him.

He threw back his head and laughed with delight. "You vixen."

She straightened her shoulders despite the abject terror on her face. "I've been called that, and worse," she announced.

Now Helen laughed, too.

The arena echoed with their merriment.

Outside Rome, A.D. 39

Aulus, a gray-haired man in excellent condition, wearing a breastplate over his long robe, raised his shield as Diana jabbed at him with a spear.

"Again, you're a little off," he remonstrated. "What is wrong with you?"

She shook her head, unwilling to say. He would be delighted to know that her betrothed was missing, for he was opposed to her marriage on all fronts. Less delighted, perhaps, that Helen was acting strangely. Distant, and guarded. Like Diana, he would want to know why.

"Let's quit for the day." He held out his hand for the spear. "Go and take a hot bath. Work out the kinks." He pointed to his forehead. "In here."

She shifted uncomfortably. For almost a year, they had worked together as Watcher and Slayer. Yet their relationship had not warmed. She had the distinct impression that he found her lacking, and that if she died, he would not grieve.

As he instructed, she went off to the women's baths, laying aside her worries in favor of a nice long soak.

She was there when her father came to tell her that Aulus and Helen had been taken by soldiers, and that they had flung a sack containing Demetrius's head onto the grounds of his family's home.

Chapter 13

As the Gilesmobile sped along, the sky suddenly cracked open and rain screamed down. In ten seconds, Willow was soaked to the skin, despite the fact that she tried to cast a spell of protection against the elements. So far, no go. As she kept trying to remind everyone, she was basically getting a C when it came to spellcasting. Kind of like Buffy and chemistry last year: more of her experiments failed than succeeded.

"Oh, good Lord," Giles said, as the rain washed over her. He flicked on his right-hand blinker. "I've got a tarp in the back. It's wrapped around a spectacular seventeenth-century crossbow at the moment. We can use it to cover the hole."

"Or she can come back here with us," Xander invited.

"Someone will have to hold the tarp in place," she said. The truth was, she was a little afraid of Mark. Rain or no rain, she didn't particularly want to share the backseat with him. Even if he was on the floor.

The car stopped. Giles said, "I'll be right back."

He crossed around to the back and popped open the trunk. Willow took advantage of his momentary absence by scooting over to his side of the car, away from the rain. They were on Route 17, near where Oz had been kidnapped, and Willow had been growing tenser by the second. With each curve they had rounded, she half-expected someone to force the car to stop and yank them bodily out of it. As lightning flashed, each manzanita bush, each stand of deer weed and white sage, hulked at the side of a road like something waiting to leap onto the hood and dive through the broken windshield—

"I have to go to the bathroom," Mark announced.

"It's pouring rain, Mark," Xander protested.

"I have to go."

"You'll get soaked."

"I gotta go *now.*"

"Just wait, Mark, okay?" Xander sounded exasperated.

Willow glanced up at the moonlight in the hills. They were near the exit where the demon trucker had attacked them.

No wonder I feel like we've gone around in circles, she thought dully. *Cuz we have.* Time was ticking away, and she knew the stats on missing persons: the longer they were missing, the lower your chances of ever seeing them again.

"Okay, all right. I'll go with you," Xander said, as Mark pushed open the rear door on the traffic side and climbed out. "To make sure you're safe," he added.

Willow was not fooled. She doubted Mark was,

either. The boy snorted and said, "I don't need an audience."

"I gotta go, too," Xander said.

Mark stayed by the car as a truck screamed past, and then another. Then he began to lope across the highway, Xander slightly behind him. There were plenty of bushes on this side. Maybe he was trying to prove a point. And maybe he wasn't.

The heat was on. The car grew maybe one degree warmer. Willow thought about all those soup ads on TV and wished she could be in one of them, right now. Or snuggling down in her room with a cup of hot chocolate and a good website.

She sat back and closed her eyes, bone weary.

We can get possessed and not even know it, she thought. *Like Oz; when he wolfs, he doesn't realize what he's doing. Like somebody who's really sick. We don't blame them if they act cranky.*

But what about when you're just afraid? Do you get to say whatever you want, then, too?

If that's true, why do I feel so bad about snapping at Buffy?

The heater and the engine made for companionable white noise.

If I can just get warm, she thought, quaking with cold. *Imagine, going to college someplace where it snows. That's always sounded so glamorous. But maybe not so much. . . .*

The heater hissed; the engine rumbled like distant thunder. She shifted, her lids heavy. Her body felt as if it weighed a million pounds.

She was in a forest. Barefoot, she wore a gauzy white dress with a pink and blue embroidered vest and a crown of matching flowers in her hair. Dandelions fluttered into the air like butterflies or snowflakes as she walked through a patch of them, cupping her hands, and softly calling: "My beast, where are you?"

Out of a thicket, rabbits bounded in terror, followed by a white-tail deer and a flurry of birds. The bushes shook.

The forest howled.

And then he leaped from the thicket, blood on his mouth and dripping from his claws.

The Beast.

He slathered and growled at her. His eyes glowed a deep blood-red crimson. She took one step back, but one step only. Then she opened her arms and stood perfectly still.

"Come to me, Beast," she urged.

The creature stared at her blindly, without recognition.

"Come to me."

Then something changed in his face. He came at her. Her lids fluttered, but she stayed where she was.

Then he knelt before her, carefully encircling her waist with his huge, hairy arms.

She sank to the forest floor and cradled his head in her lap.

In that moment, he began to transform. . . .

She stirred slightly when Giles got back into the car. She was aware of tears on her cheeks.

His door slammed.

Then he took off, tires squealing.

"Wait," she said, slowly opening her eyes.

Mark sat beside her, driving the car.

"Wait!" she cried. "Where's Xander?" She looked around. "And Giles?"

He fishtailed down the road.

"Hide me," he said desperately. "Now."

Xander groaned and rubbed the knot on the back of his head as he raised his head. He was covered with mud from his forehead to his shoe tips.

"I don't freakin' believe this," he shouted. "That little . . . little *creep!*"

He staggered to his feet and half-ran, half-slid back to the darkened road. A flash of lightning revealed that the car was gone.

Surprise, surprise.

But sprawled on the ground was a sort of a huddle. Xander's stomach tightened and he started across. A minivan speeding by nearly hit him, then slowed about fifty feet up and began to back up. It zoomed up alongside him and the window rolled down.

"Xander?"

By the dome light, he saw that it was Willow's mother. Reflexively, he pushed his sopping hair out of his eyes and tried to tuck in his shirt. Then he realized what he was doing and said, "Hi, Mrs. Rosenberg. Can you hold on a minute?"

"Xander, what on earth are you doing out here?"

"Please, Mrs. Rosenberg, drive over there," he said, pointing, and ran across the highway.

He made it to the bundle first, and rolled it over. It was Giles. Slowly he opened his eyes and sat up.

"Mark," Giles said.

"Mark," Xander confirmed. "He must have found something very useful under the seat. Like a baseball bat." He frowned. "Nothing I noticed, though."

"Ah." Giles grimaced. "I moved quite a lot of weapons the other day. Put some on the backseat. I imagine something must have rolled onto the floor."

"Oh, how nice." Xander helped him to his feet. "And for the lightning round, so to speak, Where's Willow?"

Giles turned around, must have registered the absence of both car and Willow, and turned back to Xander.

The high beams of the minivan caught them both as Mrs. Rosenberg drove up.

She leaped out of the van and ran to the two of them.

"Mr. Giles. What happened?"

Giles looked at Xander. He said, "Ah, I was carjacked, actually." He hesitated.

Xander stepped up to the plate. "By Mark Dellasandro."

"Oh, my God." Mrs. Rosenberg covered her mouth. "Willow. Was she with you?"

Giles hung his head. "I'm afraid so. I'm terribly sorry."

For a moment Xander thought she was going to scream. Then she clamped her mouth shut, closed her eyes, and took a deep breath.

"Get in," she said. "We're going straight to the police."

Xander sighed in frustration and mouthed to Giles, *Library.*

As Mrs. Rosenberg headed around to the driver's side, Xander said aloud, "Library."

Giles opened the front passenger door of the minivan. "We can't. We're witnesses. Victims. We have to report this to the police or it will go very badly."

Xander doubled his fists, wishing for all the world that he had something to hit. Giles put a hand on his shoulder. Then, silently, Giles climbed in beside Mrs. Rosenberg while Xander slid into the backseat.

Neither one was buckled in before Mrs. Rosenberg hit the turbo-charge.

Buffy sagged with frustration as she and Angel returned to her house. They had spent hours in fruitless searching. It was almost dawn, and Angel would have to stay out of the sun until nightfall. So until she caught up with the gang, she would essentially be on her own.

Gee, a nap on my own would be nice, she thought wistfully.

Together they headed for the kitchen door, Angel standing aside as Buffy hurried in.

She set down her Slayer's bag and crouched beside her mother. Joyce was asleep, or maybe passed out, her head on the table. Her handcuffed wrist looked swollen.

"Maybe I put them on too tight," Buffy said, fishing in her pocket for the key.

Angel examined her mother's wrist as Buffy quickly unlatched the cuff.

"No, it looks okay," he said, with the voice of authority.

"Okay. Let's get her into bed."

Buffy started to lift her mother over her shoulder, but Angel said, "I'm taller. It'll be easier for me."

"Macho man," she shot at him, but let him do it. She was tired. Besides, there were stairs.

She picked up her satchel and drew up the rear, touching her mom's hair, hoping she wouldn't have a hangover. Her mom was a very light drinker. Some nights she just went all crazy and had a wine cooler with dinner, and the results were very funny.

On the way through the living room, she glanced at the phone machine. No messages.

Damn. Now she was really worried.

Buffy pushed open her mother's bedroom door and helped Angel gently lay her on the bed. She took off her shoes and pulled the sheets over her, then kissed her cheek.

"Mmf," Joyce murmured.

Angel and Buffy tiptoed out. Buffy shut the door and led the way into her own bedroom.

They both glanced at the bed at the same time. Angel walked to the window and peered out between the blinds.

"I'll have to go soon."

Buffy set down her Slayer's bag and stretched, making her back crack. The trio of vampires was the only battle action they'd seen, but she felt very worn down.

"Tell me more about Helen," she said. "Tell me everything, so I can deal with her when the time comes."

Angel nodded seriously. "She's got to be stopped. But Buffy, she may be the one you can't stop."

Buffy swallowed. "Are you saying she'll kill me?"

"I would never let that happen," he said in a rush.

She tried to mimic his crooked smile, but he only peered at her and said, "Are you in pain?"

"I'm fine." She decided it was a better idea to get up

off the bed. She sat on her chair and said, "Helen. Dish."

"Helen," he said.

Rome, A.D. 39

Julian put on the full armor of a general of the Roman Imperial Army to meet the Slayer and her Watcher. Though Diana was the nemesis of his people, nevertheless she was an exalted personage who deserved his respect.

With his bodyguards, he trooped down to the deepest dungeons, past the screaming prisoners and the tedious Christians, on their knees and praying in their large group cells. Julian covered his mouth and nose with the edge of his cape as the stench of death and dying wafted around them, a miasma of torment and despair.

Pots of boiling oil added a viscosity to the mix, the fires casting shadows on the stone walls. The footsteps of the soldiers made many turn and look, torturers and tortured alike.

And then there she was. On her knees, her arms pulled tight overhead, her face was streaked with mud. There was straw in her hair. Her dress was ripped.

She saw Julian and the others, and let out an ear-piercing scream.

Julian was taken aback. He had not expected a Slayer to behave so. He was a little disappointed; he'd imagined their meeting very differently.

"Greetings in the name of the Emperor, the great Gaius, known as Caligula," he said, saluting by making a fist where his heart lay unbeating inside him, then opened his hand and extended it forward.

"What?" Her eyes were enormous. "Please, let me go."

There was a stir among Julian's guards. He crossed his arms over his chest. "Diana—"

"I'm not Diana!" she shouted. "I'm Helen! I'm not Diana!"

Julian went immediately to the cell of the Watcher. He was a proud man, well formed despite his age. He lifted his head as Julian rapped on the bars and demanded, "Why did you tell my soldiers that girl is the Slayer?"

The Watcher smiled grimly. "Why do you think?"

Julian swore. *Tricked!* He transformed himself into his true nature and glared at the man. "You shall pay. But before you do, you'll tell me where she is."

There was something in the man's eyes that gave Julian the impression that he would break rather easily.

For the second time, the vampire was disappointed.

"They tortured the Watcher," Angel said. "For days. Finally he told them that he and Diana had a prearranged hiding place in a grove sacred to her patron goddess, Diana of the Hunt. They sent troops, but she wasn't there."

Buffy nodded slowly. "So they kept Helen as bait."

Angel nodded.

The phone rang. Buffy heaved a huge sigh of relief and grabbed it.

"It's Giles, Buffy."

"Thank God! We've been looking for you guys everywhere. There's this urn, and we think it's got something in it; and so we should meet, that is you and I and Willow, if she can get out of going home; to do the research, and—"

Giles cut in, "Mark knocked Xander and me out and took my car."

Her eyes widened. "Willow. Has not been mentioned."

"Willow," Giles confirmed. "She was in the car when he took it."

Buffy closed her eyes. "Giles, where is she?" Buffy asked. "Has Mark called you?"

"There's no reason to assume that anything bad will happen to her," Giles said soothingly. "Mark's terrified, Buffy. He doesn't know whom to trust. Where to turn."

Buffy's insides constricted. "You're making me feel so much better."

"We're at the police station. We've been here for hours. Mrs. Rosenberg's with the detectives now. This is the first opportunity we've had to use the phone."

He cleared his throat. "Ms. Broadman was in earlier. Apparently she was mugged by three individuals in Halloween costumes."

"Yeah. Vamps in togas." She sighed. "Speaking of, Angel's been filling in some more blanks in the Helen saga."

"We're being released to go home. Xander assures me he won't be missed—which, while convenient, is sad commentary on his home life—"

"Giles."

"We'll meet at the library." He sighed. "I was counting on Willow to do a Net search."

"Don't look at me," she said.

"All right. Meet us there as soon as you can."

"Okay." She disconnected and dropped the portable on her bed. She covered her face with her hands. "Willow," she whispered.

"We'll find her. We'll find all of them."

She nodded mutely. *I can't let her down again,* she thought desperately. *I will never, ever forgive myself if something happens to her.*

Angel looked at the window. "Buffy, I hate to do this, but I have to go. Or I can stay here."

"No, you'll be stuck in my house all day. My mom will force you to bake with her." Resolutely, she gestured toward the window. "Do you have time to make it back to your place?"

"If I go now."

"Angel," she blurted.

"Willow's proven herself to be strong and resourceful," Angel reminded her gently. "She's held her own before."

Buffy said, "I wasn't there. When she got shot. Because I . . . was . . ."

She looked up at him, stricken.

"When I think of all the evil things I did when I was changed," Angel said softly, "it's almost more than I can handle. But you know what's worse?

"The years after, when my soul had been restored, but I did nothing. I knew about all the evils in the world, but I gave in to the luxury of guilt."

"Luxury?" Buffy echoed bitterly.

"You can't afford it, Buffy." He smiled his faint smile. "If you try to keep track of all the times you aren't perfect, you'll lose count. And no one else is keeping score."

"I'm fine," she insisted, tension coiling inside her. *Now is not the time. And this sure isn't the place.*

"Okay." He stood. "Call when you hear anything. I'm a light sleeper."

"I know," she said, then flushed. "I didn't mean that the way it sounded."

He said, "It didn't sound the way it sounded."

He left the room.

Without looking back.

Angel silently let himself out of Buffy's house and walked quickly down the street, smelling the approach of dawn. His reluctance to leave her would prove his undoing one day. Sometimes he timed it awfully close.

He thought of the misery he'd seen on Buffy's face. *What's she blaming herself for? Not being a robot? Not being on duty twenty-four seven?*

Then he saw Helen at the end of the block, resplendent in all her mad beauty.

Without breaking stride, he approached her. She held out her arms and glided toward him. Her white face was beautiful, her eyes large and startling.

"Angelus," she said huskily, rubbing her body against his. "Angel, my love."

He didn't react to her inviting movements. She drew away with a pout and lifted her chin.

"Aren't you glad to see me?"

He remembered her as they had been when he was Angelus.

He remembered himself. There was nothing inside him now that wanted her. But there had been a time . . .

"You know what I am now."

She laughed. "A vampire with a soul." She wrinkled her nose. "What an absurdity."

222

"And yet."

She reached her hands around her head, catching handfuls of lustrous hair and letting them tumble to her shoulders. "You were a wild, vicious thing when I loved you in England," she said softly. "And I loved you as no one else has. I was a wild, vicious thing in your arms. Was I not?"

He inclined his head. "Yes."

"And yet, you left me." She sounded wounded. "As everyone leaves me. Abandons me."

"I regained my soul."

"Ah." She blinked. "That would explain it. If I believed you." She put her hands on his chest. "How could you resist me? How can you resist me now? I can give you a love potion."

"Viagra?"

She threw back her head and laughed heartily. "Angelus, I've always loved your wit." She kissed his neck. "Come with me, my love. Come to my court. We'll kill Julian and I'll make you my king."

"We talked about killing Julian before," Angel said carefully, "but you told me you were his prisoner."

"We're going to take over this place," she said. "We will reestablish the glory that was Rome."

"In the glory that is Sunnydale," Angel said flatly.

"We are going to call up Meter," she announced. "With her power, we will reign supreme." She twined herself around him. "We will use the beating heart of the Slayer, and the ashes of Caligula."

Angel blinked, startled. "You have his ashes?"

"We will become one with the dark gods." She caressed Angel's face. "I would hate to see you destroyed along with the other champions of good."

She kissed him full on the lips. "It's near dawn, my

beautiful Angelus. Time to rest. Think about what I've said to you while you slumber."

She turned and disappeared into the shadows. Deeply troubled, Angel walked on.

The Yorkshire Moor, 1897

It was a glorious night for death.

The mists boiled over the landscape, rising into columns that moved and swayed like phantoms. The single coach that dared a wind-tossed midnight ride creaked and jingled as the outriders beat the horses.

In a heavy black wool cloak and shiny new boots, Angelus put the spurs to his stallion and galloped after the coach. Though his mouth was smeared with warm human blood, he lusted for more.

As the moon glowed over the sea of fog, a white shape ran directly in front of his mount. He would have run it down, except that the horse reared wildly, throwing him from the saddle.

The shape growled and flung itself at him, growling savagely and flying at his neck. He stopped it easily, backhanded it, and it was thrown at least ten feet from him.

To his amazement, it began to whimper, and then to laugh.

He got up and cautiously approached it.

At that moment, he had his first glimpse of Helen. She looked straight up at him in full vamp face and said, "Oh tell me, is it true, vampires still walk the earth?"

He was startled by her question. In the ensuing silence, she transformed into her human face, and he was even more startled by her beauty. She was exquisite, dark-haired and black-eyed, in ebony taffeta and crimson lace, roses in her hair.

"Why do you ask?" he queried, suspiciously narrowing his eyes at her.

"I've been a prisoner." Her voice was breathy, excited. "I've not seen another . . . person . . . in centuries, save my jailer."

He waited.

"He walled me up alive. Hunted every night, and forced me to feed off him," she continued. "I broke my own arm freeing myself from captivity. I spied a weakness in the bolts, and I pushed until they gave."

Sure enough, her left arm dangled at her side. Soon, however, it would heal itself.

She reached forward and grabbed his hand. "Help me, please. I shall be grateful to you from the bottom of my heart."

Her icy, evil heart.

Buffy sat on her bed for a few minutes, breathing deeply so she wouldn't lose it. Because she was beginning to lose it. She had spent too many hours on overdrive. How many times had Cordelia pointed out that hanging with Buffy was like signing your own death warrant? Even Willow had said that.

Willow wasn't Willow at the time she said that, exactly, she reminded herself.

Wearily, she stood, replenished her Slayage supplies, looked yearningly at the shower, and left the house. It was still dark, but birds were singing and twittering. Someone's sprinklers went off.

Forgot to call them on account of the rain, she told herself.

"*Slayer,*" she heard someone hiss.

She froze.

"Slayer."

There it was again.

She whirled around, every muscle in her body on alert for battle, but there was no one there.

There. Across the street.

A black van with tinted windows started rolling down the street.

Buffy ran for all she was worth toward the van, cutting an intercept course as it picked up speed. It left her in its wake; she pumped her arms and legs to keep up, knowing it was a waste of time and energy but unable to stop herself. She stared down at the empty license plate holder, then scrutinized the van itself for distinguishing marks. Found one: Sunnydale Used Kar Mart.

So they had bought it here.

A car passed in the other direction, driver craning his head at the girl running down the street after the black vehicle, drove on. Just another day in Sunnydale.

Then, in the glare of an overhead streetlight, a head poked out of the side of the van—the door must be open—and Buffy stared at a green, rubber-faced demon who was grinning a snaggle-toothed pumpkin grin at her. He gave her a little wave.

She gave him something back, not quite as friendly.

Then something tumbled out of the van, and the van sped away.

Something that looked like a body.

"Oh, God, no."

She ran.

It was the longest run of her life, although it was perhaps only a hundred feet.

The heap was a body.

"Willow, no."

She fell to her knees before she had time to register that it was the body of a guy, not a girl.

"Willow, Willow," she groaned, turning it over.

The smashed, gray face of local druggie Jordan Smyth stared back at her.

Chapter 14

WHEN OZ WAS THROWN INTO CORDELIA'S CELL, SHE didn't recognize him at first. He was filthy and bruised, and just barely conscious.

"Oz!" she shrieked.

He opened one eye. "Hey." Shut it.

"Oz, oh, my God." She knelt over him, afraid to touch him. Whipping up her head, she screamed at the darkness, "What have you done to him?"

Oz groaned and slowly sat up. "They let the dogs play with me. Wolf-baiting. Very big in ancient Rome, I guess."

Cordelia touched her hand to her mouth. "But you'll heal, right? Cuz you usually heal pretty fast."

"Or Julian will do it for me," he said. "What have they done to you?"

"You mean . . . what do you mean? About Julian?"

"He's got all these ointments and lotions." He held out his hand. "I almost lost this hand . . . doing something. He fixed it."

"My God." She looked around, then leaned toward him. "Why are they doing this? Why are we prisoners?"

"The way I figure it," Oz said, "is we're bait, primarily. For Buffy. Secondarily, we're sacrifices to their goddess. Thirdly, we're part of the floor show." When she stared at him blankly, he explained, "We're going to fight Buffy in the arena."

"Well, *I'm* not." Cordelia folded her arms.

Oz paused. "They're going to give you something. It'll make you go all crazy." He paused again. "You won't know what you're doing."

"Like when I was with Xander."

"Exactly."

We've got to get out of here," Cordelia said urgently.

"That thought had crossed my mind, also." Oz gestured to his battered body. "I've been trying to get out of here a lot. I think that's why they let the dogs use me for a chew toy."

"Then Buffy will just have to save us." She huffed. "Sooner, rather than later."

"Good thinking," Oz said. He wasn't smiling. He was deadly earnest.

Buffy got to the library just before dawn, sneaking past marauding bands of wild townspeople. From the smoke roiling beneath the moonlight, it appeared that the rain had doused several fires.

It was a simple matter to slip onto school grounds; she found herself thinking about Brian Dellasandro and his most recent journey to this very building. Probably his last journey to this very building. She couldn't even imagine what was going to happen to him after what he had done. What would happen to a lot of people, in fact.

She walked quietly on the toes of her boots, wrapping her coat around herself. She was colder inside the school hallway than she had been outside.

Through the porthole windows in the double doors of the library, she saw Giles and Xander, seated at the study table with books heaped around them. Giles was on the phone, and Xander was plopped behind the computer.

Buffy pushed in. They both looked up. They both brightened.

"Did you bring donuts?" Xander asked.

She realized she should have taken the time to eat before she left home. She was starving. A hungry Slayer was not only a cranky Slayer but a sluggish Slayer, and she did not have time to be sluggish.

However, food had been nowhere near her thoughts.

"No," she told him.

"That's not a problem, because I did. I being, on occasion, donut guy," Xander said, lifting a large pink box from behind a mountain of dusty volumes. With a flourish, he stood and opened the box, revealing at least two dozen donuts.

"Giles likes sprinkles, did you know that?" he asked. "He ate two."

Buffy selected a maple bar and bit into it hungrily.

"Tea?" Giles asked.

It was something warm. "Sure, that's nice."

"Or, a fresh latte?" Xander queried, holding up a familiar, and much beloved, paper cup of the Espresso Pump's finest.

"Oh, Xander, marry me and have my children," Buffy cooed, reaching for it.

"You're just a bottomless pit of wants and needs," he zinged back, holding up a little pink packet. "Sugar substitute?"

"No. I'll take it this way." She sipped through the little slot in the plastic lid and closed her eyes. A tiny surge jittered through her, and she blessed whoever it was that invented caffeine.

"A demon guy in the vamp van pushed Jordan Smyth out the door," she said, getting down to business. "Very much dead."

"A sad end to a sad life," Giles said.

"They bought it at the Sunnydale Kar Mart. No license plate."

"That's something. Not much," Giles said. "What did you do with the body?"

She shrugged. "Left it there. It was almost dawn. I didn't want to get caught with it. You know I have a sort of a bad rep as it is."

A silence dropped over the trio, as if they were giving Jordan the respect he had craved in life and never gotten.

Then Giles got back to it. "So what did Angel give you?"

"In terms of information," Xander said quickly, "cuz the rest, I don't even want to hear about."

"There is no rest. There can be no rest. None, okay?" Buffy said, rolling her eyes even though she felt her cheeks turning pink. She turned to Giles. "What did you ask me?"

"Angel told you more about Helen, the Betrayed One."

Buffy nodded. "A little more. He had to go, because of the sun."

"Some guys have the lamest excuses," Xander said.

Buffy ignored him. "There was this vampire, Julian."

"Yes. I know of him, of course. Since he was Helen's paramour."

"Oh." Buffy sipped her coffee and chewed her donut thoughtfully. "Paramour. We didn't get that far." She swallowed and took another bite. "All we got to was that the Roman soldiers picked her up instead of the Slayer. Diana's Watcher confessed to the switch."

"A bit of a disappointment, that fellow," Giles conceded. "That scheme was not at all approved, I might add."

"Helen went in Diana's place?" Xander asked.

Buffy reached for another donut and regarded it suspiciously. She put it down. "Maybe it's all this sugar that's wigging out the happy folk of Sunnydale. Willow's mother did a paper about it. Some guy in San Francisco even tried to dodge a murder rap by saying sugar made him all crazy."

"It was called the 'Twinkie Defense,'" Xander confirmed. "Behold, I have knowledge."

"And I am impressed," Buffy told him. She moved on. "The Watcher told the soldiers Helen was the Slayer, and since she was with him, they believed it. I guess Helen was pretty ticked off about it."

"Ouch," Xander said. "You do something like that, Giles, and I'll never buy the ones with sprinkles again."

"It's difficult to believe Diana would consent to

such a scheme," Giles observed. "To let any person stand in for her."

"Maybe she didn't," Buffy said. "We don't get her side, do we?" She peered at the stack of books. "No journals? No diaries?"

"We faxed the Vatican," Xander said importantly.

"Wow." Buffy looked impressed.

"Not the Vatican precisely, but someone who . . . works in Rome," Giles said offhandedly.

"An undercover Watcher spy?" Buffy asked, even more impressed.

"No," Giles said quickly, then pushed up his glasses. "Well, something like that."

"Now that's what I'd be good at," Xander said. "I'm stylin' in my Watcher trenchcoat and fedora."

Buffy nodded to Giles. "The Italian not-a-spy, faxed because?"

She could tell Giles was delighted that she'd asked. He was winding up for the pitch even as he perched on a corner of the study table and folded his arms.

"Well, you see, the Roman emperor of that time, Caligula, was extremely depraved. Completely mad. He was so awful he only lasted four years before he was assassinated. But in that time, he perpetrated more heinous acts than any other of the Caesars, before or after."

"Or since," Xander added.

"As Rome is no longer ruled by the Imperial Caesars," Giles said rather tiredly, "we may discount their influence in the present day."

"Or not," Buffy said. She pulled out the urn. "This thing got stolen from the art gallery."

Giles was silent for a moment. Then he said in a

hushed voice, "The Urn of Caligula. I didn't know it actually existed."

Buffy looked at Xander, knowing that, despite the urgency of their mission, Giles was about to do some more talking to find his way to the knowledge. Xander started to drum his fingers; she gave her head a little shake. He grimaced and folded his hands under his arms, maybe not realizing he was imitating Giles, and gazed expectantly at the Englishman.

"This is really quite remarkable," Giles continued, cradling the piece as he moved a hand over several of the books, then lifted one and began paging through it. "Caligula is also believed to have been a minor demon. It's said that when he met the vampire Julian, he aspired to immortality without becoming a vampire himself. He founded the Cult of Meter. She is the mother of all darkness. He declared himself her son, and it was from his desire to sacrifice to her that he was so enthusiastic about the Games. An incredible number of people died in gladiatorial combat during his reign. Also, mass butcherings—Christians thrown to the lions, that sort of thing."

"And people get so hepped up about violence on television," Xander quipped.

"What's in the urn?" Buffy asked.

"If the legend is correct, these are Caligula's ashes." He tapped the stopper. "He was assassinated, and his body burnt. The story has it that on the full moon of Meter, which occurs only once every six hundred and sixty-six years, his evil energy can be used by those who know how to wield it, for their own purposes."

"Which can now be us, for our purposes," Buffy said. "Cuz we've got the trophy."

"Yes, perhaps," Giles said slowly, "but I'll have to

do a lot of research. It's dangerous to use evil power, even against itself."

Buffy sighed. "We need Willow."

"We need Willow," Giles replied, turning away.

"Meanwhile," he said, and in that moment, he caught his foot on the leg of a chair at the study table and dropped the urn.

A smoky scent immediately filled the room. Giles whipped his head back and made a half circle away from Buffy. When he turned back, she scarcely recognized him. The expression on his face was nothing short of demonic.

"You little . . ." he said between clenched teeth. "Night and day, I watch out for you. I have no life. My friend died and I couldn't even go to him."

"Xander," Buffy said anxiously, watching Giles the way one might watch a rabid dog, "don't inhale."

"You never back me up," Xander said behind her. "You let them expel me. You let them take Cordy. And now Willow."

They both circled her. *Uh-oh.*

"Guys?" she said anxiously. "Think this through. It's not you. *It's not you.*"

"We'd all be better off if you had never come here," Xander said, coming nearer, fists clenched.

Buffy backed away from him. "Xander, calm down. I don't want to hurt you."

"Everyone dies because of you."

"No," she said, blinking.

As Xander lunged, she grabbed the urn, saw that the stopper had fallen out, and crammed it back in. Cradling it against her chest, she blocked Xander's awkward leap at her.

"Xander, stop it!" she shouted.

But as he leaped again, she gave him a light kick to the midsection. It wasn't enough to hurt him, but he lost his balance, fell against a chair, and smacked his forehead on the edge of the table. Blood welled from the cut.

Then she socked Giles hard, square in the jaw.

"Buffy," Giles murmured, staggering, his hand to his mouth. "What . . ." He gestured to the urn. "All we did was smell it. Not even that."

"What about me?" she asked as she crouched over Xander. "I smelled it."

"Wha . . . wha . . ." He was woozy but conscious.

"Perhaps being the Slayer, you're somehow immune." Giles cleared his throat. "I apologize sincerely, Buffy. You know I don't think that way. Not for a moment."

He looked down at Xander. "I'll get the first-aid kit," he said, disappearing into his office.

Xander was bleeding pretty badly. Another little guilt to add to the list.

Oh, c'mon, Summers, she could almost hear him saying. *Don't take credit for all the bad schwarma in my sad little world.*

"Here." Along with the regulation white plastic box, Giles was carrying a spare teacup with some water in it, which he set down beside Buffy's knee as he knelt beside her and Xander. He dipped a paper towel in the water and daubed Xander's cut.

"Ouuuuch," Xander groaned. "Wha' happen'?"

Giles dipped the paper towel back in the water.

There was an audible hiss.

Buffy and Giles looked at each other, then down in the water.

Forming in the center of a droplet of blood was a small black circle.

236

Giles said, "Here," absently pushing Xander in Buffy's arms. He picked up the cup and held it under the study light on the table. "This is fascinating."

"And it means?"

Giles went back into his office and returned with another cup of water and a small, sharp knife. The dull library fluorescents glinted off the metal, giving it the aura of something bigger and more dangerous.

As Buffy watched, Giles cut his finger and let the blood drip into the cup. They both bent forward, Buffy with Xander still cradled against her chest.

When the blood droplets hit the water, they hissed. The black dot formed in the center of each drop.

Giles nodded. "Perhaps it means I'm still infected."

Buffy stuck out her finger.

Giles handed her the knife. "I'll get another cup. I think I've got one more. For when company comes."

While he was rummaging in his office, Xander moaned and snuggled against Buffy's chest. He mumbled something Buffy couldn't understand.

"Xand?" she whispered. "Are you awake?"

"God, I hope so," he whispered back, and opened his eyes.

She grinned reprovingly at him and sat him up.

"Perv."

"Right. Here we go," Giles announced, coming into the room. He smiled at Xander. "Glad to see you up and about."

"Oh, I'm up," Xander said blandly. "Way up."

"Here." Giles handed Buffy a cracked white china cup with at least three chips in the rim. The handle had been glued back on.

"If this is for company, I'd hate to see what your unannounced drop-ins get."

Giles colored. "I, ah, dropped it."

Smashed it against the floor, she wanted to correct him. But no sense opening old wounds.

And speaking of opening wounds . . .

With a little flourish, she gave her fingertip a quick slash.

"Ouch," Xander said. "Are we all three becoming blood brothers?"

Buffy held her finger over the teacup. Giles watched as she forced out three, four, five drops.

The blood hissed when it hit the water. Giles and Buffy stared down at it.

The dots formed.

"So I've got it, too," Buffy said, sitting back on her heels.

"What?" Xander asked. "Black tick disease?"

"Perhaps you're simply a carrier," Giles offered.

"Good, cuz it would be real bad to have a psycho Slayer," Buffy said.

"Please, please tell me what's going on," Xander said, "and leave out all the bad parts."

Buffy thought a moment. Then she said, "You're going to live. I think."

The phone rang, and Giles went to get it.

"Angel," he said. "What is it?"

The Yorkshire Moors, 1897

In a private room in the Raven Inn, Helen laughed gleefully and threw back her head as Angelus entwined his arm with hers and they drank goblets of fresh, warm blood. Helen reclined on a chaise lounge, as she had in ancient Rome, while Angelus was curled up beside her by the blazing fire in the fireplace. They were in evening dress to celebrate Helen's kill. The death of a Slayer was a special occasion.

"To Grace," Angelus said.

"To Grace." She clinked her glass against his, then sipped. "Ah. Young. Vibrant. Slayer's blood is best."

His eyes gleamed as he peered at her over the rim. "It was a vicious kill."

"Not my most vicious, however." She lay back on her elbows. "Tell me truly, have you never heard of me?"

"I'm a young vampire," he said. "Only about a hundred and fifty. I have so much to learn." He kissed her hard. "Stay tonight. All night."

She let her head fall back as he ran kisses down her neck and collarbone, over to her shoulder. "My jailer hunts for blood even now. If I'm not back when he returns to feed me . . ."

"Let's kill him," Angelus said. "We'll run and hunt all over Europe."

She gasped as passion leapt between them. "We'll need to plan."

Giles's car gave up the ghost about half a mile from the intersection of Boundary Street and the empty canyon where Mrs. Gibson's beloved pet had been found. Mark made Willow help push it off the street, into a fenced empty lot that was half-covered with brush and tumbleweeds. Willow tried to tell herself it was a lousy hiding place and that someone would notice it right away, but after Mark put some bushes on top of the hood, it was impossible to distinguish the car from the landscape.

In the rosy dawn, he pushed her ahead of himself, toward Mrs. Gibson's house.

"No, you don't want to go in there," Willow told him. "There may be, um, bad people in there."

"Drug dealers," Mark said. "I've got a gun. I know how to use it."

Willow's hair stood on the back of her head. "Mark, you're, please don't be offended, but you're just a kid. And I'm, well, okay, a little older than you, but I'm no match for what we might find in there." She looked up. The sun had just risen, but that didn't mean too much. Angel could move around in his mansion during the day if he stayed away from any sunny places. So could other vampires, in other houses.

This house.

"I'll blow 'em away."

"Mark, the good guys don't always win," she ventured gently. "Sometimes they get killed."

For a moment he wavered. She saw his uncertainty and crossed her fingers behind her back. "So let's go back and get Giles and Xander," she said. "We'll hide you. We'll keep you safe."

It was the very most wrong thing she could have said. His face hardened and he waved her on ahead of himself without a word.

They went around to the back. The sky was washed with the rosy glow of dawn. *Someone will see us,* Willow thought hopefully. But there were very few houses in this part of town. Sunnydale Estates was a dream that had died.

Like so much did in Sunnydale.

Mark tried the back door. Willow fully expected it to be locked; when it opened at his touch, he looked as surprised as she did.

He murmured to her, "I don't want to make you go first, but you might leave me."

"What do you want me for?" she whispered back.

"I don't want you to tell them where I am."

She wouldn't insult his intelligence by promising that she wouldn't tell; instead she nodded and minced into the house.

It stank of rotting things; an odor so foul it was like something solid in her mouth. She recoiled, lumbering backward, and accidentally ran into Mark's gun. The metal jabbed into her lower back and she almost screamed. At the last second, she caught herself.

"No funny stuff," he muttered, "okay?"

"Okay, okay." Willow could hear the rising panic in her voice. *Something is dead in here, and no one knows where we are.*

Not even Buffy.

She thought of her friend and realized how truly unfair she'd been about Buffy looking for Oz. Buffy was the Chosen One, but she wasn't exactly psychic. Okay, dreams and premonitions, but they happened to her. She couldn't call them into being. She had searched all over Sunnydale for Oz and Cordy. And if she and Angel stole a kiss or two while she ran herself ragged, that should be okay, too. After all, it was all they got, all they could have.

She knew she and Oz would have something more, one day. Except, not on werewolf days.

Unless Mark freaks out and kills me, she thought, choking back a sob. *Or unless Oz is already—*

"Dead," Mark said aloud as they moved from the kitchen through an archway into the living room.

Willow jumped. "What?"

"There's a dead squirrel to our right," Mark cautioned her. "Don't look at it."

Despite the fact that he had a loaded gun pointed at

her spine, she was touched by his thoughtfulness. "Thanks."

"Someone's been living here," he said.

Willow studiously avoided the place where the squirrel must be. About five feet ahead of them was a mattress with some incredibly grimy sheets, an opened but untouched can of Spam and a loaf of white bread on top of a cardboard box, and a stack of magazines.

Mark picked up a couple of the magazines. "Jordan read this kind of junk," he said with disgust. "That's who it was. Jordan Smyth."

"Who it was," Willow echoed. "Living here, you mean?"

"He sold it to my brother." He picked up the Spam, examined it, and set it down. "The drug."

Willow stared at him.

"The drug that made him do it," he finished.

Willow gaped at him. "Some *drug* made him go crazy? You knew this all along? Why didn't you say anything?"

Mark's face turned bright red. "Because I wasn't sure."

And he's not sure now. Just like anyone who had been touched—or pummeled—by tragedy, Mark was looking for a reason why.

"Was it PCP?" she asked him.

"Angel dust?" He sighed. "I don't know. I'm not into drugs. I hate them. I tried to get it away from him. I—I—"

"It's okay." Willow swallowed hard. This kid was on the edge. She had no idea how to keep him from going over it. And only a vague idea of how not to push him over it herself.

Willow took a step forward; her shoe landing on

something small and hard. Without moving her head, she moved her foot and stared down.

It was a cell phone.

She caught her breath and covered it with her foot again.

It was dawn, and Helen slept.

She did not sleep well. For hundreds of years, she had not slept well.

Neither had Julian.

He remembered her now, in her despair.

Rome, A.D. 40

Six months had gone by since the capture of Helen and the death of the Watcher, and the countryside raged. The demons and monsters of Caligula's court scorched the earth, releasing dark magicks and freeing the hideous crawling things that dwelled beneath the soil.

The dead walked, and capered, and no one was safe.

In response—so Julian believed—the Empire went mad. Fathers murdered daughters; sons drove mothers to suicide. Strangers banded in wild, feral armies and marched on the villages of innocent people who had done them no wrong. They burned them to the ground, and slashed the throats of every man, woman, and child.

Livestock perished. Crops rotted.

Caligula went madder still, ordering elaborately staged mass executions, and delivering up the Vestal Virgins to the Games—an act that shocked all Rome. The Vestal Virgins were sacred acolytes of the temples, not political prisoners or slaves bred for sacrifice.

Caligula built the temple of Meter, and installed priests to pray to her statue every moment of every day. Caligula's sudden devotion to her made Julian suspicious. It was as if the emperor were trying to find another way to live forever, save at the fangs of his vampire confidant.

Meanwhile, Helen, the friend of the Slayer, began to despair. Her beloved childhood friend was nowhere to be found, had not made even one attempt to save Helen. Caligula was convinced that the Slayer was dead, and this drove him into a deep rage, pushing him toward more brutality.

Julian knew better. He had reports of her slaying vampires in the countryside, the wild ones who took huge risks in their eagerness to slake their bloodlust.

He came to see Helen, at first once, perhaps twice a month, enjoying the effect of total terror he instilled in her. Then, as she became accustomed to him, he began to stay longer. She was actually well informed, for a woman of her time. The lessons of Roman girls were generally restricted to spinning cloth and running a villa. Helen knew a little of the world, and had opinions.

So he would sit of an evening, sipping wine, upon occasion passing her a goblet so that she, too, might partake. At first, she would refuse, thinking that he was poisoning her, but over time, she began to insist that she didn't care if she lived or died.

Which was why he began to taunt her. At least now in Sunnydale, lying in her arms, that was what he told himself. Or perhaps it was his cruel streak which prompted him to make her cry.

At first it was easy.

"She has been seen, your Diana," he would say, stretching out his legs. "She tried to stop one of our armies from routing a village. She killed several of my best men."

"She is a goddess," Helen would snap at him, sounding ever so more uncertain.

"Then why doesn't she appear to you and save you?" Over the rim of his goblet, he watched her. He saw her fire roar to life, and he fanned it. "If you're her best friend on earth, why does she ignore your plight?"

Helen raised her head, but her expression spoke volumes about her agony. Clearly she had been asking the same questions.

"She doesn't even know I'm here."

"Oh, she knows. We have made sure she knows. In letters and proclamations read all over the Empire. Why, even in Britannia, the name of Helen is known."

She turned from him then, downhearted and mournful. The fires were banked for the night. But tomorrow, he would attempt to fan them higher.

As he prepared to leave, he examined her in the torchlight. Even in the dreadful conditions in which he found her, she was incredibly beautiful. She stirred him.

He wanted her.

He vowed he would have her.

Now, as he lay with Helen asleep in his arms, he looked down at the way she clutched her hands together, drawing blood from her own palms, the heaving of her chest as she dreamed. Her madness had grown, along with his love for her. But he knew it was clouding her thinking.

She was capable of anything, including killing him.

He didn't want to think of that, but he must. Julian was a survivor, first and foremost. And then, a lover.

He let his mind drift to the exquisite beauty,

Cordelia. A wonderful name. An excellent fighting spirit. As with Helen, it would be such a waste if she died in the arena. Diverting, however.

And the court was restless. They were enjoying the havoc rampaging over Sunnydale, but they wanted to participate more fully in the destruction of the town. After all, Nero had fiddled while Rome burned.

And Nero had been one of their own.

He looked down at Helen, and wondered what she dreamed of.

Then she whispered, "Angelus."

Buffy backhanded a monster with a human face and a human trunk, covered in red scales and with cloven hooves, and slammed her sandaled foot on its chest. With her three-pronged trident at its neck, she raised her face to the crowd.

They shouted, "Cut his throat!"

She pushed the trident straight through its neck.

It sighed and whispered, "Buffy."

As she looked down in horror, it morphed into Angel. The crowd screamed for his death.

And before she knew what she was doing, she up-ended the trident and pushed the wooden handle through his chest.

In less than a second, he was dust.

Buffy sat up and cried, "No!"

"Hey, Buffy, it's okay. You were dreaming," Xander said.

There was a pillow under her head and a throw over her body. She smoothed back her hair and said, "What time is it?"

"Half-past third period," Xander replied. "Giles put

out that 'Closed for Fumigation' sign we stole from the Bronze a couple years ago to keep pesky knowledge-seekers out of their tax-funded sanctuary."

"You shouldn't have let me sleep." She yawned and got to her feet. "But it was nice. Thanks."

He bobbed his head and gestured to a huge pile of books. "Meanwhile, Giles and I press on with the info Angel gave us."

"And?"

He showed her the spine of a large book bounded in what looked like moldy animal skin. *"The Cult of Meter and the Orphic Mysteries: A Comparative Analysis."*

"Lucky you," she drawled. "Find anything?"

"Not yet. But I'm still knee-deep in footnotes." He looked at her. "You were kind of whimpering."

"I had a dream," she told him. "I dreamed I was a gladiator. And I killed a demon." She hesitated. "With Angel's face."

Xander held up his hands. "Not riffing off the obvious here, okay? I don't play to the cheap seats. But according to Angel, Helen became a gladiator. Caligula got tired of waiting for Diana to rescue her. So he put her in the Games. She had to battle the major spookables and assorted other bad mothers. One after another. Day after day. Or rather, night after night."

"Until she became a regular killing machine," Buffy said tersely.

"Something like that, yes," Giles announced, pushing up his glasses as he rushed out of his office. "We just got a fax."

"From Rome?" Xander asked.

"Yes," Giles continued, clearing his throat. "He believes we're facing a psychoactive poison, that is, one that affects the mind." He looked at them triumphantly.

"And the poison is called?"

"Well, he didn't quite know," Giles admitted. "Also, he believes that by opening the urn, the demonic energy of Caligula has been unleashed, and only need be called upon using the proper rites and rituals to raise Meter. She's the real threat."

"Will the bad guys know that the urn has been opened?"

Giles frowned. "I'm not sure. Helen was boasting of this entire enterprise to Angel."

"Helen?" Buffy asked shakily. She didn't know Angel had spoken to her.

"She approached him just before dawn."

Near my house, Buffy realized. *She was probably in the van when they tossed Jordan Smyth's body out.*

"And just to add to the mix—"

"We have to figure this all out before nightfall," Buffy said without surprise. "Because the signs and portents indicate that tonight's the night for the bad stuff to happen."

Giles sighed and smiled grimly. "Two points for the Slayer."

"Boy, do we need Willow," Xander muttered.

Giles's phone rang again.

Chapter 15

WILLOW'S HEART POUNDED AS SHE HIT "SEND" ON THE cell phone. She had managed to bend down and pick it up when Mark cautiously drew back the dusty curtains again and peeked out the grimy windows in the living room. She hadn't quite dared to run through the kitchen and out the door. She turned the phone on without Mark's noticing by coughing to cover the sound of the beep. But she had no idea how much juice the battery had left.

Now, with the phone hidden in the bib pocket of her corduroy overalls, she didn't even know if the connection to the library had been made. There was no way to tell.

So she simply started talking.

"So, Mark," she said in a loud voice, "are we going to stay here much longer? They say Mrs. Gibson haunts her house. I'm not sure I want to find out. What about you?"

He frowned at her. "Where are the 'vampires'?

Your friends were sure the vampires would come here."

"It's daylight," she said hopefully. "Vampires can't walk around during the day."

"Oh, hah." He made a face. "That's just TV talk."

"No, it's true." She shrugged, wondering why she was arguing with him. Maybe it was good that he wanted to stay here. If Giles could hear her, help would soon be on the way.

Giles looked at Buffy. "Willow is with Mark at Mrs. Gibson's house. I got disconnected. It was abrupt. It could simply be the cell range, or—"

Buffy was already out the swinging doors.

Xander called, "Can I come, too?"

As the doors flapped behind her, she called back, "Not this time. You'd only slow me down."

Xander looked at Giles and shook his head. "She's been going to the Cordelia Chase School of Charm and Tact."

Giles shrugged. "Don't feel too badly, Xander. She says the same thing to me." He picked up the urn and turned his head to look at the clock. "It's almost lunch time. The chemistry lab should be empty . . ." He glanced at Xander.

"What's the worst thing that can happen to me?" Xander asked. "I can get expelled again?"

"We'll keep our eyes out for Principal Snyder," Giles said, gathering up a few books and putting them in his well-worn valise.

They left together, moving swiftly. Giles said sadly, "Willow's spellcasting skills would be very handy right about now. Not to mention her supply of herbs and magickal effect. It's unfortunate that her kit is in my car."

Xander snapped his fingers. "Not to worry. She restocked her locker. And I, of course, know the combination."

Giles flashed him a smile. "Excellent, Xander."

"Thank you, thank you," he said, leading the way.

Rome, A.D. 40

The sun was setting as Helen's last adversary of the day clanked into the amphitheater. The rays hit the monster's plates of armor and the long, curved blades at its elbows and knees. Fully seven feet tall, it was well armed.

Clad in a skimpy armor breastplate and carrying only a spear and a shield, Helen was barely armed at all.

The creature came at her. She knew it was not human. In the last six months, she had encountered only one real man, and he had died so quickly that the spectators had protested their boredom. Now only the most fearsome demons and creatures of the night were pitted against her. They came from everywhere, leaving caves and underwater grottoes and icy mountain lairs for Rome, eager for the riches and honors Caligula would bestow on the one who killed Helen. If none showed, Caligula conjured them up from the foul depths of the torture chambers, raising the dead, promising a new existence on earth if they would only fight her.

Each one, he fed the Madness Potion. Each one went mad with an insatiable need to kill. There was no end to it. Night after night, Helen fought for her life against beings infected with bloodlust. The crowds adored her for surviving. They jeered at her opponents. She knew vast sums had been won and lost wagering on her. Surely this monster would be the one. Or that one. Or the next.

Now, facing the helmeted creature, Helen hurt all over. She thought some ribs might be cracked. As it came at her, she executed a roll and groaned aloud.

In the gallery, Caligula did not even watch. He was too busy amusing a beautiful girl who sat on his lap and poured wine into his mouth. *Stupid cow.* The girl would be dead by sunrise, a sacrifice to his lust and depravity.

"Be aggressive!" Helen's trainer shouted from the side gate. He wore a harness of leather and a leather apron over short pants. His body was covered with scars. He was one of the lucky ones, a retired gladiator put in charge of training new victims for the Games. He had been given his freedom and a splendid villa for the results he had achieved with Helen.

Behind him loomed the vampire, Julian, the monster who claimed to love her. He wore his human face, but his eyes gleamed golden in the torchlight.

The creature in the arena slashed a spiked mace at her, and she executed another roll. Wincing with pain, she scanned the crowd, dreaming that Diana would appear and save her. It had never happened; she didn't know why she thought it would ever happen.

The thought infuriated her. With renewed vigor, she got to her feet. The crowd sensed the change in her and jubilant cheers rose up. She was the favorite. That she had survived this long was too delicious.

She hacked and slashed at the monster, catching it behind the knee with her sword. There was a seam in its armor there, and she sliced with the side of her sword. The sword slid into some kind of muscle, some kind of bone, blood the color of ocher spurting from the wound. The creature bellowed.

She sliced again, and it fell forward.

Helen ran to it, whipped off its helmet, and cut off its spiny, leathery head. Its eyes were long and narrow, like the eyes of a snake, and they fluttered shut as the creature died.

The crowd went wild.

Helen picked up the head and saluted Caligula with it. He finally took his eyes off the beautiful girl in his lap and gave Helen a cheery wave.

"Nicely done, gladiator," he bellowed. That was all.

She staggered from the arena to the side gate as they prepared to bring out the lions for the Christians, which would be the grand finale of the evening.

Her trainer was not there waiting for her. Julian stood alone.

"Don't touch me," she said.

But as he swept her into his arms and carried her toward her cell, she was too tired and too sore to protest. Her head lolled against his chest; she nearly lost consciousness, but she fought to retain control of herself as he carried her down the maze of corridors beyond the amphitheater proper.

Inside her cell, which was in the gladiators' quarters, he laid her down on a silken coverlet spread over a real bed—luxuries he had given her himself—and uncapped a jade bottle of unguent.

"I've got a new salve. Tell me where it hurts," he said.

She gritted her teeth. "I'm not going to fight anymore," she announced. "Kill me if you want, but I'm finished."

Julian bent over her, his armor golden and gleaming, his cape flowing around him. Even though she hated him, she had to admit that he was incredibly handsome. More handsome even than Demetrius, whose death she no longer mourned. She had been a captive for almost a year, and that year had hardened her.

"Your blood rises when you fight," Julian said. "Don't deny it. I see it in your eyes. You were born to be a warrior. It is a gift from the darkness that you were brought here."

She made no answer.

He chuckled. "Don't deny it. What would your life have been back on your country farm? A Roman wife, locked away in her house, losing your looks, dying in childbirth. But here, you are revered."

He began to rub the unguent into her sore muscles, removing her breastplate and checking her ribs. When he had first begun to minister to her, perhaps three months before, it had astonished her that a being as cruel and heartless as Julian could be so tender. His healing balms had restored her more times than she could count.

Despite herself, she caught her breath as he continued the massage.

"You're tired and you want to stop," he murmured. "I can make it stop."

She closed her head as flickers surged through her body. "By making me like you."

"Yes." He touched the vein in her neck. She jumped, and he chuckled softly. "I have never drunk of you, tempted though I am. And I will not, until you give me permission."

"It's not because of me. Caligula has forbidden it," she threw at him. Just as he would not allow her to drink the Madness Potion. He wanted her "pure."

He savored her terror.

There was a silence. Then Julian said, "He won't be here forever."

Helen took that in. Perhaps there was another plot to kill the emperor. There was a different one every week. All had failed, and the perpetrators had died horrible deaths.

"I won't be, either," she said, with a confidence she didn't feel.

"She has deserted you, Helen," he whispered, trailing his hand down her arm. "She has left you to this hellish existence. She knows you're here. Everyone knows you're here."

Helen said nothing.

"She let the soldiers take you in her place."

It was true. Aulus had called out, "Diana, no!" and looked straight at her, straight at *Helen*. Was this Diana's revenge for telling her secret to Demetrius? Retribution for his death?

"I can stop it, right now," Julian murmured. "I would make it very quick. And when I am emperor, you will reign beside me."

"Over demons and ghouls."

"No different than now," he asserted. He put his lips against her ear. "This would be over, my beloved Helen. The pain, the fighting, night after night. Our life together would be glorious."

She clamped her mouth shut and turned her head as tears spilled down her face.

Does he know that I'm tempted? she wondered.
She didn't dare speak.

Buffy was a bit winded by the time she reached the
deserted block where Mrs. Gibson's house sat. She
made a right into an empty lot, then jerked hard as
she made out the shape of a car beneath well-placed
shrubs and tumbleweeds. She pulled a few of the
bushes off the hood and smiled grimly.

Giles's poor car. Maybe he would finally have to
buy a new one.

She opened the door and found Willow's witchy
bag, which also contained some stakes and holy water.
She hoisted it over her shoulder and recovered the
vehicle. Then she trotted the length of the lot and
dipped down the hill, crabbing along over the soggy,
muddy earth.

"Hang on, Willow," she muttered under her breath.
"Please."

She bent over and darted as fast as she could under
the window on the right-hand side. Dropping to a
crouch, she held her breath, waiting for a sign that
she'd been spotted. None came.

Scanning the ground, she saw several sets of muddy
footprints, some of them very fresh.

Willow, please be all right, Buffy begged, reaching
for the door knob. She opened the door and snuck
inside.

Mark cocked his head. Willow's eyes ticked to the
left and she saw the remains of the dead squirrel. Her
stomach roiled. She was terrified and sickened.

"I thought I heard something," he said.

Willow swallowed. *It could be good guys or bad*

guys, but either way, I really don't want to end up like that squirrel.

Mark picked up the gun and aimed it at her.

Willow's eyes widened. "You don't want to hurt me."

"I don't want to hurt anybody," he admitted. "But everybody in town wants to kill me and my brother." Nervously he licked his lips and sighted down the barrel. "You're my hostage. If they don't let Brian go, I'm going to kill you."

"You couldn't," Willow said, her mouth going dry. "You're a good kid."

His lips quivered. "I was."

"We'll figure out how to stop . . ." She paused. "Mark, if you think your brother went crazy because he took that drug, what about the rest of us? We thought it was some kind of possession. Or a curse."

He said something so quietly she couldn't make out what it was. She took a step forward.

"Don't come any closer." He held the gun with both hands.

Cautiously, Willow held out her arms. "I didn't hear what you said."

He frowned. In his slender hands, the gun was beginning to shake. "Yes, you did. You just want to make me say it again."

She shook her head. "No, honest. I really didn't. But—"

"I put it in the water!" he shouted.

"The water? But I—"

"I poured the drug in the reservoir!"

"Oh, my God," Willow breathed, stunned. Everyone in town drank water. Good guys. Bad guys. All that tea Giles drank. The cappuccinos and lattes at the Bronze. Even her mom, who had read somewhere how important it was to drink at least two liters of water a day. "Oh . . . Mark."

"That's why he went crazy. I made him go crazy." Mark burst into tears. "I killed my parents."

"No—"

"Yes! Yes! He didn't know what he was doing."

The sobs came heavy and wracked with pain. Willow dared to come forward another step, then another.

"All those people," he said, lowering the gun. "I did it."

"Mark, you didn't know." Willow took another step toward him. Another. She felt as if she were walking a tightrope stretched between two skyscrapers. If she looked down, she would fall. The only way to make it was to keep moving.

"Don't," he warned, but she could tell his heart wasn't in it.

She put her hand on his shoulder and eased the gun from his weak grasp. Then she put her arms around him; he sobbed against her. She felt the pain striking him, harder with each sob; and she was afraid. She had never grieved like this. But if Oz was dead, she would hurt at least as much.

"I didn't mean to, I didn't," he wailed.

"I know." She patted his back and took a deep breath. *If only he'd told us this in the beginning,* she thought, *fewer people would be dead.*

"Please, Mark," she said gently, "do you know where they took my friends?"

"Who? Who are you talking about?"

"The people who gave your brother the drug. They've captured some friends of ours." She closed her eyes as things clicked into place. *The vampires have done it all. That's what Buffy's dreams mean.*

They drugged us and brought evil into our hearts.

"Jordan," he said. "Jordan gave it to him. He took my ring as payment."

Willow was shocked. Buffy had told her about Lindsey Acuff's autopsy photos. *If they found Mark's ring, and Jordan Smyth had it . . . Jordan Smyth murdered Lindsey Acuff.*

She took a breath. "All right. Let's go to Giles. He needs to talk to you."

"No." He yanked out of her embrace. "No way!"

"Yes way," Buffy said, walking into the room. She looked at Willow. "You okay?"

Willow nodded, weak-kneed with relief at the sight of her friend. "How long were you here?"

"Long enough to hear about the reservoir." She reached out a hand. "Mark, you have to come with us. You have to help fix this."

"I just want to run away," he said miserably.

Buffy nodded. "I know the feeling. Believe me, I really do. But you can't, Mark. It doesn't work. It's like the world is on some big conveyer belt, and it catches up with you sooner or later. It doesn't matter how fast you run."

"Not if I go to Mexico." He flushed, as if even he knew how silly that sounded.

Willow raised a hand. She dug into her pocket and pulled out the cell phone. Mark's eyes widened but he said nothing.

Willow started to press the numbers for the library, but the battery had died. She looked at Buffy and said, "I was hoping for a ride."

"I assume the phone here doesn't work," Buffy said.

"I didn't see one."

Buffy turned. "I'll make a quick run through the house."

"There's a dead squirrel," Willow warned her.

Small potatoes. Buffy smiled. "Thanks, Will."

Willow turned to Mark, who flopped down on the mattress and crossed his arms and legs. "I'm dead," he moaned.

"No. We'll fix it," Willow said, with a confidence she didn't feel. They didn't always fix everything. Sometimes the dark won. People died. Every one of the Slayerettes had lost someone they cared about. Buffy and Giles had endured more heartbreak than Willow thought it would be possible to handle.

Slayers died. Buffy had already lived longer than many of the Chosen Ones before her.

With a sudden shiver of fear, she called out, "Buffy?"

Buffy appeared at the entrance to the room. Her face was pale. She said, "Don't go anywhere else in the house. Just follow me straight out the kitchen door."

Willow looked at Mark. His eyes were big in his small face. He said, "Why? What's in here?"

"You don't want to know." Buffy turned her back as if she expected them both to fall in.

Which they did.

Rome, A.D. *40*

Julian finished his meal and let the body drop to the floor. He crossed to the basin held by his bruised and beaten slave girl and washed the blood from his face. She had displeased him mightily the night before, but now he couldn't recall her offense.

He gargled, spit, and left the room.

Smiling, he walked leisurely to the Temple of Meter, where Caligula was in communion with his so-called goddess. He pushed the door. It was locked. He pushed harder, breaking the lock, and sauntered in.

Caligula was on his knees, before the large statue of Meter. The goddess was a grinning fanged creature with huge, violent eyes that gleamed from the fires burning in the empty sockets. At least a dozen ruined human corpses piled beside a stone altar in her lap, faces contorted in terror and agony. Their hearts were piled atop the altar.

Such a sight was commonplace. Julian kept walking, fully expecting to be greeted cordially when he announced his presence.

Then Caligula rose, picked up one of the hearts, and placed it into the mouth of the goddess. To Julian's utter shock, the statue began to devour it with its huge stone fangs.

That's new, he thought, thrown. *How did the emperor manage that? With priests inside the statue, pulling ropes?*

"*Greetings, my son.*" The voice did not emanate from the statue. It was disembodied, inhabiting no form.

Julian crept into the shadows.

"My mother," Caligula said humbly, lovingly. "Is it finally enough? I put the Madness Potion in the aqueduct, and all Rome lies in ruins. Thousands have died in your name. Will you rise from the darkness and give me what I desire?"

"It is not enough," the voice intoned. *"I cannot rise without the Slayer's heart. Then I shall come. And you shall live forever."*

"What of my rival?" he demanded. "Will you destroy Julian the vampire?"

"Who calls me, rules me," the voice seductively promised.

"Then I call you, Meter!" Caligula shouted.

From the statue's mouth, blood geysered. It smoked and crackled, and turned a brilliant blue. Then it gushed over Caligula like a waterfall. He was bathed in it.

When the stream stopped, he threw back his head and shouted with triumph.

"You are with me, Dark Mother!" he cried. "Your evil lives in me!" He spread forth a hand, and fire emanated from his fingers.

"You are flesh with me," the voice agreed. *"Your bones shall carry my essence until I can come forth. It will be a full moon, and it will be within the season.*

"If," it added, *"I can eat the Slayer's heart."*

Caligula lowered his head. "As with all else you have commanded, it shall be done."

Though thrown, Julian seethed.

And planned.

Giles leaned over a glass beaker bubbling away on a Bunsen burner and squeezed a couple of droplets of something purple from an eyedropper. As Giles had instructed, Xander kept his gas mask and goggles on. Going psycho around big bottles of acid and gas flames would be very not good. So he was determined not to do it.

Also masked and wearing goggles, Giles had out a

couple of especially moldy books, which gave Xander hope, and occasionally he would ask Xander to turn the pages. They were thick and felt very strange to the touch. Not at all papery. *I so don't want to know what they're made of.*

"So, are we getting anyplace?" Xander asked.

"Yes," Giles said, squinting at the mixture. "I've distilled down the samples of our infected blood. I do believe I've isolated the original ingredients of the Madness Potion of Caligula."

"Oh, great." Xander made a face. "Now we'll be on *The X-Files.*"

"Caligula originally had it developed for the Games. He wanted the gladiators to put on a fine spectacle, you see. Enrage them so they would become mindless killing machines. Go on a bad trip, as it were."

"Giles, you hippie," Xander riffed.

Flushing slightly, Giles ignored him. "The Roman Empire fell because of the depravity and insanity that pervaded it. One could theorize that the Madness Potion somehow got distributed throughout the populace."

They looked at each other.

"Just like here in Sunnydale," Xander said slowly.

"Just like here in Sunnydale," Giles echoed.

"So this town is on a bad trip."

"A very bad trip."

They both gazed at the bubbling beaker.

"Yes!" Julian cried, delighted, as Cordelia sailed her spear into the target he held in front of his body. "Wonderfully done!"

"But how will she do against a real adversary?" the dark vampire woman asked as she approached them. Cordelia stiffened. "Against someone who fights back?"

Helen pulled the spear from Julian's target and aimed it at Cordelia. Cordelia bit back a cry. *That's what this bitch wants from me, fear and pleading. She's the queen of mean and I could certainly learn a few things from her . . .*

"Stay cool," Oz murmured. Flanked by demons, he stood at the side of the arena, a spear in his hand.

Helen morphed into vamp face. She bent low, raising the spear over her shoulder, and stalked Cordy. Cordelia's heart beat crazily but she kept her cool, mincing backward, never taking her gaze off the spear.

Suddenly the vampire straightened. She threw back her head and laughed, turned, and hurtled the spear at Julian.

"She's a feisty one. No wonder you fancy her," she said.

Laughing, she turned and glided away, her black skirts swishing like Morticia Addams all vogued out for the Executioners' Ball.

Julian glared after her. As Cordelia stood reeling, he snapped the spear in two by clenching his fist.

Then he smiled at Cordelia, and her blood ran cold. It was not a friendly smile. It was calculated and icy. She figured then that "fancy" was not a wacky foreign word for "like."

"Don't think I will save you," he said, clapping his hands. Cordy's hulking trainer, a man covered with scars from the top of his pin head to his thick lack of waist, strutted into the arena from the side door and bowed.

"Take them back to their cells," Julian said. "Prepare them for tonight's festivities."

"Festivities?" Cordy repeated shrilly, as the demons led her and Oz out of the arena.

Transforming into vamp face, Julian smiled at her.

"As in, let the Games begin."

Buffy put the money in the pay phone while Mark cowered behind Willow. Across the street, a gas station blazed out of control.

Not the best place to make a phone call, Buffy thought, *but the first place.*

The sun was going down, and the town was going up. In the distance, explosions shook the ground like bombs going off. Buffy had no idea what was going on, and no idea how to stop it. Right now, her little piece of the rock was saving this kid and getting Willow to the library, where she could help with the research.

"Giles," she said, as soon as she knew the phone had been picked up.

"Buffy. Thank heavens. Is Willow—"

"With me. Mark, too. I'm bringing them in. A car would be good. Yours kind of died, finally." *About six blocks back, and it wasn't pretty.*

"Died?" he asked shakily. "Where are you? I'll send Xander. We'll locate another vehicle."

She scanned the area. "I guess we could keep walking."

"No. It's not safe to go about with that boy in tow. I've turned on the local radio news and people are searching everywhere for him."

She huffed. "Look, I can deal. If we wait for Xander, we're sitting ducks."

"You can do remarkable things, it's true. But the odds are stacked against you, Buffy. You cannot fight an entire town."

Raising her hand slightly, Willow mouthed, *Reservoir*.

"Before I forget, Mark put this drug in the reservoir," she said. "It's what made everybody go wacko."

Giles was silent for a moment. Then he murmured, "Oh, Lord."

Buffy frowned into the phone. "What?"

"I'm not sure. Just sit tight."

"Quack, quack," she replied. "Over and out."

She hung up and looked at Willow. "Giles wants us to stay here and wait for Xander."

"Xander?" Willow asked.

"With wheels." She shrugged. "That's all I can reveal, even under torture."

Willow raised her brows. "Well, if we're hiding from everybody, and we don't know what the car looks like, how will we connect?"

Buffy shrugged. "Technically, we only have to hide Mark. Not everyone knows he was last seen with us. You."

"No. Just all the police officers," Willow said, gulping as a cruiser crept down the main street. She pulled Mark deeper into the shadows.

"You guys are going to get me killed," he said.

Buffy said nothing. She was watching the sun go down.

Rome, A.D. *40*

"I've found her," Julian said to Helen as he entered the cell.

Helen stared at him, all the blood draining from her face. Her lips were numb, her cheeks icy hot. She almost slipped on the straw that covered her floor.

He crossed to an elaborate chair he had brought her and lounged in it, every inch the patrician Roman nobleman.

Every inch a vicious killer.

"Here is my last offer," he said. "I am going to assassinate the emperor very soon. I entrust my existence to you, telling you that. But the world will turn upside down when that happens, and unless you are on my side, I'll have no way of protecting you."

"Diana," she rasped.

"We almost killed her." He stretched and settled into the chair. "But it takes a lot to kill a Slayer."

"She is of the gods." Helen's throat was so tight she could barely speak.

"Perhaps. But the fact remains that she is dying, and I am not. And I know where she is."

He leaned forward. "I'm going to bring her here. I can heal her. You know I can. I have healed your many wounds."

She closed her eyes and waited for what she knew she would hear.

"You know my price already," he said.

She opened her eyes and gazed at him with blinding hatred. "I will never become like you. I don't care if she dies. She never tried to save me."

"Oh, but she did." His voice was lilting, gently mocking. "She's tried many times. I suppose I failed to mention that before."

Fury rose in her, quickly followed by anguish. "You're lying."

"I'm not."

She flew at him, unable to control herself. She was a gladiator now.

He matched her, blow for blow, until at last he grabbed her by the hair and pulled back her head. She was panting.

"Ah, my lioness." He bent toward her neck.

"Great Julian," someone said behind him, and he let her go.

Helen's heart seized inside her rib cage. Two soldiers carried a still form in on a pallet, entering the cell as Julian held open the door for them. They set the pallet on the floor, and it was only then that Helen dared come near.

Diana's blond hair framed a face graying with the approach of death. She was covered with a heavy woolen cloak; blood had seeped from her wounds into the cream-colored fabric, lending it a macabre beauty.

"Oh, Diana, Diana," Helen said in a rush. Then she felt Julian's stare. "She never tried to save me."

"Then let her die." He rose. "You hold her life in your hands. The decision is entirely up to you. If you consent to join me, her life belongs to you, and you may do with her as you please. You can tell me to heal her. I'll even set her free if you desire it."

He bowed. "I'll leave you now. You need time to think. But don't take too long, sweet Helen. The Slayer's time has almost run out."

Helen raised her chin. "I'll let her die."

Julian turned and left the cell.

Helen screamed, "I'll let her die!"

Xander slipped out of the library and walked quickly into the faculty lot, blending in with the shadows. He had no idea how Giles had filched Ms. Broadman's keys, and he wished they were anyone's keys but Ms. Broadman's.

Until he found out that his nemesis drove a wicked-sleek, sable black Jaguar XKE.

"Tell me I've died and gone to heaven," he breathed, jingling the keys.

"All right," Angel said as he emerged from the shadows. "If it'll make you happy."

"Dead Boy," Xander murmured, to hide his fright at being surprised. "What the hell—pardon the expression, since I know that's a sensitive subject for you—are you doing here?"

Angel had on all the clothes that made Buffy go girly—the duster, the shirt, the black leather pants. And boots. The tude to match, with his haunted look and those cheekbones. Not that Xander had noticed his cheekbones in anything but a critical, masculine way.

"I checked Buffy's house. She wasn't there. Giles's phone was busy. So." Angel looked questioningly at Xander.

"I'm going to go pick her up right now," Xander said.

Angel looked about as happy as Angel ever did. "I'll go with."

Xander wasn't sure which was stronger inside him, relief, resentment, or alarm. After all, if Angel went psycho, Xander could pretty much count on dying.

And if they showed up together, Buffy would figure the vampire for the white knight, even if Xander was the one driving the bitchen car.

On the other hand, if a fight broke out, Angel was a good thing to have around.

"Hop in," Xander said casually.

Angel looked at him askance. "Do you know how to drive this thing?"

"Sure." Xander was miffed. He slid into the seat and hesitated, searching for the ignition switch. "I, ah, just forget a little."

"Let me drive." Angel started to open his door.

Xander jammed in the key, took off the brake, and screeched backward just like Batman in the car of the ages.

"It's coming back to me," he said.

Chapter 16

THE HOUNDS LUNGED AT THE WEREWOLF, BARKING, jaws snapping, eager for combat. Helen held them back just barely out of reach, as the caged beast swung at them and howled. It was hungry; it was raging. The very sight of it made Julian realize that, old as he was, there were still some things in the weary old world that could excite him.

Let the Games begin, he thought. He had sent one of his minions out on an important mission: to find the treacherous Angelus, and deal with him before he, Julian, came into his kingdom.

Julian knew his good and faithful servant would not fail him in this.

If only they could find the urn in time, things would be perfect. Six hundred sixty-six years was a long time to wait for another perfect moment.

One of the dogs thrust its muzzle between the bars of the cage. The wolf sprang.

The dog's shrieks would have moved a creature possessed of a warm, living heart.

Julian praised the gods that his was dead. But, staring at Helen as she threw back her head and laughed, he swore that it pounded.

Together they entered the dark sacrificial chamber, lit by a single candle. In time, if they succeeded in their plans, they would build a fabulous temple to the goddess, as Caligula had done, and sacrifice all the inhabitants of Sunnydale to her. And then, the inhabitants of the surrounding towns and cities. And eventually, every single living human on the planet.

Trembling with eagerness, Julian bowed before the statue of Meter. Helen did the same.

Julian pointed to the bloody pile of human hearts arranged on the altar. They had been cut out of the bodies they had left to rot in the house they had purchased in Sunnydale.

"Dear Meter," he said, "we have made more sacrifices in your name. Tonight we conduct the final sacrifices required for your rebirth."

The statue shifted. Its eyes blazed.

One of the hearts on the altar began to beat, and the ground trembled.

Julian thrilled. This hadn't happened before. Twice, they had tried to raise Meter, and twice they had failed.

"My essence has been released into the world," a disembodied voice proclaimed. *"I am here."*

"Then rise, Dark Mother!" Julian cried, opening his arms. "Take your place with us!"

The earth trembled again, more violently. *"I cannot. The ashes containing my essence are still required,"* a disembodied voice echoed throughout the chamber.

"But you just said your essence has been—" Helen began, then kept her silence as Julian elbowed her.

"Whoever has the urn must have opened it," he murmured to her. "But it's not enough."

"We can give you the heart of a Slayer," Julian promised. "Tonight, on your special night. Will this be enough?"

Twice before, they had tried to raise Meter with Slayer's hearts, but without the ashes.

"The ashes," the voice insisted. *"The heart as well."*

The earth shook harder.

It's Meter, struggling to rise, Julian thought. "It shall be done," he said.

Buffy paced as she, Willow, and Mark waited for Xander to show. Smoke made her eyes water and the stench of burning oil coated the inside of her mouth. It was impossible to see more than a foot or two in any direction. How could they ever expect Xander to find them?

He may have already passed by us, Buffy thought.

As if on cue, the hulking shape of a car pulled up to the curb. It idled, the beams barely visible in the murk. Buffy thought she heard the click of a door.

Mark called out, "Here!"

"Who's there?" a deep male voice called. Definitely not Xander. And not anyone she knew.

"Sssh," she warned.

"You'd better answer," the stranger said. "We're cops."

Mark shouted, "You won't take me, you crazy bastards!"

"It's the Dellasandro kid," the voice cried out.

Like some kind of scene in a badly lit movie, more cars roared up, their high beams highlighting the boiling smoke. Doors slammed as figures raced toward them, their flashlights beaming crazily.

"Willow, get him out of here," Buffy said, just as someone rammed into her from behind.

"Hey, back off!" She whirled around with a roundhouse kick, anticipating a solid connection, when a hand grabbed her around the ankle, then its owner jumped forward and scooped her up, preventing her fall.

"It's me." He put her down.

"Angel." She tried to squint through the smoke. "What—?"

"And me," Xander said. "C'mon. The Jag's around the corner. Wherever the corner is."

A fist smashed into the back of Buffy's head. She stumbled into Angel.

As if they were performing their tai chi exercises together, both moved forward with one outstretched fist and one clenched against their chest. When Buffy found a target, she double-punched it, fists pummeling a solid object she guessed was a face.

The object dipped out of range and she heard the distinctive sound of a human body collapsing to the ground.

One down. How many to go?

"Xander, how ya doing?" she bellowed.

"No clue," he shouted back. "Ow! Hey, ouch! Um, just fine."

"Willow?" Buffy yelled.

There was no answer. Buffy hoped that was good news.

Then she was surrounded by forms in the smoke who must have homed in on her voice.

She felt a cold hand on her shoulder.

"Angel?" she said.

The hand squeezed.

Angel shouted, "Buffy!"

"What?" she asked blindly.

Then it came: the unmistakable sound of a dusting. The unearthly scream of a staked vampire, who then exploded into ash.

Buffy froze. Her lips moved but no sound came out. She couldn't breathe. Someone hit her, but she barely registered it as she swayed, disbelieving.

"Angel," she whispered. Then she called, "Angel? *Angel!*" It was a shriek of pure terror. *Not here. Not now. Not this way.*

"String him up!"

"Buffy?" It was Xander. "Buffy, help!"

A wind whipped up, sudden and fierce, and the smoke tumbled over and over itself, like a carpet rolling up. It thinned, and Buffy lurched unsteadily as she ranged over the throng and found no trace of Angel. And no evidence of Xander, either.

Then she looked up.

A rope tied around his neck, Xander was being hoisted up by two men who had climbed onto a lamppost and thrown the rope over the arched portion of metal. As he clutched at the rope and kicked, Xander's eyes were bulging. His face was scarlet. He was strangling.

Wordlessly, Buffy fought her way through the mob, kicking savagely, pushing burly men out of her way as if they were paper dolls. They had lost interest in her. Xander was the prize now.

"Xander!" she shouted.

"It's the boy. Kill him. String him up!" an old gray-haired woman screeched, waving an old black pocketbook over her head.

Buffy made her way to the base of the lamppost. A tall, dark man swung a baseball bat at her, but she dropped to her knees and the bat sailed high. She rammed her elbow into the back of his rib cage, using his momentum against him, and he made a half circle, then shouted as the bat continued through and smacked the other side of the streetlight.

She snaked up the metal column and onto the pole, reaching the first of the two men. Before he realized what she was doing, she grabbed his ankles and jumped, pulling him straight down. As he fell, she lunged for the column, climbed up, and rammed into the other man, who had been sitting astride the curved section. He flailed to keep his balance, then fell.

The rope around Xander's neck went slack, but this was not good news. The crowd below started grabbing and shouting; if they got hold of him, they would probably tear him apart.

It's the madness, Buffy reminded herself. *It's not them. But they look so evil. . . .*

"Sorry, Xand," she said, reaching a hand toward him as she straddled the pole. He reached up his hands—*good thinking*—and she grabbed them, giving the rope some slack. He started coughing and gasping; she got him around the shoulders and pulled him up until he could loop his arms over the pole.

He jerked behind himself with his head. "Ow, my neck muscles." Then he looked down. "Did they get Mark?"

"I don't know. I think Willow got him out of here."

She surveyed the scene. There was a building about ten feet away, and a long pole extended at an angle from the roof like some kind of flag pole. The building was on fire, but other than that, it was perfect.

As he swung up beside her, she said, "Give me your rope."

"It's all yours. Forever."

Together they worked the knot at the nape of his neck, loosening it until Buffy could slip the opposite end through it and untie it. Then she doubled it up a couple times, gauging its length, and nodded to herself.

"We need an anchor, something to catch onto that building somehow." She held out her hand. "Give me your shoe."

"My shoe." He frowned. "Why *my* shoe? Why not yours?"

She looked at him. "Okay, okay," he said.

He reached down and yanked off his shoe. Buffy tied the rope around it, swung it around over her head, and whipped it out toward the outcropping flag pole.

The rope wrapped around it on the first try.

"And now . . ." Xander said uncertainly.

She tugged hard on the rope, making sure it was secure. "We go hand over hand."

"And we know we won't fall because . . ."

Buffy shrugged. "We don't."

"I knew that."

"Me first. Test case," she said. She looped their end of the rope around the overhang and knotted it well. Gave it a tug. It was holding on the other end by virtue of Xander's shoe.

"Okay." She took a breath. Then she swung out and

started moving hand over hand along the makeshift suspension bridge. The crowd beneath howled. It would take them no time to shinny up and either grab Xander or loosen the rope. So she redoubled her efforts.

The building was blazing, but she found a few red-hot bricks to lean against while she took her weight off the rope. Urgently she gestured for Xander to get a hustle on; the natives were beyond restless.

He took longer than she did, but not as long as she might have expected. In short order, he was standing beside her, cringing as flames shot through a broken window and nearly singed them both.

"Yow." He flinched and pulled his elbows in. Sweat poured down his face. "Now what?"

She looked down. "We could jump."

He stared at her. "Ha ha. You're such a kidder."

"We could burn to death."

"I'm still laughing like a hyena." His voice was rising. He was getting scared.

"Look." She pointed to a jagged section of the roof that wasn't on fire. "Let's try that, get to the roof, run across and look for a way down."

"Sounds like a plan. Or not," Xander said gamely.

Willow slowly staggered along. She was tired and she hurt.

He's going to die, and it's going to be my fault, she thought miserably. They were a long way from the school, and no matter how badly she wanted to keep going, she was going to have to stop.

"Where are we going?" Mark demanded. "We should have stayed with Buffy."

"It'll be okay," she said.

278

Then a car screeched up behind them, and Willow took off, dragging him behind her.

"Will!"

It was Xander. And Buffy. In the Jag.

In no time at all, they reached the school. The four bolted inside the main building and careened down the corridors to the library.

Buffy skidded to a stop, the others tumbling in after her. There was no one there. Books were piled in huge, leaning-Pisa stacks and the computer was beeping plaintively. Other than that, the place was tomblike.

And thanks to her tenure on the Hellmouth, Buffy knew from tombs.

The double doors swung open, shut, and Giles walked into the library, an enormous book lying in his arms. He was muttering to himself in Latin, if Buffy knew her dead languages.

Which I don't.

"Hey," she said, stepping into the light. The others followed suit.

"Buffy. Willow." He nodded at Xander and Mark, then looked back at Willow. "Your parents are worried sick."

She reached for the phone, then stopped. "My mother won't ever let me out of the house again."

Giles sighed. "And frankly, I've sore need of you. But it is your decision."

"I can't call," she said tightly. "I can't let them get in the way."

"Unfortunately, I concur," Giles said. "Too much is at stake."

He surveyed the group. "Where's Angel?"

"Yeah," Xander said. "Where's Dead Boy?"

Buffy swallowed hard and said nothing.

Giles shrugged. "Well, I'm sure he will along momentarily."

Mark stepped forward. "I'm sorry I hit you, Mr. Giles. And stole your car."

"Thank you. Apology accepted."

The boy hung his head. "I put the . . . the stuff in the reservoir."

"Yes," Giles said, but there was an edge to his voice. "So Buffy told me. But where did you get it?"

He said softly, "I was mad at Brian. He took a ring of mine to pay for some drugs. He told me Jordan said they'd make him study better. I got really ticked. I found the little bottle in his room and I hid it.

"I was going with friends up to the reservoir. We were going to wait until it closed, and then we were going to camp out." He looked embarrassed. "We were trying to spot Sunni. So we could take pictures and be really famous. I threw the bottle in. I didn't open it or anything. But it must have come uncapped."

He added dejectedly, "There was hardly anything in it."

"I guess it was enough," Xander put in.

"Xander," Willow reproved.

Mark started to cry. "I killed them."

Giles said, "Are you speaking of the sacrifice?"

Mark moved closer to Willow, and she put a protective arm around him. "What are you talking about?"

"It appears that to activate the Madness Potion— which is the drug that Mark put into the reservoir, one must offer up a blood sacrifice," Giles elaborated. "A human sacrifice."

Buffy, Willow, and Xander stared in horror at the boy, whose face went chalk white. He swayed a little and said, "In the reservoir?"

Giles watched him closely. "Yes."

"I didn't do anything like that." He looked as if he were ready to bolt. Giles's glance ticked toward Willow and she gave the boy a reassuring pat.

The boy nodded. "I would never . . . I didn't kill people the way my broth—" He bit off his words and stared down at his hands.

"All right, then," Giles said. "Willow, please access the police files. I'm sure there's been an unsolved murder or accident, which occurred that day near the reservoir."

"Which could be considered the sacrifice," Buffy said slowly.

"This might take a while," Willow said, pulling out the chair. "I'll need to sort through all the recent murders to find one you like."

She began typing.

Then she said, "What about missing persons? Here's someone reported missing. Her husband works at the reservoir."

"What's her name?" Buffy asked.

"Ida Bitterman."

"I saw him up there," Buffy said, remembering the man who had told her to get a raincoat and a weapon.

"Make a note," Giles said.

Rome, A.D. *40*

They were alone. Helen sat transfixed on the floor, watching Diana's shallow breaths. The torches flickered and began to smoke, casting shadows over her pale face. Her cheeks were large hollows; her eyes were sunken. Death was slowly embracing her; Helen felt his cold, menacing presence and wrapped her arms around herself.

Diana groaned softly. Her chest rose; unconsciously, Helen took a breath and held it along with her. She began to feel dizzy. Still Diana's chest did not fall.

Helen gave a little cry and leaned forward, touching the blanket over Diana's chest. Then she flattened her palm and pushed down very gently. Diana exhaled with a gasp.

Helen kept her hand on her chest, wet with blood, and waited for the next breath. When it didn't come, she leaned over Diana and whispered, "Breathe, damn you."

"She is dead, and you have waited too long," Julian said behind her.

"No," Helen wailed, shuddering.

Julian unlocked the cell and walked in. He squatted on the other side of the Slayer and pressed his fingertips to her neck.

Diana stirred uneasily and took a sharp, deep breath.

He took Helen's hand in his and turned it over, caressing it with his fingertips. His touch was incredibly gentle; she had not expected that in him. He trailed slowly up her arm, moving silkily, and she looked away. In all this grief and fury, she would not be moved by his touch.

"Say the word, Helen. She's almost dead. I will be the most ardent lover. I will be faithful to you forever. Can you expect that of any mortal? More to the point, will you ever taste love with one? You'll die here like an animal.

"But I'll hand you the world, and you shall be its queen."

She raised her chin and tried to save herself. "I have tasted love."

"Demetrius? But, little Helen, he was the one who told us about Diana."

She went numb. "That cannot be true."

"It is. He was in the employ of the emperor. And you saw how he was repaid."

Beneath their hands, Diana groaned again and whispered, "Helen."

"Her thoughts, as she is dying, are of you," Julian said. "I give you her life, if you wish it."

He took Helen's other hand and slowly stood, easing her up. Advancing slowly, he circled around Diana's body, turning Helen toward him.

"It's time," he whispered.

She closed her eyes. *Diana, Patroness of the Hunt,* she prayed. *Though I take on evil form, preserve my soul. Preserve my innocence.*

But she had no innocence. She had told Demetrius exactly what this monster wanted to know. The gods had paid her back for betraying Diana's secret.

The soldiers had taken Helen in her stead.

Julian growled like a wild beast. Eyes still shut, Helen whispered, "No."

Sharp daggers pierced her neck.

With a gasp Helen came to life, jerking awake. Julian stood over her, a torch in his hand. He wore his true face.

His beautiful face.

"Oh," she said, reaching a hand to him.

He helped her stand. Caressed her hair, her shoulders, her face. Languorously, she let her head fall back.

"How is it with you, beloved?" he asked.

"I hunger." She was ravenous. She opened her mouth to bite him and he laughed, wagging a finger at her.

"Your first blood must be of the living," he said.

His hands on her shoulders, he turned her around and pointed to the body on the floor.

"I gave you her life in return for your change," he reminded her.

Helen laughed and fell to her knees beside the Slayer. "Then I'll take her life," she said gleefully.

Her face changed, and she drank.

Rapturously.

"According to legend, they kept the capture and death of the Slayer a secret," Giles said. "Helen's transformation as well."

Willow had found no murders at the reservoir within the last year, never mind the last month. However, Mr. Bitterman's wife had not been found.

"Keep trying," Giles urged her, as Mark, Buffy, and Xander followed him back into the chemistry lab.

Mark looked awed as Giles mixed and stirred.

"The next evening, Julian arranged a banquet. He announced that Helen would battle a new assailant as entertainment."

He raised a test tube and pushed up his glasses and

he judged the color of the contents, which were a very pale blue.

"It was a sham. The demon she was to fight was a confederate of Julian's. At a prearranged signal, Helen transformed and together they attacked the emperor. He managed to elude them, but they hunted him down and drowned him in the Roman aqueduct. Julian instructed that his body be burned and he intended to keep the ashes, believing them to be possessed of magickal energy. Which apparently, they are. By using them in the ritual to raise Meter, Julian fully intended to become emperor of a demonic empire."

"But he didn't," Willow said, "unless we got a-bridged textbooks for ancient history."

"He didn't," Giles concurred. "They didn't know then that when a Slayer dies, a new one is called." He cleared his throat, and glanced at Buffy. "The new Slayer attacked almost immediately. In the ensuing confusion, the ashes went missing. I can only conjecture that Julian and Helen are here because the Urn of Caligula made it here to the Hellmouth. Perhaps Willow will be able to trace their rediscovery."

"That might be really useful," Xander said. "I'll go tell her to do that."

"Good idea," Giles said. "Take Mark with you."

"No," the boy protested. "I want to watch you."

"It may become dangerous. I am not precisely sure of what I'm doing," Giles said.

The two left. Giles looked at Buffy and said, "I know you're worried about Angel."

"No time now," she murmured. "Keep talking. Tell me everything you know."

He regarded her for a moment, then resumed mixing and pouring. "Almost overnight, the chaos which had reigned supreme over the Empire evaporated. The new emperor, Claudius, routed out the vampires and demons. They were nearly eliminated, all but a few."

"It evaporated, why?"

"An excellent question, and one whose answer is appalling, I'm afraid." Giles was quiet for a moment. Then he said, "My source material indicates that to reverse the effects of the Madness Potion, two components are needed. One is an actual antidote, which I am trying to create here."

"And?" Buffy prodded.

Giles looked down for a moment. Then he took a deep breath.

"The author believes that killing the emperor in the aqueduct served as a sacrifice, which the gods accepted as worthy. They then reversed the curse."

Buffy stared back at him. "So someone has to *die.*"

There was a long silence. "Yes. To be more precise, the person who instigated the curse."

A beat. "Whoever poured the potion in the reservoir in the first place," Buffy whispered.

They stared at one another.

Chapter 17

In the library, Willow said to Xander, "No mystery with the urn. It was unearthed during an archeological dig. An Italian antiquities expert said it was of no particular historical value, so they decided to donate it to a charity auction. Some guy bought it for the equivalent of a hundred dollars.

"Later on, another antiquities expert decided it was priceless."

Xander snorted. "Experts. You gotta love 'em."

Willow continued, reading off the screen, "It became part of a traveling collection up for sale on consignment, which is how it came here."

"Helen and Julian must have gone all crazy when they heard about it," Xander said. "Figured this was their lucky century."

Willow nodded. Then she looked around. "Hey, where's Mark?"

* * *

Buffy said to Giles, "So we have an antidote." She gestured to the test tube. "Nice blue."

Giles angled the test tube. "Chamomile, believe it or not."

"Like the tea?" She wrinkled her forehead.

He tapped the tube. "This Madness Potion is not a poison in the strictest sense of the word. It's a synergist blend of various herbs and oils which stimulate one's mental and psychic states."

He thought for a moment. "Upon occasion, we seem to have run into some of these components. I had chamomile tea bags. There's also a small amount of rose in the mix. I broke a bottle of rose water in my kitchen. Either they stimulated us to anger, or they calmed us down, depending upon their strength."

Buffy picked up a gas mask and gestured to the urn. "Well, you're proof positive that this stuff calms people down."

Buffy had worn the mask while Giles uncorked the urn and went berserk. Then she'd waved the tube in front of his nose, he calmed down enough to drink some of it, and then he reverted completely back to his calm and collected Giles self.

However, he was still infected. He had cut himself and let the fresh drops of blood spill into a beaker. They had still hissed and shown the black dots.

"Because there's also a curse involved," Giles had explained. "It's not simply a physical thing."

It made sense to Buffy. He and Willow used wards and spells against physical manifestations of the supernatural all the time. But that didn't mean they had contained the source.

Which leads us back to the matter of the sacrifice, she thought.

"I can't kill a little boy," she blurted, "and neither can you."

The chem lab door opened and Willow and Xander ran in. "Mark's gone," Willow said. "We can't find him anywhere. He must have wigged."

"And now our previous discussion is moot," Giles murmured.

Xander walked along the lab bench with all its elaborate equipment. "Any progress?"

"Yeah," Buffy said slowly. "Giles found the antidote."

"I see. Good show," Xander returned, imitating Giles's accent. "So, were you going to make more of that stuff, or are you setting up for a rousing round of Mousetrap?"

"I'm truly surprised that such a tiny amount of the stuff could create such astonishing effects," Giles said, clearing his throat. "But I shall prepare some more antidote. We'll take it to the reservoir and pour it in. That will ameliorate the effects."

Xander said, "Not to mention calming everybody down, at least temporarily."

"That was the jist of what I said," Giles murmured.

"I knew that." Xander rubbed his hands. "Okay, Dr. Frank N Furter. Just tell me what to do."

Buffy sat huddled on her lab stool as Giles went through the elaborate process of creating more of the antidote. Angel still did not show. Her mind kept repeating the terrible sound of the staking, a sound that usually brought a smile to her lips. She remembered the cold hand on her shoulder. The sound of his voice, so near.

"All right," Giles said finally. "I think I've mixed a

sufficient quantity. We need to get to the reservoir. Perhaps we should take the urn, too."

"But if we get attacked, Helen and Julian may snag it," Buffy pointed out. "We don't know if there's still power in it or not."

"They may somehow already know we have it," Buffy told him. She looked at Giles. "And vampires can come into the high school without an official invitation, if you get my drift."

"So we take the urn," Xander said, raising a finger. "New topic: transportation. The Jag—"

"Buffy's mother dropped off their car," Giles cut in. "She's gone to stay with the Rosenbergs."

"Oh." Willow made a face.

"We're finished here. We've got to get going," Buffy said.

They left the building. In the faculty lot, Buffy thought she saw a shadow against the chain-link fence. *Mark?* Her heart leapt. *Angel?*

"The Jag's gone," Xander said. Then he said guiltily, "I think maybe I left the keys in it."

"Maybe Mark took it," Willow ventured.

"Well, I hope he can handle it. It's a big boy's car." He flushed as Buffy and Willow gave him a look. *"Person's* car. A big person's car. But not as in large."

Moving swiftly, the four of them climbed into Joyce's car. As Giles sat behind the wheel, Buffy scanned the area.

"Anything amiss?" Giles asked.

"I think it's okay," Buffy said to Giles. "I thought I saw a shadow, but nothing's carjacked us. So far."

Giles drove the car out of the faculty lot and onto the streets of Sunnydale. Behind Buffy, Xander nervously drummed the armrest. Buffy scanned the landscape, which was dotted with clumps of people still under the influence of the Madness Potion, standing atop cars and bashing in the windshields while others cheered them on, looting, fighting.

Then the van turned onto Route 17. Sagging with exhaustion, Buffy thought of the many nights her mother waited at home with no idea where her daughter was. She pitied the Rosenbergs. As soon as they were finished with this, they'd drop Willow off first thing.

Buffy closed her eyes to rest, leaning her head back on the headrest.

She jerked awake at the scream of police sirens. She stared into the rearview mirror as Xander muttered, "Oh, my God."

There had to be at least a dozen police cruisers behind them; and in a long parade behind them, at least twenty civilian vehicles. All were bearing down on the minivan.

"We've been spotted," Giles said.

"Punch it," Xander said. "Floor it."

"I am." Giles glanced in the rearview mirror. "Damn it." He looked over at Buffy. "If something happens," he said quietly.

"Reservoir, got it." She patted his valise, which contained the two flasks of antidote.

The sirens were gaining on them. A car pulled abreast the van and a voice blared over a microphone: "Pull over. We are armed."

Willow lowered her voice and began chanting. The cruiser kept up with the car. Tight-lipped, Giles kept driving, while Buffy peered around him at the police officer. So far, he hadn't drawn his weapon.

"Plan B is?" Buffy asked dismally.

"I slow down, you jump out with my valise, and get to the reservoir," Giles said. "Dump in the antidote. Hide the urn."

She waited. When he didn't go on, she said, "And what about the other part? The sacrifice and the curse?"

"Pull over *immediately,*" the police officer boomed.

And now his gun was out. Buffy glanced at Giles, who nodded and said, "Plan B."

"No," Willow cried. "Give my spell a chance."

"I will shoot," the cop said, taking aim at the front tire.

Willow took up her chant again. *More Latin,* Buffy guessed. It seemed all the really good spells—except for the Restoration of the Soul—were in Latin. She crossed her fingers that Willow pulled it off, then nervously uncrossed them in case doing so made for some kind of jinx.

Suddenly a dense fog tumbled toward the car, rushing head-on like an enormous ocean wave. Buffy braced herself in case there was something in it, while Giles continued to drive, steely-eyed. Willow's voice rose excitedly.

"Keep going, chica," Xander urged her.

The fog engulfed both them and their pursuers. Giles turned off the car lights, muttering, "I should have done that in the beginning," and sped on.

"Giles, I think Plan B is still our best bet," Buffy insisted. "You're going to be forced over."

She gathered the valise against her chest and opened the car door. The fog rushed in, icy, damp fingers molding themselves over her face and body.

Giles swerved off the road and onto bumpy terrain.

Buffy nearly tumbled out, but she kept her grip on both sides of the door. There was a dizzy moment; then she plunged from the van, rolled over on her shoulder, then executed several more rolls over the muddy ground.

Remaining off the highway, Giles put the van in reverse and drove backwards in the dark and the fog. Sirens screamed past them. Then he turned off the car.

"Um," Willow said, but Xander highly approved.

"This is called silent running, Will," he informed her, finding and holding her hand. He gave it a pat. "At least, when it's submarine movies. We're eluding their sonar, so to speak. They don't have any way of knowing where we are."

"Except that I can't maintain this spell for much longer," she said.

"Oh." Giles sounded surprised. "In that case—"

He never finished the sentence. There was a terrible wrench of grinding metal, and then a single shout and the sounds of a scuffle. Xander's door was next, yanked out, and huge, rough hands grabbed him and dragged him out of the van.

"Willow!" he shouted. "Run!"

"Get the girl!" a low, gravelly voice bellowed.

"Hey," Xander protested. "You can't do this! We're Americans!"

"We're not," the voice replied.

Then a damp cloth was clamped over Xander's nose and mouth, and he felt himself passing out.

"No." His eyes rolled back in his head. His own voice was an echo as he went somewhere else.

* * *

Buffy half-ran, half-climbed up the steep slope toward the reservoir. The fog was gone; she saw dozens of taillights heading out of town and wondered if Giles and the others had managed to outrun the convoy. The two flasks and the urn in the valise had survived her leap out of the car. That was something.

Wet branches whipped her face as the wind picked up again. She forced them out of her way, then ducked down to get her bearings. *Not far now.*

Using outcropping bushes and rocks, she pulled herself up the slippery slope, a slight thrill of triumph washing over her when she spied the concrete steps that led from the base of the dam to the top. With a burst of speed, she hustled on up to the base.

She took the steps two at a time. The gate was still unlocked from the last time she'd been here—evidence of the chaos that had taken over the town—and it squealed loudly as she pushed it open and dashed to the water's edge.

Crouching, she opened the valise and pulled out one of the two flasks. In the moonlight, the liquid inside looked not blue, but yellow.

She popped open the cork.

"Let this work," she breathed, her own version of a spell, or a prayer, or both.

At that moment, shapes flew out of the darkness and charged her. Buffy set down the flask, straightened, and made a one-eighty, pummeling a leathery, winged demon as it swooped down on her, claws slashing her forearms until she headbutted it and kicked it in the midsection. By then, several vampires had surrounded her. Staying focused, she took note of each as she dealt first with the tall, bald one on her right, then the one in the middle, then the one to her left. Three remained; by dropping to her knees, she made two of them collide with each other. The effect would have been comical if she'd had time to laugh.

Crouching, she broke off a length of branch from a manzanita bush and ran it through the third vampire as it flung itself at her. The dusting was startling as it exploded in midair.

She sprang to her feet, fully prepared for the next onslaught, when a blond male vampire stepped from the shadows and said, "Slayer, wait." He had a British accent.

"What, you guys need to catch your breath already?" she asked, scanning her perimeter. More demons stepped from the shadows. More vampires. Lots and lots of them.

"No, but *he* does." The vampire pointed toward the reservoir.

Buffy hazarded a glance. About twenty feet from shore, a small figure flailed in the water. It disappeared beneath the surface, then popped back up.

"Buffy!" Mark called. "Buffy, run!"

She clenched her fists and glared at the vampire, who shrugged. "Not our doing. If you willingly accompany us, we'll let you rescue him. Or we can continue the battle while he drowns."

Nothing inside her believed him, and she sure as hell wasn't going to cooperate once she saved Mark. But she said, "Agreed."

Buffy pushed her way past the vampires and demons. She couldn't spot the flask she'd already opened and put on the ground, but the valise, which still contained the second flask and the urn, lay at the water's edge. There was perhaps a three-foot drop from the embankment to the lake itself. Taking a deep breath, she made a show of taking off her jacket and dropping it over the valise. Then she scooted it with her foot over the edge, covering the splash with a jump of her own.

As she had anticipated, the water there was shallow. She caught at the valise and pulled it along with her as she dashed thigh-deep through the chilly water, then scooted off and began to swim.

Mark had gone under the water again. She felt inside the valise and found the second flask. Uncorked it. Poured it into the water. Hoped one was enough.

Still holding the valise, she swam as hard as she could for Mark.

It was easy to find him from his splashing and struggling. She got him in a lifeguard hold and said, "Take it easy. I've got you."

He clamped his fingers around her arm and pulled, trying to break her grip. "Let me go. I have to die. I poured it in."

She flushed. She should have realized a smart kid like him would have figured that one out. She kept her grasp around his chest and shook him gently. "No. No one is dying."

As he struggled, his face went under and he came up, sputtering and coughing.

"Slayer, we're waiting."

The blond vampire stood observing at the water's edge. Buffy sized up the situation: maybe alone, she could swim deeper into the lake, try to make a break for it on the other side. But weighed down with Mark, there was no chance.

"Buffy, let me go," Mark begged. "If I die here, I can save people."

"No, they aren't going to kill you." She winced and hoped that was true. Rule #217 of the Slayer's Handbook: *Thar be no honor among vampires.*

However, sometimes life surprised you.

Buffy got to the shallows and looped the handle of the valise over an outcropping bush as surreptitiously as she could. Then she helped Mark straggle along. The blond vampire reached out a hand and Buffy ignored it, making her way up the embankment unassisted. Then she turned and helped Mark.

"Why'd you let me do that?" she asked the vampire.

"You would have damaged some of my followers," he replied simply.

"How'd you know I would come back?"

He shrugged. "I didn't. But I would have retrieved you." He pointed to the winged demon.

He clapped his hands. "Chain her."

"Oh, please." Buffy rolled her eyes as two vampires came forward with a heavy set of handcuffs separated by a length of very thick chain.

"Hercules himself could not break these," said the vampire. "However, you are a Slayer, and another matter."

At his nod, the two vampires clamped the cuffs around her wrists. Then someone came up behind her, grabbed her head, and clapped an evil-smelling rag over her nose and mouth.

Mark shouted, "Don't hurt her!"

Unfortunately, Buffy struggled.

Therefore, pain was in the equation.

* * *

Buffy snapped awake inside a metal cage. Her hands were chained on either side of her, the chains bolted to the floor. Not the newest of experiences for the Chosen One, but not her favorite, either. No matter what Angel said about handcuffs.

Angel . . .

Outside the cage, in a cavern dimly lit by torches, Helen was leaning over her, fully vamped out in a black metallic corset, a chain mail skirt, and—oh, yeah, her vamp face. Her eyes glittered darkly. Buffy saw at once the madness there.

"The Slayer," she hissed, leaning over Buffy. "I should kill you now."

"That pleasure has been reserved," Julian said, coming up behind Helen and putting his hands on her shoulders.

Helen stiffened. "It is my right and privilege."

"I have something in mind for her. Something that will thrill you beyond words."

Her face contorted into anger, which he could not see. But Buffy could.

"Oh?" the vampire said between clamped fangs.

He smiled indulgently. "Yes."

As he walked away, he looked for the dark vampire to follow him, but she remained with Buffy. Julian shrugged and disappeared into the shadows.

Helen looked down at her prisoner with contempt, and trailed her fingers along the chain link.

"I will kill you," she said simply. "I don't care what Julian wants. It is my right."

"Who died and made you Slayer slayer?" Buffy snapped, pulling on her chains. The bolts held. It was a professional job.

"Diana did." Helen leaned over as if she were talking to a child. "Let me tell you something. In the battle between good and evil, good must inevitably lose. Evil acts. Good reacts. Therefore, good is always one step behind. It can't keep pace."

"No," Buffy said. "I don't believe that."

"You believe that you will die fighting evil," Helen continued, pressing her face into the chain link. Blood rose along the diamond pattern, but she gave no indication that she felt it at all. "And there will be more evil after you. The next Slayer will die. And the next."

She straightened and stared down at Buffy; in the muted light, she looked like a Grecian statue, cold and haughty, hard and unyielding.

"And they say *I'm* mad."

"Evil doesn't create," Buffy countered. "It only destroys."

"I was created by evil," Helen retorted.

Buffy tried to move her hands, but her chains held. "You were created by despair. You thought you had been abandoned."

Helen's lip curled. "I had been."

"Slayers don't work that way." Buffy yanked on the chains. "Slayers risk everything to save people."

"Save your breath. And your energy. For the arena."

Helen turned her back on Buffy and glided away.

"She didn't abandon you!" Buffy shouted at her. "She died for you!"

Helen made no answer. Then she stopped and made a slow half-turn.

"Are you forgetting that I killed her?"

Buffy stared straight at her. "I'm sure she understood. I'm sure she's forgiven you."

Helen snorted. "You're such a child."

The vampire started to leave, then paused. "Angelus," she said softly. "Have you seen him?"

She doesn't know, Buffy thought. She kept silent.

Stiffly, Helen moved into the darkness.

After leaving the Slayer, Helen went to Cordelia's cage. They had removed the one called Oz before darkness had fallen.

The girl was doing pushups. Helen said, "Hello, dark beauty."

Cordelia ignored her.

"You know that we intend to put you in the arena. And that you will die there."

"Bet me," Cordelia said, raising herself up and down. "Heavily."

"If you kill the Slayer right now, I will spare you. And I will keep Julian from you. She's chained down, and it would be a simple task."

Cordelia only grunted. Then she stopped, pushed back into a sitting position and said, "I wish I had the energy to laugh in your face."

Helen visited the little redhead next. She smiled gently at her and said, "Greetings. Are you being treated well?"

"For someone who's being held against her will by vampires, I guess, yes," she said nervously. "Where's Buffy?"

"She is the subject of our discussion." She smiled. "I'd like to offer you a trade. Your life for hers." She showed her the sacrificial knife. "All you must do is cut out her heart. She is restrained. She cannot fight you."

Willow gaped at her.

The vampire stood. "Now. There will be no second chance."

The redhead remained silent.

Helen swept away.

"Greetings, my handsome one," Helen said to Xander.

Xander swallowed. *Why is it the monster chicks always think I'm hot?*

"You understand that you have been brought here to die."

"Well, I didn't before. Thanks for the update." He scowled at her.

She chuckled. "I can prevent it. I will prevent it."

He did not stop scowling. "Then I'm happy."

"If you kill the Slayer this moment. While she is helpless."

Xander stared at her. He finally said, "Are you nuts?"

She shrugged and moved away.

"Watcher," she said to Giles. "I have known many Watchers. The vast majority of them cracked under pressure. They told me everything I wanted to know about their Slayers. Habits, haunts, weaknesses, delights. After that, it was a simple matter to hunt them down."

Giles gazed at her levelly. "I sincerely hope that you are lying to me."

Her smile was slow and lazy, the smile of an immortal being who knows she has all the time in the world . . . and her captive does not.

"We intend to sacrifice you to Meter," she said. "We will torture you slowly, and your death will be hideous. The pain will be unbearable. I will spare you that, if you will kill the Slayer. Right now. She cannot fight you."

"Angel was right," he said slowly. "You are mad."

In the temple chamber, Julian knelt before the beating heart on the altar and said, "Meter."

"I yet live," the voice replied. *"But I have no form. The ashes rest beside the lake. Fetch them, and I will come forth."*

"The reservoir," Helen said, and clapped her hands in delight. "Who shall we send?"

Someone was coming.

Xander took a deep breath and braced himself. He had faced death many times and, well, it still scared the hell out of him. But sometimes—on a good day—he could keep his cool.

A flashlight beam shined in his eyes.

"Harris, it's Willy."

"Why am I not surprised you're involved in this?" Xander drawled, glaring at the smarmy bartender.

"Listen. I'm gonna bust you out. I got a key. You get the hell out of here and go to the reservoir. There's some ashes there, somewhere. They're magickal, or something."

"The Urn of Caligula?" Xander asked.

"Yeah, whatever." Willy looked incredibly freaked. "Get rid of them."

"Get rid of them how?"

He fished out a ring of keys and unlocked the padlock on his gate.

"Just go. Figure it out on the way." He handed Xander another set of keys. "These are for my car. The Pontiac Trans Am around the side. Has a dent from where my girlfriend was, ah, trying to park it."

Xander took the keys. "How do I know you're on our side?"

"Harris, have you seen these vampires? They are not good people," he said earnestly.

Xander stared at him for a beat. Then he shook his head, and ran for all he was worth.

Chapter 18

I<small>N HER CAGE</small>, B<small>UFFY WAS WAITING FOR THEM WHEN THEY</small> came for her. Julian and Helen were surrounded by other vampires and demons, decked out in their Sunday best, including togas, big, poofy ball gowns, and Victorian top hats. Laughing and talking, they advanced like some ghoulish Mardi Gras parade to her cell.

Cowards. Big Mama Helen liked to threaten to take her out, but the vampire had brought a fairly decent-sized army of bodyguards with her.

"Slayer," Julian said, dressed like he wanted to play Pontius Pilate in the school Christmas pageant. He laid his fist over his chest, then extended his hand straight out in front of himself. "I salute you."

"That makes my day," Buffy said.

"Put on this armor." He showed her a molded breastplate that gleamed and shone.

"I'm finally going to look like a real superhero," she

drawled, giving the breastplate the once-over. "Nose cones and all."

The vampire guards tittered and Julian grinned. Helen looked pissed off.

"Listen to me," he said, still smiling. "If you try to escape, we will kill all your friends."

She took that in. Nodded, not at all surprised. *They always pull the friends card on me.*

Which was why, she knew, most Slayers had no friends.

At a signal, a tallowy, blue demon very much like the one Buffy and Angel had fried came forward and unlocked her cage. Then a vampire brought forward a bolt cutter and detached Buffy's chains from the concrete floor.

Both stood aside for her to exit.

"To the arena," Julian said delightedly.

"Don't I get to shower first?" Buffy grumbled as she strapped on the breastplate.

A scream is a wish your heart breaks . . .

Buffy's nightmares had come true.

"The arena" was a vast, underground amphitheater which had been recently built, to judge by the untouched quality of the stone wall and the graduated bleachers. Between the sections of bleachers, cut like pie wedges, long red runners stretched from the very top row, about a story high, down to the wall that separated the battlefield from the peanut gallery. There were a few white statues of naked people here and there, many of them dying agonizing deaths, lots of skulls—possibly real—and oversized stone vases brimming with roses and other flowers. Not Martha Stewart's best work.

Overhead, the rough ceiling of the cavern was lost to darkness. Torches blazed and smoked, towering over the curved rows of ghoulish spectators, some of whom Buffy recognized from the parade to and from her cell. They were eating and drinking, snapping their fingers at nervous-looking people dressed in revealing togas who dashed around like hot dog vendors at a baseball game.

Standing below a small platform in the center of the arena, Buffy was decked in the truly awesome body armor. It gave an entirely new definition to the word "uplift." They'd also given her a thigh-high skirt that was constructed of strips of leather, and matching leather boots that came up below her knees.

If I live through this, she thought, *I'm keeping these duds for next Halloween.*

"Friends, vampires, countrymen!" Julian said above the clamor as everyone got comfy. He appeared from the side door and strolled to the center of the arena, voguing, it seemed to Buffy, in a very brief sort of toga with a purple robe that swept the sand. In his blond hair, a gold circlet of leaves gleamed as he moved. Buffy thought for a few seconds about attacking him, but guards surrounded Julian before she had a chance.

In her Calisto clothes and a large, heavy golden crown, Helen was seated in an ornate golden chair on a platform to the far right of the arena, and there was an empty chair beside her.

Julian continued with the warm-up. "Tonight we celebrate the birth of our dark mother! After centuries of sacrifice, we will bring her forth with the death of a Slayer!"

The crowd went crazy. "Hail, Julian!" someone shouted. Another voice joined in, until it was a chant.

Julian let his head fall back as they cheered his name. *What a waste,* Buffy thought. *He really is a honey.*

"What do you think of that, Slayer?" he asked her beneath the shouting.

She shrugged. "I'm thinking I should get a percentage of the gate, plus a cut of the T-shirt sales."

He smiled. "I've never met a Slayer like you. I truly regret the necessity of your death."

"I feel your pain." She hefted the sword they had given her. *Quite a weapon. Sharp. A little on the heavy side. I shoulda whacked him when I had the chance. Of course, I would have needed a stake, too.*

She scanned for wooden objects. "After all you guys die, they could turn this place into a dinner theater," Buffy said. "No one ever gets tired of *Fiddler on the Roof.*"

"To the last, scrappy and proud," Julian said. He held out a golden goblet. "Speaking of pain, I offer you a potion that will numb your body. You will be unaware of injuries."

"Thanks, but I'm just saying no." Buffy hefted the sword. "And I'm really hoping your death is chock full of fruity, delicious pain in every slice."

"If it had been you back in Rome, instead of Helen, we would already rule this world," he said quietly, in a voice only she could hear. He leaned toward her. "I am an ardent lover, Buffy Summers. An excellent companion. Say the word, and I will change you here and now."

"Still saying no," she said, "but if you weren't evil and despicable, well, truth here, I would still say no."

"Very well." He clapped his hands and held out his arms. "We shall worship our mother!"

Some kind of flute music filled the room as vampire women in filmy gowns with grapes piled in their hair pranced down the runners. Then the crowd rose and sang, their arms outstretched, as vampires carried a large platform suspended on poles, and on it, a very tall statue of a sort of demon-woman with empty eye sockets and totally righteous fangs.

Possibly Meter, Buffy thought. *Or else the goddess of PMS.*

"The Slayer shall do battle until she cannot fight. Those who wish to challenge her for the sport may do so. But they are forbidden to kill her. We will cut out her beating heart and mix it with the ashes of our forefather, Caligula. And then we will feed Meter this precious bounty, and the goddess will rise."

Ashes? Buffy thought with alarm. *Do they have the urn?*

"Monsters, demons, and gladiator vampires all await the glory of defeating the Slayer in battle. Let the wagering begin!"

The whole place erupted into furious talking and shouting as Buffy was led by two fully armored whatevers to the left side of the arena. A large set of double gates—*wooden* double gates—creaked as something behind them pushed to get out.

Buffy moved her neck in a slow circle and squared her shoulders in preparation for her first opponent. She had a thought: *If they really do have the ashes, I can't let myself die.*

Talk about pressure.

* * *

Xander located the Trans Am and got to the reservoir in record time. A record for him, anyway, since he had never driven there before.

He pulled up to the gate, saw that although the two sides were pulled together, they weren't locked, and pushed his way through. Then he drove the car past the parking lot and as close to the lakeshore as he could.

He got out and stepped into the oozy mud caused by the rain. He had no idea where to look for the ashes. They could be anywhere.

Just then, a chubby man came out of a building. He was carrying a flashlight and he hailed Xander. The name on his jacket said *Jake Bitterman*.

That name rings a bell, Xander thought, on alert. *Something Willow said about him. Or his wife.*

"Evening," the man said. "May I help you?"

"Oh." Xander pasted on a big fake smile. "Yeah. A friend of mine dropped a pottery thingie here. A small vase, about yay big?" He gestured with his hands, carefully watching the man.

"Hmm. Whereabouts?" Bitterman said, looking disinterested. Xander didn't let down his guard, though.

"I'm not sure."

"Well, it's a big lake. Do you know about where she dropped it?"

She? I didn't say my friend was a she. Xander upgraded to DefCon 3 and kept working the friendly, casual angle.

"Not sure. I think I'll call her on my car phone and ask for more details," Xander said.

The man put his hand in the pocket of his jacket

and pulled out a gun. "Stop right there," he told Xander.

Damn it. I hate it when my gut instincts are right, Xander thought, as his heart went into high gear.

The man turned and waved. The door slammed open. Mark Dellasandro came out first. At least six vampires trailed after.

Xander said, as innocently as possible, "What's going on?"

"Willy called," Bitterman told him. "Somehow he had the impression your people knew where the urn was left. Screwed up, as per usual. We had a couple dozen of our boys up here, still couldn't find it." He sounded disgusted.

Mark ran to Xander. Xander patted the kid and eased him aside. He said to Bitterman, "What's your deal in all of this?"

Bitterman smirked. "Like Willy, I'm working for the new owners," he announced. "They had me put a little something in the water a while ago."

Xander stared at him. Then he said slowly, "Your wife is missing."

"Yup." He rubbed his hands and said to the vampires, "Said she'd clean me out if I divorced her, so . . ." He shrugged carelessly. "Julian explained that I had to make a sacrifice to activate the Madness Potion. Best news I had since the bitch filed the separation papers."

Mark looked up at Xander and whispered. "But *I* put the potion in the reservoir."

"Let's spread out," Bitterman said to the vampires. "If we don't find the urn in the next, oh, ten minutes or so, we'll send for more reinforcements. The Games have already started, and if the Slayer's heart stops before we get those ashes down there, there'll be hell to pay."

As they were herded toward the lake, Xander whispered to Mark, "Giles was surprised that that small of an amount of the potion made everybody nuts. It looks like source Bitterman was what caused all the ruckus. Do you understand what I'm saying?" He touched the boy's shoulder. "You're not to blame."

"So if I had drowned, the curse wouldn't have been lifted," Mark said. He burst into tears as he stumbled forward, pushed by a vampire.

"Looks like," Xander muttered to himself. "And it also looks like we have a new contestant for 'Let's Make a Sacrifice.'"

The excitement was at fever pitch by the time Buffy faced her third opponent, a clanking giant armed and armored to the gills, which puffed and gasped beneath its eyes. The onlookers kept betting, changing their bets, exchanging money.

Soon the giant's head lay at her feet, and the crowd thundered with applause and whistles.

Buffy's worn sword was replaced with a fresh one. Blood of various colors smeared her leather-covered shield.

More combatants were paraded out, sometimes singly, sometimes in pairs. Defeating each one in turn, Buffy was beginning to tire.

After another hour or so, Helen gestured to Buffy. "You see how it was for me? Night after night, for over a year?"

"You mean, just like how it is for a Slayer?" Buffy shot back.

Helen looked irritated. Julian patted her hand and she drew away from him.

"No worries, beloved," he said. "Tonight, all will come right. We shall begin a new golden age of evil."

"If we get the ashes," she retorted.

Hear that, Mable? They are ash-free. Buffy could have danced all night . . . or maybe for thirty seconds.

He chuckled. "We will. Willy has assured me that our pigeon is flying to the roost this very moment. The boy knows where they are."

Willy? Huh? Buffy was puzzled. *Boy? What boy? Mark?*

"Let's make this more interesting," Julian went on. He clapped his hands and said, "Bring out the prisoners."

Buffy's lips parted as Willow and Giles were paraded into the amphitheater. Both were chained. Both had been beaten.

Willow looked at Buffy with hollow, frightened eyes.

"Where's Cordelia? Where's Xander?" Buffy called to Giles.

Giles shook his head. "I don't know."

Julian grinned. "The boy's on an errand," he informed them.

So, Xander is "the boy." One question answered. Just about a million more to go.

Cordelia was brought in, dressed in battle gear similar to Buffy's. She was led to the dais by a badly scarred man dressed in leather. Julian leaned forward and chucked Cordelia under the chin.

"Do you wish to fight the Slayer, my lovely girl?" he asked in a silken voice.

"Yeah, right." Cordelia pulled her head away and gave her hair an angry shake.

"Well, you'll fight her nevertheless," Julian said. He smiled at Helen. "I believe you have concocted a special potion for tonight?"

She smiled prettily. "One for each of them."

A pretty girl dressed in a gauzy robe stepped forward with a gold bowl in which lay four glass vials decorated with jewels.

"The Madness Potion of Caligula," Julian announced. "Enhanced for this evening's festivities by our queen!"

The spectators broke into delighted cheers as Julian displayed the bowl.

He handed it back to the girl. She carried it over to the scarred man, and selected and uncapped one for him. He took it, grabbed Cordelia's head under his forearm, and dumped the liquid into her mouth. As she struggled, he covered her mouth and nose, forcing her to swallow.

The transformation was instantaneous. Her eyes narrowed. Her mouth curled. When the scarred man handed her a sword, she ran straight for Buffy.

Buffy hesitated, nothing inside her wanting to harm Cordelia. She dodged her first blow, but the second glanced across her armor.

Buffy was shocked. Cordelia would have seriously hurt her if she hadn't been wearing armor. This time, she wasn't as cautious about avoiding Cordy, but Cordelia still managed to dart out of range.

As four demon guards grabbed vials and rushed Giles and Willow, Oz was dragged in by a phalanx of vampires and demons. Fully wolfed out, his arms and legs were manacled; there was a huge collar around his neck, attached to an even thicker chain, and one around his waist.

He threw back his head and howled, struggling to get free.

"Oz!" Willow screamed. But Buffy knew Oz didn't understand. He didn't recognize Willow's voice, or Willow for that matter. Under the influence of the moon, he was a savage, feral beast, nothing less, and nothing more.

At a signal from Julian, the vampires very cautiously unchained Oz. With a growl, he sprang at Buffy. She ran backwards and flung herself to the ground, and he sailed over her. Raging with frustration, he whipped around and charged again.

She figured she could dodge him one or two more times, and then she was going to have to actually fight him.

Then the demons forced Willow and Giles to swallow the Madness Potion.

I'm knee-deep in the hoopla now, Buffy thought.

This time, when her friends got possessed, there were no words. No name-calling. No accusations. There was madness in the eyes of Cordelia, Giles, and Willow, and nothing else.

They charged her at the same time, though without any set plan or strategy. They were too far gone for that.

Giles approached, punching with his fists. Buffy held her sword away, unwilling to use it. At a signal from Julian, one of the demons grabbed her Watcher and put a spear in his hands. The shaft was wood, the tip, some kind of serious-looking metal. He stabbed at her, his mouth drawn back so far he looked like a vampire.

Oz charged her from behind. Buffy knew that all she had to do was drop and roll, and Oz would impale himself on Giles's spear. If the injury wasn't severe enough to kill him, it would probably enrage him so much that he would kill Giles.

Can't let it happen, she told herself, *no matter what.* She stayed where she was, in the middle.

At the reservoir, Willy said to Bitterman, "You said no more killing. That's what you said."

Willy was the bringer of reinforcements. A bunch of scummy lowlifes—what passed for friends on Willy's planet—had spread out around the reservoir, searching with flashlights for the urn.

Bitterman shrugged at Willy as he raised his gun and aimed it at Xander. "And *you* never lie, either."

"These kids . . . he's kind of my friend," Willy said, his voice rising.

Gee, we never knew you cared, Xander thought acidly. *All those missed opportunities for exchanging secret pal gifts.*

"You're just afraid the Slayer will come after you," Bitterman said to Willy. "Don't be. She's going to die tonight."

"See what I mean?" Willy said, holding out his hands. "More with the dying." He turned to Xander. "They told me they'd spare your life if I cooperated." He flushed. "Honest, kid. So tell them where the urn is, okay? Don't be a hero."

Xander said, "What makes you think I know?"

"Well, you said . . ." Willy frowned and scratched his head.

Bitterman rolled his eyes. "When they find out how badly you screwed this up, they're going to rip your lungs out."

Willy ticked his glance toward Xander as if to say, *Let's make sure they don't find out.*

Xander's heart pounded. He blinked. Willy gave him an imperceptible nod.

Mark pressed his face into Xander's side. He was trembling.

"If you're going to do it, get it over with." Xander's voice was deadly calm.

And then rage took him over. Red-hot fury, indescribable anger. *Kill the bastard. Kill him.*

With a roar of fury, he charged Bitterman just as Willy shouted, "Hey, wait a minute!"

Bitterman shouted.

The gun went off.

Mark crumpled to the ground.

"We found it!" someone bellowed triumphantly.

In the arena, Giles sprawled in the sand, gasping. Willow lay on her back. Cordelia whimpered.

With a growl, Oz swiped at Buffy with his front paws. But he was limping badly from a wound she had delivered to his hindquarters. Grimacing, she grazed him on the forepaw, leaping backward as he howled with fury.

"You'd best simply attack," Julian called to her. "You're only succeeding in enraging him."

He was right. She executed a halfhearted slash across his chest. He straightened, shrieked, whirled on her, and fell face-forward to the ground.

"Death!" the crowd yelled, as money changed

hands. They made thumbs-down gestures. "Cut off their heads!"

Helen looked expectantly at Buffy. She didn't even blink.

"Why should she? There's no incentive," Julian said. "If she knows she's going to die anyway."

Behind them, the statue of Meter moved. The mouth opened. A strange, echoey voice said, *"I thirst."*

The ground rumbled beneath Buffy's feet. She took a moment to look down. The audience gasped. Some murmured, *"Venite,* Meter."

Helen said to Julian, "Where are the ashes? We can't kill her until we have them."

Julian called over the pretty girl in the guazy robe and asked angrily, "Has anyone gotten through to Willy?"

"He's not answering his cell phone," she said.

Buffy snickered to herself. Julian narrowed his eyes at her and said, "Don't assume anything, Slayer."

At that moment, a chubby man in a jacket appeared, standing between two sections of the top row of bleachers.

"I got it," he announced.

"Excellent, Bitterman," Julian said. "Let me see."

As Buffy watched, the man walked down the aisle. He held the Urn of Caligula in both hands. Buffy tried very hard not to wig.

That's the ballgame.

With an awkward bow, Bitterman handed the urn to Julian, who took it and said, "It has indeed been opened." He walked to the statue. "Meter, darkest of mothers, is this what you require?"

The statue's eyes glowed with an eerie blue light. Then fires erupted within them, burning brightly. *"Yesssss. And the Slayer's heart."*

Beating, not stirred, Buffy thought anxiously.

Helen rose from her chair and pointed at Bitterman. "Kill him," she ordered the guards.

"No. Halt!" Julian cried. He frowned at Helen. "My dear, he's the one who activated the Madness Potion in the lake. If he dies, the potion will cease to work." He studied Buffy. "Even if an antidote is created and used."

Good guess, Buffy thought, revealing nothing.

"As will the potion we have been using here tonight, if *you* die, my queen," Julian added, almost as an afterthought. "Since you mixed it."

She paled.

Julian smiled.

"I know that you went to each one of the Slayer's friends, and offered them their freedom if they would kill her in her chains."

"No," Helen began, but he silenced her by raising his hand.

"You underestimated their loyalty to her. These people would die for the Slayer, and for each other."

"Lunacy," Helen snapped.

"Perhaps. But I have arranged a more interesting test of loyalty and friendship," Julian said. He clapped his hands. "Bring in the vampire."

Naked to the waist, wearing a leather gauntlet that extended from his shoulder and was strapped over his chest, Angel was brought into the arena.

Helen cried, "No!" and leaped to her feet. Julian put a hand on her arm and held fast.

"If you kill him, Slayer, all your friends go free. If you refuse, they die. Horribly."

"No," Helen said. "I will not permit this."

"You will watch," Julian commanded. "Or I will have you walled up again, Helen. Don't think I won't."

At his signal, the platform was surrounded by demon and vampire guards.

The amphitheater was abuzz. Boos and cheers mixed in a chorus of reaction to the scene played out in the arena. In the din, Buffy stared at Angel, able only to register that he was alive. She ran to him and put her arms around him, holding tight.

"I thought you were dead. I heard you get staked."

"I got one of the guys Julian sent to get me," he told her. "Then they knocked me out and dragged me away."

She rested her head on his chest. "We won't fight."

"Buffy, if you have to kill me, do it."

"Part them," Julian commanded in a ringing voice.

Two vampires roughly pulled them away from each other. Angel looked over the head of his handler and stared hard at Buffy.

Then he hefted his sword.

Chapter 19

As attention focused elsewhere, Jake Bitterman took the opportunity to get the hell out of the underground sports arena, or whatever it was. He jumped in his car with every notion of leaving Sunnydale as fast as possible, and never coming back.

This is way, way more than I bargained for.

He headed for Route 17, which would take him past the reservoir, and every vestige of his life. Including the body of his wife, submerged in the water.

Angel and Buffy circled each other, silently concocting a plan. She knew they were on the same page, and he knew it, too.

So this is the actual Greek tragedy I'm starring in, she thought, remembering that long-ago talent show where they accidentally upstaged themselves.

"Stop this, Julian," Helen said fiercely.

"You unfaithful bitch," the blond vampire flung at her. "I know you went to him. I know you planned to have him take my place. I have eyes and ears everywhere."

"No," Helen said, looking guilty as hell.

That's my cue, Buffy thought. She stared at Angel. Her face hardened. "You've been with her?"

Angel laughed low in his throat and morphed into vamp face. "You're just a Slayer, Buffy. Helen's the queen of my kind."

"Angelus," Helen breathed. "I thought—"

"You bastard!" Buffy shrieked, laying it on thick. "I'll kill you for that!"

She went on the offensive. Pulling no punches—*in case Julian needs convincing*—she rammed her fist into Angel's face. She thrust her sword directly at his chest. He parried it, with difficulty, and aimed his sword for her neck. Nicked her.

Hey, she protested silently.

"We've done this before," he said, panting.

"And I won," she retorted.

Then she extended the weapon directly in front of herself, charged him, and ran him through.

He cried out, caught at the gushing wound, and fell to his knees.

"A stake!" Buffy shouted, holding out her hand.

Julian prepared to toss her a sharpened wooden spear.

"No!" Helen shouted.

She grabbed the spear and leaped off the platform.

"Slayer, I knew it would come to this," she said, morphing into vamp face. "I would be the one to kill you."

The ground rumbled.

"Make haste," the voice of Meter insisted. *"The time grows short."*

As vampires swarmed all over the reservoir, Xander and Willy carried the limp, bloody form of Mark Dellasandro back to the Trans Am and got the hell out of there.

"Call nine-one-one," Xander said.

Willy sat in the back with Mark's feet in his lap. "My cell phone isn't working. I think I forgot to recharge."

"We'll go to the hospital," Xander said.

"Did you hear what that vamp said? You're supposed to be sacrificed tonight. Maybe if you don't show, everything will be okay."

Xander gave him a look. "You know, I would love to harbor delusions of grandeur, but hey, I'm donut guy. I'm sure if I don't show, they'll just sacrifice someone else."

Willy shrugged. "Yeah, I s'pose you're right."

"Anyway, Bitterman got away," Xander added as the car fishtailed around a bend in the road as they headed for Route 17. "So Sunnydale is going to be cursed forever."

"So they win," Willy said nervously.

"We'll see."

Xander kept driving.

Buffy slashed at Helen with her sword, and Helen blocked it again. The arena was crazed with frenzied onlookers, some begging Julian to stop the fight, others urging the combatants on. Buffy had no idea how long they had fought. But neither could seem to gain the upper hand.

"Isn't this getting boring?" Buffy said. "Want to try Rock, Scissors, Paper?"

Helen grunted and came after her again, hacking and slashing. Her face was streaked with blood. Buffy's was, too. Blood had pooled in the sand, and Buffy started to feel a little woozy.

Okay, maybe I was a little cocky, she thought. *Maybe it's time to pump it up.*

The fires in Meter's eyes flared as the statue heaved and shifted. The ground beneath their feet shook, and everybody got all excited and wiggy about it.

Buffy turned and saw that Angel had revived somewhat. He was looking hard at her. Then he shifted his line of vision. He was staring at the Urn of Caligula, which Julian had set down beside his feet. His attention was riveted on Helen.

Buffy nodded at Angel.

He leaped toward the platform, lunged for the urn, and grabbed it just as Julian realized what was happening.

"Buffy!" he shouted, tossing it to her.

She caught it.

"Tag, I'm it," she said to Helen.

Helen shrieked and charged her. On the defensive, Buffy backed up, until Helen slowed and cried, "Not the fire!"

Buffy blinked. She looked at Angel. Then she smiled at Helen. She walked backward to the statue. Its mouth opened and it clacked its fangs at her.

Buffy dodged them, murmuring, "Oh, my, what big teeth you have."

Then she climbed onto the statue and held the urn directly in front of the fire in the statue's right eye.

Julian and Helen held their breath.

Buffy looked at Angel, who moved his shoulders. "Go for it," he said.

Buffy threw the urn into the eye.

At once the entire room began to shake. The statue writhed and shouted, *"Who dares?"*

In a fury, Helen attacked, showing Buffy no quarter. Then she whirled on Angel, jabbing at him with her spear.

"Keep back, assassin," she said to him. "This fight is between us."

"It doesn't matter anymore if you kill her," Julian said to Helen, glowering. "So you might as well."

Helen went berserk. She hacked and slashed, completely losing track of what she was doing.

Buffy whistled. "And you were the baddest of the bad? Hard to believe."

But then, suddenly, Buffy found herself on her back, and Helen straddling her. She didn't know how it had happened. But it looked like she was going to die.

"I've killed better Slayers than you," Helen hissed at her. "Nobler. More dedicated."

The words shouldn't have distracted Buffy, but they did. As the killing blow descended, she thought, *Darn it. She's going to kill me after all.*

A sharp, hot wind whistled through the arena. Buffy smelled somethng very sweet, very nice. Her vision clouded for a moment, and everything appeared to be golden.

And then her muscles were filled with fresh power. Energy surged through her. She didn't even know what she was doing; she couldn't see, couldn't hear. She was no longer sure where she was.

Then, as if from a very long distance away, she heard Helen scream, "Diana!"

Buffy's arms jerked forward.

The sound of a dusting vibrated around her.

When she blinked her eyes open, a pile of dust lay on the sand, and Helen was gone.

Julian morphed into full vamp face.

He came at Buffy. In Meter's voice he said, *"You are the destroyer. You must die."*

The arena went silent.

Then, like a single entity, everyone rose and came for Buffy and the others.

The arena came alive.

The curse of Helen's madness potion was lifted, and Willow knew who she was.

Settling deep within herself, finding a place of calm inside her terror, Willow whispered:

> *"By the light and the heart of the earth,*
> *"I forbid all evil spirits my bedstead and couch;*
> *"I forbid you my house and my home;*
> *"I forbid you my flesh and blood and body and*
>   *soul.*
> *"I irrevocably forbid you entrance to my mind*
>   *and my thoughts;*
> *"My fears and my strengths;*
> *"Until you have traveled over every single hill and*
>   *vale;*
> *"Forged every stream and river;*
> *"Counted all the grains of sands on all the shores;*
> *"And every star in the sky.*
> *"I forbid you."*

Then a voice shattered her calm, booming throughout the arena as she staggered from the impact:

"Who dares to challenge Meter?"

Willow caught her breath. She went deeper and repeated her incantation.

"Enough! Stop or you will be destroyed."

Willow took a breath, and dove straight down into her own soul.

The earth beneath her feet shook violently.

Willow found other words inside her, words in languages she did not know.

They were weapons of the light, handed down through the ages in places and dimensions she had never been. But as she let the confusion and chaos swirl outside herself, she allowed the spells and wards to come into being through her being.

Evil is forbidden.

Evil is denied.

The earth shook.

The voice of Meter shouted, *"Stop or you die!"*

All over Sunnydale, the earth shook. Accustomed to earthquakes, the townsfolk darted under the transoms of their houses and watched their light fixtures shake. Pictures dropped from walls and mirrors shattered.

At the Sunnydale Reservoir, more leaks sprang in the badly constructed dam.

Willow knew what was happening.

She kept chanting.

She knew Buffy was fighting off demons and vampires while the others tried to get free of the chains.

She knew Oz was severely wounded.

But she kept herself open to the words of light.
I forbid you, I forbid you, I forbid you.
Something listened.
Something gathered.
It grew. It drew strength from her.
The arena began to crack apart.

As Xander drove, the ground rolled like an ocean. Huge slabs of earth and rock jutted up. There was a deafening, thunderous crack, and then water was rushing everywhere beneath the moonlight.

"The dam's broke!" Willy shouted.

The water rushed down the valley. It took with it avocado and citrus groves, hundreds of heads of cattle, several vampires, and poured onto Route 17. It completely engulfed Jake Bitterman, the necessary sacrifice to end Sunnydale's nightmare.

It spilled onto the highway, causing numerous accidents, and splashing through a power substation, shutting down a third of the town's power.

And Xander lost control of the car as it was swept along. His head slammed against the steering wheel, and as he lost consciousness, he thought he was starring in a movie about the parting of the Red Sea.

Buffy shouted, "Willow, wake up! *Move!*"
Willow opened her eyes and looked around.

It was like a scene in a horror movie. As the amphitheater shook to pieces, a full-scale battle raged. All around Willow, vampires exploded and demons bled. There was a long, stringy arm on the floor, its fingers flexing spastically. A head at her feet, the eyes gouged out.

Cordelia, returned to sanity, was fighting beside Giles. Both were armed with stakes, and they were both in the process of taking out vampires. Oz lay in a heap, bleeding badly, but Angel had staggered to his feet and was protecting him.

It was only a matter of time before the demons and vampires overwhelmed them.

Buffy was fighting one on one with Julian. They appeared to be evenly matched, but Buffy was obviously tired. With a cry, Willow moved to help her.

Then she heard Cordelia scream.

The vampire she was battling had just pushed her onto her back, and he had raised a sword over his head. Willow dashed up behind him and drove her stake into his back.

He exploded into dust.

Cordelia said, "Thanks," and got to her feet.

Another vampire attacked. Together, Willow and Cordelia dusted that one, too.

Then Willow realized that Giles was in trouble. An enormous demon with leathery wings was swooping at him, taloned claws ripping at his arms and chest. Giles was a mess of blood and cuts.

Willow looked down at the little pile of dust, grabbed up the sword that lay in it, and ran to help Giles. She slashed at the wings of the monster; it renewed its attack, cutting a deep gash in Willow's arm.

"Willow!" Cordelia screamed again.

A hulking, hideous monster stepped over Oz.

A vampire managed to land a rough body blow on Angel.

Julian cut Buffy's arm, and she almost dropped her sword.

Too many, Willow thought. *Which one do I help?*

"Willow," Buffy bellowed. "Move your butt!"

And Willow did. She stopped thinking, stopped assessing, and moved into full battle mode. Her body did what her mind had done, seeking the light, filling with determination. It didn't matter how many there were. What mattered was the one in front of her.

And the next one.

And the next.

Huge blocks of rock fell like bombs from overhead, slamming into friend and foe alike. Willow looked worriedly at Oz, who was still inert. Everything in her wanted to shield him, but she realized that if she and the others were defeated, he would die anyway.

Then the ground began to crack. In her ear, Buffy shouted, "Jump!"

Willow leaped across the fissure. Then she cried, "Oz!" and jumped back across it, to help Angel and Giles as they dragged Oz toward the rapidly growing crack.

"Go back, Willow," Angel told her. "We can do it."

"Cordelia!" Willow yelled. "Come on!"

Cordelia, in the process of backing away from a hairy white creature, threw down her sword and ran toward Willow. Together they sailed over the split, just as it pushed outward on either side, becoming a huge chasm.

Of the bad guys, only Julian and a couple of vampires were on the Slayerettes' side of the chasm. Before Willow could react, Angel and Giles took the two vampires out.

Buffy and Julian faced off. His face was incredible; beyond vampiric, a mask of shadows and hollows. His golden eyes gleamed like pinpoints in two black holes, like the statue's. His hands were claws; his skin pure white, strips of it peeling off. Blue veins criss-crossed his features, pulsating like overfull tubes of paint.

The thing that was once Julian circled her. He growled and hissed, his eyes flickering, his hands drawing into taloned claws.

Then he saw the golden bowl on the floor and picked up one of the vials of Madness Potion. He stood for a moment, uncapping it, and then he said, "Ah, yes. A sacrifice."

Without warning, he whirled on a vampire guard and pierced its eyes with his nails. As the vampire screamed in agony, Julian ran to the wooden gates and smashed them with a single punch.

Great minds think alike, Buffy thought. *Now the wood is nice and jagged, just the way we Slayers like it.*

Julian staked the screaming vampire. It exploded.

"I have made my sacrifice," he announced. "I have initiated the curse of the Madness Potion. Now you will die under the frenzy of my blade."

He swallowed it.

His eyes glazed.

And then he exploded into dust.

Buffy stared. "Well, that was kind of an anticli-max," she said.

On the other side of the chasm, the roof caved in. Tons of rock slammed down on the last vestiges of the demon court, crushing vampire and monster alike. The shock sent Buffy and her friends sprawling.

Then, on top of the rubble, the floor of the Alibi crashed down in bits and pieces.

Buffy said, "That wasn't."

Epilogue

THREE DAYS HAD PASSED. SUNNYDALE BEGAN TO TAKE stock. The flood damage was astronomical. The dead were mourned.

And Xander was back in the hospital.

Buffy stood with Giles, Willow, and Oz around his hospital bed and made a face at him.

"I swear, what is it with you, Harris? Do you have a crush on a nurse or something?"

"I like the food," he said, indicating the mush on his evening tray. "So," he said to Giles, "what's the official explanation for a town gone mad?" He held up his hand, then winced. "Let me guess. PCP."

Giles inclined his head. "PCP it is."

Xander rolled his eyes. "So unoriginal. What about Julian? What was his deal?"

Giles perked up. "So far as we can ascertain, Helen had mixed holy water in with the Madness Potion. We're not sure what her plans were, but they obviously included getting rid of at least one vampire in the arena."

"Hence, kaboom," Oz said. He smiled at Willow, who gave him a very careful squeeze. Though werewolves healed fast, they didn't heal spontaneously.

A nurse bustled in and scowled at the large group.

"Visiting hours are over," she announced frostily. "And next time, please limit yourselves to two visitors at a time."

"Jawohl, mein Fraulein," Xander said under his breath. Then he murmured to Buffy, "She's the one I'm crushing on. Sue me, I love bossy chicks."

The nurse stood meaningfully beside the door.

Buffy looked down at Xander. "You did a good job up there. I didn't follow up on the blood in the bathroom. Maybe I could have stopped this all a lot sooner if I'd found out it belonged to Bitterman's sacrificed wife."

He winked at her. "It's on my résumé. I'm sure it'll help me snag that job at Happy Burger."

"We've gotta go," Willow said. "I'm going to help Oz MP3 a new Dingo song he wrote."

Oz smiled faintly. "What can I say? They missed me."

"Well, thanks for stopping by, everybody," Xander said. "Now it's just me and Hindu TV, if I know my Sunnydale Hospital channel selections."

Buffy turned and left with the others. They were halfway down the hall when she heard sobbing in one of the rooms.

Glancing at the others, she walked soundlessly to the door and peered inside.

In his hospital bed, Brian Dellasandro wept bitterly, his arms around Mark. Mark was crying just as hard, as a woman who resembled them looked on helplessly.

"That's their aunt," Willow said, coming up beside her.

"How's he going to live with himself?" Buffy murmured. "Knowing he killed his parents. That people are dead . . ."

"They're going to see a therapist," Willow added. "But I think it will take a lot more than that for Brian to forgive himself. Even if it was a drug."

"But it was also a curse," Oz said. "So how come everybody wasn't affected? How come you weren't, Buffy?"

Buffy looked at Giles.

"A predilection for violence?" he asked quietly. "Something within some of us which responded more readily to evil?"

"One man's evil is another man's good intentions," Oz said.

"I researched Julian," Giles said. "In life, he was a great man. A philanthropist. He was also opposed to the owning of slaves. A shame, that when he was changed, it was so extreme."

Giles murmured softly, *" 'The evil that men do lives after them. The good is oft interred with their bones.' Julius Caesar.* By Shakespeare."

"Gwenyth Paltrow's boyfriend," Buffy filled in, but her throat caught.

She walked on, somewhat apart from the others.

Willow caught up with her. She swallowed and looked uncertainly at the Slayer.

"Hey," Buffy said.

"Hey." Willow took a breath. "What will it take for

you to forgive me? Cuz I was mean to you even when I wasn't drugged."

"Willow," Buffy said, and she began to break down. "Will, it's my fault that you almost died. I—I was with . . ." She caught her breath and turned away. "I failed you."

"Buffy, you're not perfect," Willow said. She flushed. "I guess I expected you to be, though, and that sure wasn't fair."

"I . . ." Buffy ran her hand through her hair. "That doesn't matter, Will. Fair doesn't enter into it. I'm the Slayer."

"There are sins of omission, and sins of commision," Willow said. "It's a lot harder to forgive yourself for something you *didn't* do. Because that kind of blaming never ends." She made a face. "We can all do better. But if we try, that's what matters.

"I think that's something we're supposed to learn, anyway."

Buffy closed her eyes. "It's just . . . every time someone gets killed, I think I should have prevented it. I mean, how can I go Bronzing and to the movies and all that stuff, when I know we're on a Hellmouth?"

"Because you're not a god," Willow said. "Slayer, sure, but also a human being."

Behind them, Oz said quietly, " 'To err is human. To forgive, divine.' "

"But people die when I make mistakes," Buffy murmured.

"But you save a lot of other people," Willow said. "Back during the big battle? I started to get overwhelmed. Then I realized that if all I did was freak, I wouldn't be able to help anyone. But I was injured and tired and scared. I didn't do very well."

"But we won," Buffy said.

"We won," Willow agreed.

The good that you do, she thought. *Oh, Buffy, I hope it lives after you.*

After all of us.

"Want to talk?" Willow asked in a small voice. "Over coffee? Oz will wait."

"Coffee," Buffy said warmly.

The two friends moved quietly away from the others.

About the Author

Nancy Holder is the award-winning *Los Angeles Times*–bestselling author of forty-two novels and more than two hundred short stories, articles, and essays. She has won four Bram Stoker Awards for her supernatural fiction, including Best Novel for *Dead in the Water*. Her work has been translated into over two dozen languages. With her frequent collaborator, Christopher Golden, she has written many Buffy projects, including the *Sunnydale High School Yearbook, The Watcher's Guide,* and *Immortal*. Her solo Buffy-Angel efforts include *The Evil That Men Do* and *Not Forgotten*. She is currently finishing *The Watcher's Guide, Vol. 2*, written with Jeff Mariotte and Maryelizabeth Hart.

Holder is an avid swimmer and lifelong horror aficionado. A native Californian, she lives in San Diego with her brilliant and beautiful daughter, Belle, and their intrepid dogs, Mr. Ron and Dot.